THE
ULTIMATE RIP-OFF:
A TAXING TALE

The
Ultimate Rip-off:
A TAXING TALE

Iris Weil Collett

Next to being shot at and missed, nothing is quite as
satisfying as an income tax refund.
— F. J. Raymond

THOMAS HORTON AND DAUGHTERS
26662 S. New Town Drive / Sun Lakes, AZ 85248

Dedicated to Dana

PREFACE

A supplementary text to your public finance, taxation, accounting, or auditing classes in a suspense thriller format. Would be ideal for an MBA program or law school which has a light coverage of taxation or accounting. Could be used in IRS training programs for beginning agents.

Mix fraud, crime, politics, and taxation together to get a better way of learning the taxation process. If used as a supplement to a taxation course or a public finance course, this gripping novel provides a painless way of learning many taxation principles. This suspenseful novel puts taxation concepts into words a novice can understand and enjoy. Jeff Burke, an Ollie North–type Special Agent of the IRS, goes beyond the law to find several taxpayers who are evading taxes.

He survives four attacks on his life as he uncovers a major plot by an IRS official and a rare coin enterprise to rip off $758 million in income tax revenues in order to finance the building of a neutron bomb.

Featuring sleuths who handle net worth statements and financial records the way most detectives handle guns, the humorous characters put taxation concepts into real-life individual and business decisions. Along the way public finance concepts and political controversies, contemporary individual and corporate tax planning, tax fraud and avoidance, and the life of IRS employees are elucidated in a way both students and instructors will find gripping as well as informative. Much more explosive than the Iran-Contra affair. Never dull!

CHAPTER 1

You can have a lord, you can have a king, but the man to fear is the tax collector.

— Ancient Iraqi Proverb

The radio was on and a soft tune filled the room. Carl liked to work with the background of a radio. He did not consciously hear the news reporter begin the hourly report, but Carl looked up from the sheaf of papers in front of him when he heard his name mentioned.

"Folks, here are the latest predictions of Carl Strovee —

"Madonna shall divorce for the third time and wed David Letterman.

"David Eisenhower will beat Joseph Kennedy II in the New Hampshire primary.

"The Houston Astros will win the World Series.

"New Zealand will win the America's Cup a second time."

Carl lit a cigarette and leaned back in his chair. "Dammit!" Carl exclaimed to himself. "How can I work on predictions with the IRS on my back?"

The letter had arrived yesterday addressed to Carl Strover — they had even misspelled his name! Millions had heard of Strovee the Swami through his books and newspaper columns on astrology. This would be the second year in a row they had audited his return.

Carl had first gained prominence when he accurately predicted the date — within two days — of the third Arab boycott. In fact, many of his predictions had been accurate. He had predicted that President Carter would be elected president, that David Eisenhower would win a Senate seat, that Don Johnson would win an Oscar.

The letter indicated that Agent Yvonne Talbert had arranged for an office audit of Carl's last two tax returns. "Please bring the document or minutes that indicate that the stock you sold was Section 1244 stock," the letter had stated. Carl had claimed a $50,000 ordinary deduction and a $3,000 capital loss on his tax return for the sale.

Carl thought, "How much money have I hidden from the government? Doesn't everyone cheat on their income taxes?" August 15th, 3:00 p.m., at the Federal Building, Room 2001 was the information in the letter. Two days before his birthday. A great birthday present! Carl would be 35. He was still single.

And Henry had not been in town yesterday. Henry Silverman, his accountant, had helped Carl set up a system of hiding about forty percent of his gross receipts.

"Simple," he had said. "Many of the receipts which you receive are cash payments. When you prepare a personal horoscope for a client, he pays you with a check or with cash. Many clients do not wish anyone to know they deal with an astrologer.

"We'll keep two sets of books," Henry had said. "One set is for the IRS and the other set is for your personal benefit. Remember, most of the payments by your clients are not deductible by them, so they will not keep a record of their payments."

"Gee, I'm in the 45% tax bracket already," Carl reflected. "What more do they want? Even hiding 40% of my cash receipts, I'm still paying 27 cents out of each $1 to pay for the lousy government welfare programs. Why Henry had given me a copy of *Take It Off!*, published by no less than Playboy Press, which provided more than 1,000 tax deductions most people overlooked. Had Ralph Nader not predicted that the average taxpayer works three months out of the year for the govern-

2

ment? In the 45% tax bracket, I work almost five months out of the year for the federal government."

Carl flicked the ashes off the end of his cigarette and smiled gently as he thought. "Ironic. Much of my work is fraud and I'm systematically cheating the IRS. How do I make predictions? Some of it is luck, but most of it is merely reading everything. My nearly photographic mind allows me to put together various pieces of information into believable predictions. But much of my success is guaranteed by making enough predictions so that some of them come true.

"Thank goodness people are forgetful. They don't remember that I predicted that Carter would not run for re-election, the Great Salt Lake would dry up, there would be a depression in 1985, and an earthquake would make Chappaquiddick Island disappear. Where was my mind when I made those turkeys?" He sipped some whiskey from a glass on his table.

Henry's telephone service had indicated he would be back around 10:00 a.m. today. "Better call him," Carl spoke to himself as he turned down the radio. He was fuming with impatience. "I surely hope he is in and I don't have to speak to that blasted recording again. I'm always tempted to shout obscenities into the phone and leave the number of the local police department." He stubbed out his cigarette and lit another one. He dialed the number again.

"Hello, are you paying too much in taxes?" was the pleasant response at the other end of the line. "We can show you how better records and some planning can save you money."

"Yes, this is Carl Strovee. Could I speak to Henry?" Carl spoke in a high, almost soprano voice.

"Just a moment, Mr. Strovee."

Each time Carl called and received Henry's standard question — "Are you paying too much in taxes?" — he was always impressed that Henry did not miss a chance to advertise his trade.

"Hello, Carl, this is Henry. What scheme do you wish to try this week?" Henry asked in a low, polite voice.

"How to beat an IRS audit."

"What?" was Henry's puzzled response.

"They're auditing me again. I got a letter yesterday. They want to see information about the Section 1244 stock. You know, from my corporation that went bankrupt. I got an ordinary loss rather than a capital loss."

"Now don't panic, Carl. Everything went smoothly last year, didn't it? You didn't even have to attend the conference. It's probably just a routine audit. How many times have you been audited?"

"Three times."

"Three years in a row?"

"No, they skipped one year," replied Carl.

"I thought so. They are not supposed to audit anyone more than two years in a row if no adjustments are made, although they can examine up to the last three years' returns on any one audit."

"Let me read you the list of things they want."

"Why don't you just bring the letter in around five o'clock this afternoon. That will give me a chance to review your file."

"Goodbye," responded Henry about the same time there was a dull click at the other end of the line. Henry put down the phone, frustrated. He clenched his fist and softly pounded the desk with it. His calculator rattled on his desk. Henry certainly did not appreciate this unpleasant news. Carl Strovee was vulnerable. "How much was he ripping off from the government?" Henry wondered. "About forty percent. Trouble. Maybe it is a routine audit."

Henry Silverman was not a certified public accountant. He was a public accountant. He had dropped out of City College after he had taken enough courses to sit for the CPA exam. He sat for the CPA exam several times, but could not seem to pass it. Why does an accountant need to know about calculus, linear programming, and the rest of that junk? Then they passed a requirement that you had to have a college degree in order to sit for the examination, so Henry gave up on the CPA examination. Not that Henry was dumb. He had a sound knowledge

4

of accounting, especially tax accounting. But he did not have the capstone — the CPA certificate.

The CPA certificate was the cream on the top. It was the dream of every accountant. The exam was tough. Only about 10% of the candidates pass the entire exam on their first sitting. Two and a half days of accounting, auditing, taxation and other sophisticated matters. The certificate was the union card to work with one of the "big-eight." In the late '70s the Metcalf Report indicated that the eight biggest accounting firms had a "stranglehold on the profession and obligingly twist accounting principles to suit their corporate clients." Most accountants heatedly denied these charges.

The accounting profession is different than the legal profession. Whereas the legal profession is made up of smaller firms with many small practitioners, the accounting profession is dominated by eight large CPA firms which have branch offices in most major cities.

Henry had not worked with a "big-eight firm." They would not hire anyone without an accounting degree. He had worked with a smaller firm in New York City. He had been lucky even to be hired by the small firm. His uncle got him the job, somehow.

Henry did not fit the patterns of an accountant. Contrary to the popular impression that most accountants are white, male and Catholic; Henry was black and Protestant. He felt that clients often treated him with condescension because of his color.

Henry soon quit the small CPA firm in New York when it became evident that he would not pass the CPA exam and therefore had no hope of ever moving up in the firm. He went to Washington, D.C., and set up his own shop without a union card. He was lucky he did not have his CPA in the early days.

He had survived by advertising. In those early days a CPA could not advertise. It was against their Code of Ethics. Actually it was a way of preserving their caste system.

But Henry had advertised and advertised. He was able to find write-up work and eat. Write-up work was the scorn of

CPAs. Write-up work was demeaning and difficult. But someone had to keep the detail records for small and medium-sized companies. Just as armies travel on their stomachs, industry would grind to a halt without recordkeeping.

Henry knew he was intelligent because he had passed the Treasury examination while in New York. A CPA or lawyer was automatically admitted to practice before the Treasury Department. Other persons have to take and pass an examination which is given annually. Passing the exam requires detailed tax knowledge. Henry passed the exam on the first try. Henry liked taxes.

Being admitted to practice before the Treasury Department had been a problem when he moved to Washington. A person admitted to practice is prohibited from using any title such as tax accountant or from advertising in any fashion. In effect, true tax experts were not allowed to advertise, whereas the unscrupulous tax "experts" were allowed to advertise their wares. Thus, he had to drop his status as an enrolled person when he moved to Washington. He had to advertise in order to eat.

Adversity had been helpful to Henry in the beginning. Two events moved him into his present consulting firm. First, early in 1977 the Supreme Court gave lawyers the right to advertise. Within a short time CPAs began to advertise. Now it was not uncommon to see full-page ads in the *Wall Street Journal, Barrons*, and other publications extolling the virtues of this or that CPA firm.

Second, with the increasing use of computers in tax and accounting work, Henry's prospects had dimmed. In desperation Henry began to advise clients about various shaky and shady techniques. He suggested techniques that did *not* appear in *Accountant's News* and *Tax Tricks and Techniques*. Henry began to advocate fraud.

Every "red-blooded accountant" knows the classic verbiage of Judge Learned Hand, a very famous tax judge:

Over and over again courts have said that there is nothing sinister in arranging one's affairs so as to keep taxes as low as possible. Everybody does so, rich or poor; and all do right, for nobody owes any public duty to pay more than the law demands: taxes are enforced extractions, not voluntary contributions. To demand more in the name of morals is mere cant.

Henry's techniques went beyond the fine line between tax avoidance versus tax evasion. Tax avoidance is fine under the law, but tax evasion may result in free room and board in a federal penitentiary.

Henry knew that any attempt to avoid taxes was not a criminal offense. Attempts to avoid, reduce, minimize, or alleviate taxes by legitimate means are permissible. Anyone who avoids taxes does not misrepresent or conceal. Such a taxpayer merely shapes events to reduce, defer, or eliminate his tax liability. Upon the happening of events, the taxpayer makes a full disclosure. For example, the creation of a bona fide partnership in order to divide the income among several individual partners is okay.

On the other hand, Henry was aware that evasion involves subterfuge, deceit, camouflage or concealment in order to color or obscure events. A taxpayer may not make things seem other than they are. The willful attempt in any manner to evade or defeat a tax constitutes a criminal offense — a fine of not more than $100,000, or imprisonment not more than five years, or both. For example, the failure to report taxable income from a second job would be evasion. "The difference between tax avoidance and tax evasion is like the difference between a lightning bug and lightning," was Henry's favorite statement.

Henry was an excellent speaker. He now traveled a great deal giving unadvertised seminars on tax fraud techniques to high-tax bracket taxpayers. His fee was steep; each individual had to pay $1,000 for his eight-hour seminar. But his advice was worth it.

His most profitable flim-flam was advising taxpayers how to set up their own church. Such a scheme can relieve a taxpayer of the federal income tax, the state franchise tax, and local taxes. An individual can become a minister for $10 and can even purchase for a fifty dollar "offering" a mail-order Honorary Doctor of Divinity certificate from the Worldwide Life Church, Inc., a California corporation. For an offering of ten dollars per month for recordkeeping purposes, this same organization will send a Church Charter and tax-exempt status.

The taxpayer can appoint his wife and daughter to be the church secretary and treasurer. Then the taxpayer can put his $20,000 paychecks (less approximately $3,200 of federal taxes) into a church fund recorded by the church treasurer. Next the church can buy or rent a house for their minister to live in. Estimate $4,000 a year for this amount. Our minister is entitled to a living allowance for himself and his family. Estimate another $8,000. Add $2,000 for phone, utilities, and insurance. The minister will need a car to perform church work. This car can be used for personal work. Approximate $3,000. At the end of the year, our taxpayer can apply for a refund of the $3,200 withheld. Thus, his entire salary is tax-free.

Henry knew that this religious tax shelter was as porous as a leaky boat.

Another technique which Henry advocated was setting up an apocalypse trust. A trust is a special entity established by an individual with someone called the trustee in charge of operations of the special entity. Under this apocalypse arrangement, a taxpayer transfers to a trust all of his assets and assigns his lifetime services to the trust. For example, a dentist might transfer his place of business to a trust. The beneficiaries are generally the taxpayer's family, with the grantor retaining broad powers over the income and principal of the trust. The trust collects all of the taxpayer's income and deducts all of the taxpayer's expenses. The purpose of this arrangement is to shift income to taxpayers in lower tax brackets as well as to avoid the estate tax. Obviously the IRS was opposed to such an arrangement, but such opposition did not stop taxpayers from trying it. Henry knew this was a leaky tax shelter, but it pulled in the bucks for him.

Henry recalled an old quick silver technique for wealthy individuals, which involved fictitious transactions in the London silver market. Suppose a businessman or entertainer has taxable income of $300,000.

He obtains a "loan" of $3,000,000 from a commodities broker, supposedly to invest in silver bullion in London. Of course, the broker does not obtain the three million dollars because the loan is phony. The phony loan is to bear a 10% rate of interest.

The $3,000,000 in silver is allegedly bought and "interest" payments on the phony loan are actually made to the broker by check, $300,000 over a year's time. The taxpayer deducts the interest payments from his taxable income, bringing his income down to zero.

Then the taxpayer arranges for the broker to sell the nonexistent silver for future delivery one year hence, at a profit equal to the imaginary interest payments. Thus, the interest payments to the broker return to the taxpayer, less, of course, a brokerage fee to the broker for the phony transaction.

The net result of this flim-flam was to turn a large taxable ordinary income into a similar capital gain that was taxed at a favorable tax rate. The bottom line: Had the taxpayer not taken the interest deduction, his tax liability would have been approximately $190,000. Whereas, the capital gain tax would have been approximately $100,000 — a tax *evasion* of approximately $90,000. Of course, the Tax Reform Act of 1986 stopped this scam by gradually eliminating the consumer interest expense deduction and favorable capital gain treatment. Capital gain treatment reappeared in 1990 to help the depressed real estate industry.

Henry did have one characteristic of an accountant. Although he had a neatly trimmed black mustache, Henry was very conservative. He subscribed to such newsletters as *The Duff Times*, *Inflation Survival Letter* and *Mick's World Currency Report*. He had been the one who introduced the scheme to avoid taxation using the standard gold content of the dollar. He encouraged several individuals to file their Form 1040 but pay no taxes. They then asserted that they were not required to pay taxes because the symbol "$" means "dollars" and its meaning for purposes of the tax law is the same as for the law describing the content of the dollar. The taxpayers maintained that they received no such "dollars." In essence, the taxpayers argued that a dollar is not a dollar because its purchasing power had declined and because paper currency cannot be converted into gold. Henry's idea lost in court.

This type of scheme did lead Henry into his latest adventure. He was publishing a private newsletter informing his readers how to evade taxes. The annual subscription cost for "How to Cheat and Defraud the IRS" was $900. He published it under a pseudonym, I. M. Clever.

The need for a pseudonym was obvious. Henry had once been arrested on an indictment alleging a violation of federal income tax laws. He had been accused of knowingly preparing a false letter in connection with a tax matter. He had beaten the rap, but it paid to be cautious when dealing with the IRS.

Henry frowned, irritated by the call from Carl. He returned to the incomplete partnership return in front of him. He was working on the Schedule K items. With corporate marginal tax rates higher than individual rates after 1986, the flow-through type entities had multiplied over the years. Sitting on Henry's untidy desk was his dog-eared copy from *Taxes—The Tax Magazine* of an article entitled "Some Early Strategies for the Methodical Disincorporation of America After the Tax Reform Act of 1986: Grafting Partnerships Onto C Corporations, Running Amok with the Master Limited Partnership Concept, and Generally Endeavoring to Defeat the Intention of the Draftsmen of the Repeal of General Utilities."

CHAPTER 2

The mere fact that a taxpayer chooses one road in preference to another, in order to avoid the hot sun of taxation, is no reason to deny he actually traveled the first road.
— Hugh C. Bickford

Jeff Burke awoke on his side in pain. It was Monday and he did not wish to get up. But he had missed work on Friday and Jake was expecting him this morning.

Jeff liked to play softball — until Thursday. Jeff liked to pitch softball — until Thursday. Jeff was pitching in the top of the third inning. One out, with a runner on first. His team was the Sentry Superstars.

The batter hit a sharp line drive which struck the ground once and then bounced wildly and hit Jeff directly in the crotch. Surprisingly Jeff picked up the softball and threw the runner out before collapsing.

One hour later he was resting in a bathtub of cold water with sore, swollen plumbing. On Friday morning he was sitting in the doctor's office. The office was filled with old people. What has Medicare done — made the doctor's office a retreat of the "old fogies." Jeff did notice the pretty, blondish woman with an overworked look leave the office about 20 minutes into his long wait. Other than that event, the only stimulating items in the office were the magazines, all of which were three or four months old. He tried to read some stories in *Esquire*, but could not keep his mind focused on the words.

Two hours he had to wait. Then thirty seconds with the doctor with a sullen, narrow face. Jeff winced when the fat, nimble hands explored his swollen private parts. The doctor put two fingers in his crotch and requested a cough. Boy did that hurt. The doctor mumbled, "You're lucky to have anything left. Wear jocks and keep an ice pack on them."

"Just great," Jeff thought. "An ice pack on my testicles!" Jeff made a mental note to have the doctor audited as he left the doctor's office. Jeff worked for the IRS, and he knew that many medical doctors earn a very high income. A doctor might keep vital income records personally in order to avoid letting employees know about his business. Some doctors have a constant turnover of clerical help to accomplish the same result. Thus, fees may be collected without the employees' knowledge, and omitted from the doctor's records. A nice way of avoiding taxes.

"Wonder how he invests his money?" Jeff thought. Jeff recalled that the IRS Audit Guide indicated that many doctors are active investors in securities, bonds, rental properties, oil properties, and especially real estate. The Audit Guide was, of course, the "bible" of a good agent. If he gives prescriptions for the druggist next door, I bet he has a kickback arrangement with the druggist.

The Audit Guide indicates that doctors often have kickback arrangements with druggists on prescriptions, with opticians on prescriptions for glasses and frames, or with specialists on referrals. "I'll destroy his golden goose," Jeff mumbled to himself as he slowly maneuvered down the several stone steps. A plump, smooth-faced woman leading a snotty little kid into the doctor's office gave him a bitter look.

The sky was overcast and looked as if it might snow. "Tough," Jeff thought, "all I need to do is have to walk on ice and snow in this condition." His breath misted in front of him as he walked slowly toward his parked car. Jeff somehow maneuvered his body into his dirty car and drove toward his apartment. He stopped at an Eckerd's drugstore and purchased two jock straps.

*   *   *

Jeff slowly got out of bed. He had slept badly during the night. Each time he moved, he ached. He gingerly tucked his sore organs into his jock support, thinking he was possibly lucky he'd broken up with his delightful girlfriend, Shirley, because he could forget about a sex life for awhile. The split-up had been extremely painful to Jeff.

Jeff was a Special Agent. Criminal violations of the Internal Revenue Code are the responsibilities of Special Agents of the Criminal Investigation Division (CID). The Intelligence Division of the IRS had its beginning on July 1, 1919, as the brainchild of Daniel C. Roper, the Commissioner of the then Internal Revenue. These silent investigators have caught many tax evaders as well as put many top criminals in prison. Such notorious organized crime figures as Al "Scarface" Capone, Frank Costello, Waxey Gordon, Bernard Goldfine, and Johnny Torrio (the father of modern gangsterdom) were sent to prison by the work of Special Agents. It was the IRS, not the FBI, who toppled the empires of such political bosses as Huey Long of Louisiana, "Nucky" Johnson of Atlantic City, and Tom Pendergast of Kansas City.

He had been a Revenue Agent before asking for a transfer. The main federal snooper in the tax force is the Revenue Agent. A Revenue Agent provides a routine examination of taxpayers. A Special Agent is called into action when fraud is suspected by a Revenue Agent, or local and state police officers make a "drug bust."

He remembered the tone in Jake's voice Thursday. "Jeff," Jake had said, "I believe we have a crooked IRS agent in a critical position. There are probably other taxpayers involved in this fraud so I need your help." Jeff knew that Special Agents investigate taxpayers, not other agents. No other information was given, and Jeff had made an appointment to see Jake at 10:00 a.m. Monday in Washington.

Jeff had known Jake at Penn State. Both had earned their degrees in accounting in "Happy Valley." Penn State is located in State College, Pennsylvania, and is equally inaccessible from all parts of Pennsylvania. "Happy Valley" probably originated because there is absolutely nothing to do except study and go to bed with your wife — assuming you could find a wife.

During their junior year at Penn State Jake and Jeff had often double-dated. Jeff's girlfriend, Jane, had been a pleasantly plump brunette — chubby but cuddly. In between football games and dorm room necking sessions, Jeff had learned some psychology, because Jane's major had been psychology.

Jake Anderson started out as a strike-force agent. Sometimes called "bird-dog" agents, their so-called strike-force investigations often resulted in fraud charges. Although "bird- dog" agents are regular Revenue Agents, their basic function was to uncover possible criminal activities.

Strike-force agents have been known to work undercover close to the criminal activities. They hang around racetracks and gambling casinos. They pose as gamblers, pimps, dope peddlers, elevator doormen, and any other position that will uncover hidden revenues. They may tap telephone conversations or open people's mail. They look for "juice." "Juice" is the slang for revenue from taxpayers. Revenue is the lifeblood of the IRS and the federal government.

One strike force, code named "Operation Bird-Dog," descended upon the Ali-Quarry fight in Atlanta in 1970. These agents recorded the license tag numbers of the ringsiders. A number of expensive, custom-built cars costing as much as $40,000 turned up on the list. These lists were then forwarded to IRS officials around the United States, and the owners' income tax forms were audited.

IRS files indicated that the roaring Twenties had seemingly returned to Atlanta. The styles of the Twenties prevailed with the males challenging the females for the extreme in dress and brilliance of color, wearing wide-brimmed hats, double-breasted jackets, two-piece suits with coats to the knees; some wore full-length minks.

Jake was now a member of a little-known, elite group of agents, called Internal Security Inspectors. Their targets were dishonest Treasury Department employees, as well as government officials and employees. After Watergate, Koreagate, Iranscam, Nixon's backdated gift, Congressman Wayne Hays' Waterloo with the sex-payroll affair, and the confirmation of Lyndon Johnson's two hundred vote fraud, a special unit was established to look into the conduct of any government official.

Before he resigned, Nixon got into trouble with his taxes. Johnson and other politicians donated their personal letters and papers to charitable organizations. They took sizable charitable deductions based upon the fair market value of the donations. With a Republican president in office, the Democratic Congress changed the rules to allow a deduction only for the actual cost of the paper or letterhead.

Nixon tried to beat the effective date of the new law change and donated his Vice-Presidential papers to the National Archives. Critics asserted that Nixon's lawyer backdated the deed transferring the papers.

Later in the election campaign between Carter and Ford, Carter made taxation reform one of his major campaign issues. Then within his first year in office Carter showed an insignificant tax liability on his tax return. A large investment tax credit from the purchase of peanut machinery reduced his tax burden. An astute politician, Carter made political hay by "donating" $6,000 to the IRS. His reasoning was that everyone should pay *some* taxes. A comedian during this time wondered out loud how you could trust someone who volunteers to pay extra taxes with a smile.

Jake was an Internal Security Inspector. If Jake had found fraud by an IRS employee, he would need a Special Agent to follow up fraud with any outside taxpayers. Jeff figured that Jake needed his help in the taxpayer investigation. Once fraud is discovered by a Revenue Agent, he should suspend his activities at the earliest opportunity without disclosing to the taxpayer the reason for the suspension. The agent, however, should take the necessary steps to determine that there is fraud before asking for a Special Agent.

At 9:45 a.m. Jeff was slowly making his way toward the main entrance at 1111 Constitution Avenue. He had made reasonable time coming from Baltimore to Washington. Three arches rose two stories to the architrave. The seven-story concrete, limestone and marble structure was the IRS's national office building. It was in the Federal Triangle complex of government buildings in Washington, D.C. Built in 1930 at a cost of ten million dollars, its design was inspired by the Somerset House on London's Strand — the structure which housed Britain's tax collection agency. How soon they forget, Jeff thought, recalling the Boston tea party.

Jeff signed in with the guard and walked through the security checking machine. With the high crime rate in D.C. and the possibility of a certified lunatic bringing a bomb into the federal buildings, all federal buildings had armed guards at the entrances.

Jeff entered a vacant elevator and jabbed the button for the fourth floor. He saw a reflection of his windblown, short hair and brown mustache on the shiny, smooth wall of the elevator. He smiled back as he patted his hair down. When the elevator jerked to a stop, he walked down the hall to Jake's office. As an Inspector, bespectacled, pipe smoking Jake seemed to enjoy involvement in criminal investigations and repeatedly got involved in cases which ultimately were referred to a Special Agent. That's probably why he was placed on the bird-dog squad.

Jake looked up from his computer console. "Hello, Jeff. How are you?" With a fussy movement he removed his wire-framed glasses.

"Terrible," nodded Jeff. "Got hit in the family jewels Thursday night with a softball."

"Bad on the sex life, isn't it?" smiled Jake. "How's your softball team doing?"

"Lousy — we've won about half our games. We need more hitting. What do you have for me today?"

16

"I may have another hot one for you," replied Jake. "Have a seat."

Jeff settled into a straight back chair.

Jake gulped a swallow of coffee from a styrofoam cup and gestured with his pipe toward the folder in front of him. On the left side of his desk was the Service's standard Zenith personal computer. They had been introduced in the mid-eighties.

"Richard Onner is our target," Jake said crisply. "He is a computer expert working in our National Computer Center in Martinsburg, West Virginia." He replaced his glasses on his hawk-like nose.

After a short pause, Jake continued. "We received an anonymous tip about Richard about a year and a half ago that he was living beyond his means. The anonymous letter indicated that he was probably taking bribes."

Jeff recalled that few taxpayers knew about the IRS's formal informer's program. But rewards range from 1% to 10% of the taxes and penalties collected by the IRS as a result of tips. Agents affectionately call such rewards a "fink fee." Ex-wives or husbands, jilted girlfriends, and disgruntled friends and neighbors create approximately 160,000 tips per year.

One of the most famous cases involved an oral surgeon's nurse who informed the Special Agent's office in Los Angeles that her employer-dentist was keeping two sets of books. The dentist went on vacation. With the cooperation of the nurse, a dozen Special Agents examined more than twenty thousand patient charts in order to determine the dentist's true income. The nurse then helped obtain a confession from the dentist.

Our heroine was not rewarded for her "good deed." The nurse was blacklisted by the medical and dental professions in the area. She was unable to find similar employment and had to leave the city.

Another famous anonymous tip from a businessman in New York involved Virginia Hill, a woman who was "involved" with organized crime. She shocked the Kefauver Committee by attributing her wealth to the fact that she was "the world's best lay." Congress initiated a probe of Virginia's role

17

in organized crime, and she eventually died after swallowing twenty-eight sleeping pills in March 1966. An informer must, of course, ask for the reward. It will not be given automatically. A special form must be filled out. Approximately one of every six claims is approved. Of course, the informer normally remains anonymous from the person he is reporting. Then the informer has to pay taxes on the fink fee. The IRS carefully checks their returns in the subsequent tax year.

Jeff had about twenty unpaid informants. The confidentiality of an informant must always be protected. Even if ordered to reveal the identity of an informer in court under the threat of a contempt citation, the IRS agent should remain silent.

Only his Section Chief knew the identity of Jeff's informants. The informers' names were listed on a three-by-five-inch index card in a sealed envelope. The envelope was to be opened by his Section Chief only if Jeff were missing or in personal danger.

Informers have been known to break laws in order to obtain information. Jeff had paid an informant $7,000 recently in order to obtain tax information about a Bahamian official. Many tax shelter rings have dummy Bahamian corporations. The informer had photocopied the contents of the official's briefcase while he was with a woman arranged for by the IRS informer. The information had been very damaging to the taxpayer's tax battle with the IRS.

In the past Jeff had used several women informers to learn about the sex lives of several prominent businessmen. Using an informer to "bug" a possible tax evader was not uncommon. The "bugging of the Democratic headquarters" in the Watergate complex was not an isolated incident. Had not "landslide Lyndon" bugged Goldwater during their political campaign? Johnson and Kennedy had tapped on a wholesale basis.

Jeff asked, "Who is the informer?"

Jake smiled owlishly, "We don't know who the squeal letter is from; however, the handwriting and perfumed paper would seem to indicate that the squealer is a woman. Probably an ex-girlfriend."

At first I thought the charge had no substance. However, I talked to Onner's security broker and his banks and examined the records of his transactions. I'm convinced he is not reporting all of his income. But I don't know from whom he receives the income or how he receives it or why.

"He has gambled away about $15,000 over the past year and has lavished about $20,000 on his current girlfriend.

"I used the net worth analysis on him and he is not reporting about $32,000 of income. Here, look for yourself." His eyes were bright with excitement. Jake handed a computer printout to Jeff.

On the computer sheet was the following:

Confidential — Net Worth Analysis
IRS Personnel
Richard Onner 241-56-7682

Net Worth (end of year)	$39,000
Net Worth (beginning of year)	−27,000
	$12,000
Nondeductible expenditures	+48,000
Reconstructed income	$60,000
Reported income	−28,000
Unreported income	$32,000

Jeff knew immediately that this information was damaging. The indirect net worth method has even been upheld by the Supreme Court as a valid technique for conviction for tax evasion.

Jeff looked up and responded, "Do you have any ideas of the possible sources of income?"

"Nope. He has no wealthy family member so nontaxable gifts or an inheritance is out of the question. He drives a Porsche and spends money as if it's going out of style. He must be involved with some other taxpayers. That's why I need your help.

"I have not contacted Onner so he is unaware of the fact that he is being investigated. Of course, I must prepare a report which goes directly to the Commissioner's office since we are dealing with such a sensitive individual. I plan to send the letter tomorrow. I have told no one else."

Jeff looked at his watch and then said, "Okay, I'll check him out. You file your report with the Commissioner, but let's keep it under wraps. There may be a simple explanation, so we don't wish to damage Onner's reputation with some false charges. Keep me informed as to any more developments. I'll drive out to Martinsburg tomorrow." However, Jeff knew that once an IRS agent had embarked on an indirect, time consuming method of computing income of a taxpayer, he did not wish to waste such efforts. Some tax revenues must result from such efforts, or he would receive criticism from his supervisor.

"Have you made an extra copy of Onner's tax returns?" Jeff asked, knowing the answer already and wondering why he had even bothered to ask.

"You bet," responded Jake, handing a file to Jeff. A phone started ringing in the next office.

He rose to leave. As Jeff turned and left, he was thinking about how efficient Jake was. The phone was still ringing as he passed the door to the next office.

Jake was finishing the computer letter to the Commissioner outlining the suspicious facts concerning Richard Onner before Jeff made his way slowly out of the elevator into the sunlight. There were many bureaucratic rules within the IRS.

CHAPTER 3

Let us not make the income tax so high that the man whose money we want to use in business prefers not to take the risk.
— Wendell L. Willkie

Martinsburg, West Virginia, is about seventy miles west of Washington. Located at the head of the Shenandoah Valley, this city houses the National Computer Center of the IRS. The "Martinsburg Monster" is the nickname of the enormous IBM computers in a multi-story brick and glass structure. These high-speed electronic digital computers have more than a thousand miles of master tapes which contain the tax records of all U.S. taxpayers for the past three years.

Opened officially in 1961, this computer complex is the heart of the IRS's tax administration. A taxpayer files his tax return with his regional service center. A scanning machine feeds the data from the return into a computer and records such information on a magnetic tape. Uncle Sam collects about $225 billion in income taxes on 95 million individual tax returns each year.

These magnetic tapes are sent to the National Computer Center. Each reel contains about 15,000 tax returns. At the Center the information is posted by a computer to each taxpayer's master file. The master file includes data about the taxpayer for a three-year period. The master files are kept up to date through weekly updating. The tax return tapes and the

21

output tapes prepared at the Center are returned to the various regional centers.

At the regional center the tax returns are checked for mathematical accuracy and completeness. The reported income is compared with Form 1099s coming from employers, banks, and so forth. The computer also checks to see whether deductions, interest, dividend income, royalties, and other items fall within normal ranges. A Discriminant Function System (DIF) picks certain tax returns which have the greatest likelihood of error, cheating, and potential tax deficiency. There is always a chance that the return will be audited. In fact, about 2% of all tax returns are audited. The more complicated a return and the higher the taxable income, the greater the chance of an audit.

Richard Onner was employed as a computer operator at the National Service Center. He was a competent employee. In fact, he was downright cocky about his computer ability. He had worked at the Center for five years, but knew he had probably reached the extent of his advancement within the IRS.

Richard was divorced. His first marriage had ended because he liked to run around. His first mistake was now costing him $500 per month in alimony payments. "But at least it's deductible," Richard rationalized.

Richard thought of himself as a Don Juan or maybe a young Robert Redford. He was currently living with Tish Scarbourg. She had the gift of gab but no sense of reality. She was very attractive. Besides, the busty, robust blonde was great in bed.

Richard and Tish were lying in bed relaxing.

"When can we get married?"

Richard turned over and noticed his tanned body in the mirrors on the ceiling. Tish bounced up and down as the water in the waterbed settled back. He reached for and lit a cigarette. After the first puff he said, "You really know when to hit a man."

"Well, this is the only time I can get your undivided attention. Between computers, hang gliding, and coins. . ." She didn't finish the sentence.

Richard tried to stifle a yawn. "How much money do you earn at the advertising agency?"

"What?"

"How much money do you earn per year?"

"What's that got to do with marriage?"

"Just answer the question."

"About $28,000," Tish replied in a loud voice. "You should know, you spend part of it."

"If we get married, we'll have to pay more taxes. There is a marriage penalty."

"You're kidding me."

"Nope; our more enlightened society *and* the sometimes puritanical tax laws no longer frown upon cohabitation — uh, living together. Where two individuals have comparable incomes, they pay less taxes by living together without marriage. We can enjoy the blessing of love while minimizing our contributions to the federal government."

"Please talk in simple language."

"If we get married, you and I will have to pay more taxes. We are better off filing separate tax returns. Marriage will force us into higher tax brackets. Plus our combined general tax credit will be less."

"Isn't that good?"

"A tax credit reduces your over-all tax liability dollar-for-dollar."

Tish snapped, "What a heck of an argument against marriage, especially after I gave you such a good time." She turned over, a trifle peeved.

Richard did not mention one advantage of marriage. The IRS generally cannot obtain testimonial evidence from one spouse for use in the prosecution of the other spouse. Of course, Richard did not tell Tish everything.

"Sweet dreams, dear." Richard looked at her bottom in the mirrors. As if Tish had eyes in the back of her head, she abruptly pulled up the sheet. Richard yawned again. She was a pretty blonde thing.

23

Richard stubbed out his cigarette and turned off the brass lamp. The soft patter of the rain on the windowpanes was the last thing Richard heard before he fell asleep.

*   *   *

When Jeff Burke got back to his office in Baltimore after an uneventful drive from Washington, he was greeted with some bad news. One of his cases was settled in court in favor of the taxpayer.

The story had begun about two years ago. One of his informers had provided Jeff with a short list of some high-priced prostitutes. One name was a real pro.

Jeff obtained a search warrant and while searching her luxurious apartment found a small piece of gray luggage which was completely filled with stacks of money. The sight of all that money had made the back of his neck tingle and a chill go down his spine. When counted, the money totaled $50,055. Jeff also found her "John book."

When confronted, she shrugged her shoulders and indicated that the money was gifts from several gentlemen friends. Gifts, of course, are not taxable. At this point Jeff had Collections slap a jeopardy assessment on her for the entire amount and took her money.

A jeopardy assessment is used when the tax is already due and payable but the activities of the taxpayer jeopardize its collection. This procedure is used where the IRS believes that the taxpayer may remove or transfer the property, the taxpayer may quickly depart from the United States, the taxpayer may conceal herself or her property, or do other acts which might frustrate collection of the tax liability. The procedure is often applied to suspected criminal offenders involved in gambling, narcotics, or other illegal activities. Property may be seized by the IRS pending determination of the issue in the court.

Jeff was able to calculate her income. He obtained laundry lists from her laundry. She had made the mistake of renting her sheets and changing her sheets after each customer.

Her "John book" indicated a rate of $200 per date. She had a first-class operation! The laundry lists indicated that she had two dates per day at $200 per date, three weeks per month, twelve months per year — less, of course, appropriate expenses for her sheets. The IRS computer showed that she had not filed tax returns for the previous four years.

Jeff thought he had her. But she hired a smart tax lawyer. She voluntarily filed tax returns for the four years involved. On the fourth she reported gross income of $51,000. Although there was a substantial tax due on this amount, she indicated that she had already *paid* $50,055. She asked for a *refund* of $44,000. Obviously, the IRS refused to give her the refund.

She went to court. The issue before the court was whether a refund was due and not the propriety of her tax returns. The judge accepted her tax returns at face and ordered the IRS to refund her money *with interest*.

Jeff was depressed. He had worked on this case for about one year. There was consolation; the length of a usual fraud case was about two years.

Jeff sighed deeply and turned his attention to the Onner problem. The returns appeared to be okay. Jeff chuckled when he saw that three years before Onner had claimed a dependency exemption for an unrelated woman with whom he lived that year. Onner had also used the special head of household rate in computing his income tax. An individual who is a member of a taxpayer's household for the *entire* year does not have to be related to the taxpayer in order for the taxpayer to claim the individual as a personal exemption.

But Jeff recalled that there had been a court decision only last year which disallowed the dependency exemption and head of household rates for the breadwinner of an unmarried couple. The court held that cohabitation was illegal under local law. The decision had lacked any evidence as to habitual sexual intercourse. In other words, the taxpayers had not taken any avowals of celibacy. Jeff wondered if Onner and his girlfriend had taken such an avowal or whether the act of living with his claimed dependent violated West Virginia law.

The telephone on his desk buzzed softly. The switchboard operator indicated that Yvonne Talbert was on the other end. "Hello, Yvonne."

"Hi, Jeff. Thought I would remind you that the conference with Carl Strovee is on Wednesday at 3:00 p.m. Could you be here at 2:00 p.m. to go over the details? I believe we have a fraud case, but my blasted supervisor is putting pressure on me to close the case."

"Is he the 'switch hitting' ESP freak who makes all those weird predictions?" Jeff asked.

"Yes. I hope he can predict how many years he will get when we put the noose around his neck. See you on Wednesday."

"Goodbye."

Jeff, of course, knew what Yvonne meant by "pressure from her supervisor." Yvonne was a Revenue Agent and they worked under unofficial quotas with respect to the number of cases she must close and the amount of tax revenues she obtains. Most taxpayers were unaware of the fact that an agent wanted a short audit, collecting as much revenue as possible.

Yvonne had once told Jeff that her supervisor kept a computer record of the number of closed cases and the new revenue collected by each of his agents. Thus, each agent had to produce.

In public the IRS always denied that there were quotas. But they existed. Promotions were slow for those agents who fell below the norm. Obviously, from any one taxpayer a Revenue Agent had to find at least enough "juice" to cover his salary.

By the time Jeff was finished with his paperwork it was 6:30 p.m. He drove over to Calvert Street to Flesher Printing Company. A gloomy sky hung over the skyline of Baltimore. Mr. Flesher was a "numbered" or "jacketed" case. After the department had decided to follow through with a fraud case, it was given a number. Each Special Agent had four or five "numbered cases." Each Special Agent also had six or seven nonnumbered cases. These latter cases had not reached the stage that fraud or a criminal activity was a certainty.

Flesher Printing Company was involved with the football cards racket. The print shop had been under surveillance by Jeff for three weeks. Maybe tonight Jeff would be lucky.

Jeff thought the print shop did the printing of the tickets for the numbers racket in Baltimore. A printer always prints several practice runs before beginning a printing job. Jeff had been checking the garbage dumpster in the back of the shop for three weeks. An agent's life is not always pleasant, Jeff was thinking, as he rummaged through the garbage. Tonight Jeff found a handful of spaghetti. Certainly not enough for a fraud conviction!

There was an important difference between a *civil* conviction and a *criminal* conviction. In a *civil* tax prosecution where the IRS has assessed a deficiency, the taxpayer always has the burden of proof. The taxpayer must prove that the IRS is wrong. The taxpayer must prove that he owes no deficiency. In other words, the taxpayer is presumed to be *guilty* until he proves himself *innocent* since the taxpayer's filed return is a self-declaration of income, expenses and deductions.

But the burden of proof is upon the IRS in a *criminal* or fraud prosecution. The IRS must prove that the taxpayer willfully intended to defraud. Intent is hard to prove. Or the IRS must prove the criminal activities. Here, the taxpayer is presumed to be innocent until the IRS proves him guilty beyond a reasonable doubt. Jeff was trying to obtain evidence for a criminal prosecution.

Intent is very hard to prove. That's why many Special Agents feel that they have higher status than anyone else in law enforcement.

Consider the function of an FBI agent. He only has to prove that a car was stolen in one state and found in another state. The FBI agent does not have to prove that the person willfully intended to cross the state line.

Jeff recalled a favorite joke of Special Agents. Compared to a Special Agent, an FBI agent couldn't track an elephant with a nosebleed over fresh sand. In the past there has been competition and friction between the IRS and the FBI. Often the IRS would prepare income tax cases against underworld figures, murderers, political bosses, and other criminals who were otherwise untouchable by the FBI. The FBI would get the credit and publicity, and the IRS was left with only resentment.

For example, Jake "Greasy Thumb" Guzik, treasurer of the Al Capone gang, was one of the many top gangsters caught by Special Agents. "Greasy Thumb" got his nickname from the green stain on his hands from counting cash. Handwriting experts convinced a bank cashier to "spill his guts" about "Greasy Thumb," and he was indicted, convicted, and sent to prison for five years.

On the way home Jeff fortified himself with a sausage pizza at the Pizza Hut. That night while watching Johnny Carson, Jeff fell asleep sitting on his ice pack. He dreamed about sliding down the snowy ski slopes in Snowmass, Colorado. At the end of Fanny Hill he fell into the icy-cold Frying Pan River. He had skied at both Aspen, the Victorian town, and Snowmass several years earlier. He had also gone fly fishing in the river near Basalt. When he awoke the next morning he was shivering.

CHAPTER 4

People who squawk about their income taxes may be divided into two classes. They are: men and women.
— Anonymous

Jeff was up very early and had gulped down only one cup of hot tea for breakfast. Since 8:00 a.m. he had been sitting in his car watching the entrance to a modest brownstone on St. Paul Street.

It was now 9:10 a.m. and he was bored. Rob Fowler was under surveillance. He was a suspected "runner" for the football betting racket in Baltimore. A runner is the person who goes around collecting the bets placed during the day.

At 9:11 Rob emerged from his house with his companion. She was both old and fat. Rob was a tall, lanky, young black man with a short hairdo with a part carved into the right side. His trademark must be silk shirts, Jeff thought. He had on a bright red silk shirt this morning.

Twice a week Jeff had to follow Rob. Other agents followed Rob on the other weekdays. There was a problem. For two weeks no one had been able to follow Rob because he was a "crazy" driver.

Rob and his "lady" got into a light tan, 1991 Plymouth. All the runners drove this same type and color of car. This caused havoc with surveillance operations.

The tan Plymouth took the same route as the previous mornings. Rob dropped off his "lady" at a plumbing outlet.

Out to the Beltway the Plymouth moved. Jeff had to "run" two stoplights along the way in order to keep up with the tan car.

The traffic was still heavy on the Beltway. Jeff mumbled, "I'll get you today." The target car stayed in the right lane for about four miles. Up ahead was a Budweiser beer truck going about fifty miles an hour. This caused Jeff to get too close to Rob. Traffic was bunched up. All of a sudden Rob swerved left across two lanes. His car almost took off a bumper on the car next to him.

Jeff could do nothing. There was no way he could get across to the far-left lane because he was hemmed in. Rob sped away. Rob had won again.

Jeff cursed. In two days, he reminded himself, he would have a search warrant and search Rob's house.

Once Jeff was satisfied that he had really lost Rob, he shrugged and turned around and headed for Washington. As he had promised, he would check on Richard Onner.

After by-passing Washington, Jeff listened to the chatter on his CB as he passed through Germantown, Brunswick, and Sandy Hook, Maryland.

When he got to Shepherdstown, West Virginia, he knew he was close to Martinsburg. He had not yet decided what to do. Maybe he would go to Antietam National Battlefield and finesse Onner. A pothole in the road and the resulting pain in his groin reminded Jeff that he did not wish to walk around on a hilly battlefield.

Jeff followed the signs to Martinsburg. No one had yet prepared a bank deposit analysis on Onner. Jeff felt that Onner was not dumb enough to deposit any unreported income in a bank. But he would canvass the banks anyway.

Jeff stopped at a telephone booth near a Best Western Motel and copied down the names and addresses of the banks in Martinsburg and Onner's telephone number.

At each bank Jeff talked to the manager and showed him his Special Agent badge. Most of them gulped, then smiled and said, "Yes, sir?"

The life of a Special Agent can be dull. Some of the most important evidence that an agent can obtain during an investigation will be found in banks and other financial institutions. Jeff was thankful for his accounting background.

Agents must examine bank records such as canceled checks and bank statements. Extremely important are the teller's daily record sheets which are maintained by the bank but are not made available to the taxpayer. Teller's cash receipts will disclose transactions where the taxpayer cashed checks to obtain money for a deposit or himself. Such an activity is contrary to normal business practice and may indicate that the checks were not reported as income.

There are two types of bank canvassing. Jeff could either write the bank or make a personal visit to the bank. Under both ways, a summons letter should be prepared and presented to the bank official. Jeff had not prepared the necessary letters but the bank officials did not ask for anything.

A bank may ask for a service of a summons before permitting an examination of a taxpayer's accounts. "Thank goodness the officials didn't ask for a summons," thought Jeff. He knew that the Fourth and Fifth Amendments do not shield information voluntarily given by the taxpayer-depositor to his bank. Also, a taxpayer is not entitled to advance notice of the IRS's intention to examine the bank records. Between 1982 and 1993 agents were required to give a taxpayer at least 20 days written notice before examining third-party records. Because this law was so restrictive, it was changed in 1993.

Sometimes Jeff had to go through the bank records himself. That was a time-consuming, boring task. Often, investigative aides were used to go through tedious book records. When many banks' records were involved, Jeff often photographed the records. This could be accomplished with the use of a portable microfilmer. The managers of both banks seemed to be willing to prepare the appropriate schedules. They were willing to reproduce Onner's checks from their Recordak film. Jeff didn't complain.

Onner had a checking account at one bank and a savings account at another bank. Jeff asked the managers to prepare a schedule of Onner's transactions for the past three years. He left his business card, asking them to send the appropriate schedules to his Baltimore office.

At both banks Onner had a safe deposit box. Jeff asked for copies of the safe deposit boxes' access records, which show dates and times of entry along with the signature of the person entering the box. These dates and frequency of entries may be important, for they may coincide with the dates of deposits to or withdrawals from other accounts.

For many years the IRS could not enter a safe deposit box without getting the box holder's permission. An agent would have to contact the box holder and get his consent to inventory the contents of the box in the presence of the box holder. If the taxpayer objected, the agent could only write up a memorandum of the refusal.

But individual privacy bit the dust in 1977 in the Citibank case. The U.S. Court of Appeals in New York held that the IRS had the legal right to break open a taxpayer's safe deposit box in order to search for valuables *without giving the box holder the right to object*. Jeff wondered what was in the safe deposit boxes.

Banks are excellent sources of leads for Special Agents. Leads are often found in the Treasury Currency Reports made by banks to their Federal Reserve Bank. These TCR's may disclose large cash deposits and withdrawals. Banks get about 100,000 summons a year to provide customer records to the IRS.

Treasury Regulations prescribe certain bank record-keeping and reporting requirements. Regulations are four volumes of administrative interpretations prepared by the Treasury Department that explain the legislative Internal Revenue Code. Customers' identities must be maintained and checks must be microfilmed. Domestic cash transactions exceeding $10,000 and transportation of money exceeding $5,000 in or out of the U.S. must be reported.

In one situation Jeff became interested in a report of two deposits by a Report of Currency Transactions furnished by a Federal Reserve Bank. There were two bank deposits of $20,000 each in old, crumbled, tissue paper-thin one hundred dollar bills. The condition of the money suggested that it had been stored in an unusual place for a considerable period of time. Jeff caused a summons to be issued directing the bank to identify the owner or owners of the deposited money. Here the bank refused to provide the identity of the owner. In court the bank won. The Court said that a summons seeking the identity of a taxpayer, rather than details concerning an already identified taxpayer, was generally not enforceable under the Internal Revenue Code. The IRS does not always win.

But the IRS won in another situation. Another agent was investigating the possible income tax violation of an individual who had deposited $45,000 in deteriorated $100 bills into a Kentucky bank. The IRS issued a summons requiring the bank to provide the identity of the depositor. The bank refused to comply, but eventually the Supreme Court upheld the summons. The IRS got their man.

After eating a hamburger and drinking a milkshake at a Burger King, Jeff drove to Onner's townhouse. He observed the townhouse for about thirty minutes. He then telephoned Onner's number, but no one answered. He then walked through the private courtyard to Onner's door and rang the doorbell twice. He left.

Jeff watched the door for fifteen minutes more. He then returned and rang the doorbell again. When no one answered, he quickly picked the lock and entered through an atrium filled with plants. He pulled on some thin rubber gloves.

Jeff normally did not break and enter without a warrant. Anything he found would *not* be admissible in court. Besides, if discovered, he could be in trouble. But maybe he could locate some leads as to how Onner was getting his money.

As he entered the living room of the townhouse he noticed the natural wood beams on the ceiling; the door casing and woodwork were of natural wood also. The townhouse was furnished quite nicely. Several expensive-looking paintings were on the wall. There was an antique corn sheller on an old Singer sewing machine. On a coffee table were a *U.S. News & World Report*, a *Coin World* newspaper, *Consumer Reports*, *Hang Gliding*, and *Photoplay*. On the wall was an enlarged photograph of someone hang gliding.

In a bookcase Jeff noticed the book *How to Do Business Tax-Free: A Guide to Tax Havens*. Jeff rummaged through the letters and papers on a small desk and found the typical bills, a notice of the forthcoming meeting of the Martinsburg Coin Club, and a copy of a newsletter entitled "How to Cheat and Defraud the IRS" by I. M. Clever.

Jeff glanced at the first tax technique discussed in the newsletter. It dealt with silver coins. The author suggested that retailers might wish to sell their merchandise for dimes, quarters and half-dollars minted before 1965 with a 90% silver content. Such coins sell for more than twice their face value.

The article indicated that an Oklahoma Volkswagen dealer was offering the best deal anywhere featuring the popular new Rabbit with a price tag of only $4,720 — if paid for with these silver coins.

The car dealer would pay his wholesaler with fiat paper money for his car inventory. The dealer could avoid income taxes because his income is measured in silver coins at face value while his expenses are measured in fiat paper money. Jeff jumped when Onner's phone began to ring.

Jeff pulled out a small note pad and wrote down the name of the newsletter, the author, and mailing address. He could probably collect some "juice" if he could somehow get a list of the subscribers to this trash. He carefully replaced the note pad in its proper location.

As he put the newsletter back on the table he noticed an ad in the "classified" section:

Sue IRS Agents or other Governmental officials who violate your Civil Rights. To file a $25 suit without a lawyer send $30 to TPE, P.O. Box 2815, Turkey, N.C., 28393 for full information about affidavits, case law, etc.

Jeff felt a chill on his skin as he remembered that he had illegally broken into Onner's apartment. The phone stopped ringing and Jeff moved on into another room.

Jeff was impressed when he walked into one of the two bedrooms. There was an unmade king-size waterbed with mirrors on the ceiling and a bearskin rug on the floor. In the mirrors Jeff saw how funny he walked trying to avoid pain from his injury. He also made a mental note to lose a couple of pounds.

Jeff froze in his tracks when he heard a key enter a door lock. Luckily, it was the next door neighbor entering his townhouse.

Jeff got a light blue Kleenex from the bathroom and quickly moved to the front door. He took off his gloves and used the Kleenex to open the door. Quickly and carefully he went outside, pulling the door closed and wiping off the doorknob. A car drove into the parking lot as Jeff made his way towards his Chevrolet. Off he went with a jump start and a sigh of relief, thinking he would try to find a motel with an indoor swimming pool. Not likely in this town. "What do I want to eat tonight? Maybe I'll shoot some pool."

*　　*　　*

Richard Onner was flying like a bird. He was strapped in a harness fastened to a dacron sail. Richard had worked two Saturdays and today was his day off. He was defying gravity, flying without an airplane. He saw high, fast moving white clouds above his head.

Soaring like a bird, looking around at the earth, a thrill of excitement traveled through his body. Richard had been hang gliding since he was 15.

His rig of dacron was fitted with an aluminum and stainless steel frame which was thirty feet wide. His glider contained two hundred square feet of sail in its fifty pounds. A bird flew by as Richard made a right turn.

The chances of a hang gliding participant being injured are greater than those for any other sports participant. Hang gliding caused 81 deaths and 2,000 injuries between 1989–1991. Accidents are more common among experienced hang-gliders who fly higher, go farther, and take greater risks than novices.

Richard's father had been a glider. He was killed when a gusty wind blew him into a cliff in the hilly Vermont area. Most deaths and injuries were caused by pilot carelessness, flights during gusty winds, lack of preparation for landings, and tricky air turbulence.

Richard was very careful today. But he was unaware of the intruder who had entered, searched, and left his townhouse.

*　　*　　*

Jimmy Callaway was the Commissioner of the Internal Revenue Service. As the Commissioner, he reported to the Secretary of the Treasury. He was the boss of 92,000 employees, working in more than 1,200 offices. He was responsible for the administration of all tax laws.

The IRS receives about twenty-one million telephone calls and prepares about two million tax returns per year. It receives more than ten million tax returns in the month of March alone.

The IRS is only one of eleven sections within the Treasury Department. The IRS manual indicates the following purpose of the IRS:

... Encourage and achieve the highest possible degree of voluntary compliance with the tax laws and regulations and to maintain the highest degree of public confidence in the integrity and efficiency of the Service. This includes communicating the requirements of the

36

law to the public, determining the extent of compliance
and causes of non-compliance and cause all things need-
ful to a proper enforcement of the law.

There are seven Regional offices and fifty-eight district offices for carrying on the above lofty mission.

Each of the seven Regional offices is supervised by a Regional Commissioner. Each Regional office in turn supervises
the work of six to eleven district offices.

The Commissioner of the IRS is a political appointee.
Jimmy was the token Southerner in the current administration. He was a tall, boyish-looking man. His black hair was
slightly graying at the temples. A carbon copy of the perennial
politician.

Callaway was a product of the "yellow-dog" era in North
Carolina politics. The term "yellow-dog" was used to describe
the situation in the South whereby Southerners would vote
Democratic no matter who ran on the ticket. People would
pull the Democrat lever even if a yellow dog were the Democratic candidate.

Eisenhower and Nixon had changed some of the voting
habits of white Southerners. But Southerner Carter and his
born again campaign sweep of the South and Reagan's
Iranscam affair had solidified the Democratic grip on the South
for many years.

Callaway was born in Lizard Lick, North Carolina. A small
community in Wake County, it was named by a passing ob-
server who saw many lizards sunning and licking themselves
on a rail fence.

Being from a safe district, he became a powerful senator in
the North Carolina legislature. A shirt-sleeves campaigner, he
was as comfortable making the rounds of the political bar-
rooms as he was in the corporate boardrooms. He dominated
the Senate where few Republicans were allowed to enter. He
simply trampled down any opposition.

Although a Democrat, he was conservative. Callaway was
a cotton baron, a banker, and a businessman. He was an early

supporter of Carter and was rewarded with a middle-level position in Carter's administration. He hung on in Washington after Carter. He was later appointed Commissioner of the Internal Revenue Service by President Keeney. Callaway had the one requirement for the position: he was a lawyer. There had been only one non-lawyer to hold this position.

Callaway briefly skimmed the letter in front of him. He had an important meeting with Congressman Blackman.

Personal

Honorable Jimmy Callaway
Commissioner of Internal Revenue Service
1111 Constitution Avenue
Washington, D.C. 20220

Dear Commissioner Callaway:

Per IRS Directive #2031, I am reporting that Richard Onner, a computer employee with the IRS in Martinsburg, W.V., is under surveillance for possible income tax evasion. A net worth analysis indicates about $32,000 of unreported income per year.

I have asked Special Agent Jeff Burke (Baltimore) to help with this investigation.

Sincerely,

Jake Anderson
Internal Security Inspector

JA:ddt
cc: Jeff Burke

Commissioner Callaway left immediately for his meeting with Congressman Blackman. The Congressman was still a powerful legislator. Congressman Blackman was the Chairman of the important House Ways and Means Committee.

This Committee was the beginning of all tax laws. Even the President of the United States had to introduce tax laws through this Committee. This Committee controlled the inflow of *all* Federal revenues.

Although extremely powerful, the Chairman of the Ways and Means Committee had even more power until the late 1970s. This was the time when Fanny Foxe took her infamous swim in the Tidal Basin. This event destroyed the effectiveness of the then Congressman Wilbur Mills.

Congress stripped some of the power away from the Chairman of this Committee. The succeeding Chairmen, Congressmen Al Ullman, Dan Rostenkowski, and Congressman Blackman, never became quite the kingpin ex-Representative Wilbur Mills was.

What was the news report that he heard last week? Some ex-politicians had indicated that they had created a Politicians' Anonymous. Each time an ex-politician felt the urge to run for public office, he could dial a number and then P.A. would send over Fanny Foxe and they could jump into the Tidal Basin together.

His black limousine was waiting for him when he got downstairs. His personal chauffeur drove him to "the Hill." Yes, the "perks" had come back after Reagan.

CHAPTER 5

I don't suppose we will ever get to the point where people are pleased to pay taxes.

— Lyndon B. Johnson

Wednesday morning had been nonproductive for Jeff. He had driven over to see the "Martinsburg Computer Monster." The clean, clinical-looking buildings with the multi-level floors impressed Jeff. There were false floors under which there was vacant space filled with miles of electrical cords and other necessary equipment needed by the computers. This hidden space was kept at a cold 60° temperature. The temperature in the rooms was kept at a constant 76° with a 55% humidity.

Jeff talked to a friend and saw the organization and operation of the computer center. He had seen Richard Onner from afar, but had not talked to him and had not asked anyone about him.

During the uneventful drive back to Baltimore, Jeff decided that he would have to wait for the bank summaries to arrive. Maybe Jake Anderson could come up with something.

Jeff returned to Baltimore in time to meet Yvonne Talbert at 2:00 p.m. Yvonne had a round fat face and had a few gray hairs in her wavy brown hair. She was forty-fiveish.

"Hello, Yvonne," Jeff said as he interrupted Yvonne in deep thought. "What do you have for me today?"

Yvonne shifted in her chair and said enthusiastically. "Glad you came, Jeff. This is one you'll like. I believe I have it sewed up. Do you want a cold drink?" pointing to a small refrigerator in the corner.

"Nope. Trying to keep my weight down. Haven't had any decent exercise in about a week. You heard about my accident, didn't you?"

"Jeez, sounded bad. Getting any better?"

"Guess so," responded Jeff.

"Carl Strovee will be here at 3:00 p.m. I believe his representative is Henry Silverman, a public accountant. Silverman is a con artist. He's a cocky punk." Yvonne was noted for her bluntness.

Yvonne took a drink from a can of Coke and continued. "I audited Strovee's tax return last year. Couldn't find a dime. But I just knew he was ripping us off.

"I canvassed the banks here in Baltimore, but my bank deposit analysis of him did not show anything unusual. Then I read some biographical advertisement about him. He is from Valentine, Nebraska. I asked our Omaha office to check the banks in Valentine.

"Bingo! His retired mother has a bank account in Valentine, and he has been depositing money into her account. Using the bank deposit method, I added together all of his bank deposits, and deducted the gross income on his tax return. There was a big difference. In the past three years he has been hiding 35–45% of his gross income."

Yvonne paused, took a measured drink from her Coke, and then continued. "My supervisor is trying to get me to assess the tax with civil penalties and close the case. I wish you would make a preliminary examination. Until the criminal aspects are settled, will you be responsible for the direction taken by the investigation? I'm willing to keep it open. I believe we can nail him."

"Okay, but let's see what happens at the conference at three o'clock."

The Strovee case was following the typical scenario of a fraud investigation. A taxpayer submits his tax return to the IRS and it goes through the IRS computer. For one reason or another, the tax return is selected for audit. The higher the taxable income, the greater chance of an audit. Or perhaps the return is selected at random. Or the IRS might decide to concentrate on taxpayers in a particular profession.

For whatever the reason, the audit procedure starts when a taxpayer gets a letter from the IRS informing him that his return is to be examined and specifying whether the examination is an office or field audit. There are basically two types of office audits — a correspondence audit and an office interview audit. A correspondence audit is carried on by mail between the taxpayer and an office auditor. It is most often limited to the verification of minor items, whereas in an office interview audit the taxpayer is asked to bring his supporting records to an IRS office where he is interviewed by an Office Auditor. A field audit is used for business returns and complex individual returns. Here the Revenue Agent comes to the business premises to conduct the audit.

A Revenue Agent had suspected Carl Strovee of tax fraud. Yvonne Talbert had asked an Intelligence Officer in Omaha to check for possible bank accounts in Valentine. The Omaha office had found his mother's bank account.

With some incriminating evidence on hand, Yvonne still needed someone from the Intelligence Division to investigate the case. Jeff was being asked to continue the investigation.

Henry Silverman had encouraged Carl Strovee not to attend the conference at three o'clock. From experience Henry knew that the individuals sometimes become indignant and belligerent when their integrity and honesty were being questioned. Even worse, taxpayers sometimes have a severe attack of foot-in-mouth disease and provide too much information to the agents. Talking too much raised areas of examination that the agent was not even considering.

Henry knew that with an agent, you had to be friendly and answer the exact question asked. There was no reason to provide extra information which might complicate what might otherwise be a simple problem. Henry had never dealt with Yvonne Talbert. But he had heard that she was a "bird dog."

Carl had not heeded Henry's advice. He was going to attend the conference. Carl and Henry arrived at the same time and they walked together to Room 2001. Carl was very skinny, with bleached hair, wearing a diamond earring in his left ear.

Yvonne and Jeff were already in the room when Carl and Henry arrived. Yvonne walked over and closed the door which bore a bright blue "Do Not Disturb" sign.

Yvonne introduced herself to Henry and Carl. Yvonne then said, "Mr. Silverman and Mr. Strovee, I wish you to meet Jeff Burke."

Jeff shook hands with Silverman and Strovee and Jeff noticed that Strovee's hand trembled slightly. They all sat down at the conference table. Silverman's facial features were large and prominent. Strovee had some effeminate gestures.

Henry Silverman was the first to speak. "May I see your identification?" he asked in an imperious and confident manner.

Both Jeff and Yvonne nodded agreement and reached into their coat pockets for their identification. They knew that Henry was experienced and had asked the proper question.

Henry merely glanced at Yvonne's Revenue Agent card but he looked downcast when he saw Jeff's Special Agent badge. Henry now knew that this would be a tough encounter. Why did Carl have to show up?

"Gentlemen, I would like to talk to my client alone for a second," Henry said dryly. Henry walked over to the door. Although Carl looked surprised, he followed Henry out the door.

Once Carl had closed the door, Henry looked directly into Carl's eyes and said, "This Jeff Burke is a Special Agent. This means they suspect you of fraud. I wish you would leave and let me handle the meeting. If you stay, you'll make my job much more difficult."

Carl narrowed his eyes and said, "Look, I'm staying. I don't give a damn how difficult I make your job. I'm paying you enough money. I'm not going to let you sell me down the river. We're in this mess together; if I go down, you go too."

Henry knew that Carl was right. If Carl's boat sank, Henry would go to the bottom with him.

"Okay, but don't lie. If necessary, refuse to answer on the grounds that you may incriminate yourself. Remember the Fifth Amendment."

Henry shrugged, turned around, and went back into the room. Carl followed him, closed the door, and sat down.

Yvonne immediately asked for a Form 2848. Henry handed Yvonne a copy of the "Power of Attorney," signed by Carl, giving Henry the right to represent his client.

Yvonne had a Form 4700 Supplement in front of her which is often used by inexperienced office auditors. This form has many questions to ask the taxpayer, with a spot to check "yes" or "no" for each response from the taxpayer. But Jeff and Yvonne had decided not to go down this standardized list.

With the formalities aside, Yvonne spoke to Henry in a soft voice. "Could we see the back-up for the Section 1244 Stock?" Henry handed Yvonne the minutes page. Yvonne presented Henry a receipt for the sheet. "We wish to keep the minutes until next Wednesday."

"Is that necessary?" responded Henry in an angry tone.

"Yes, Mr. Silverman. You are aware that the election for Section 1244 stock must occur at the creation of the corporation."

"True, but the minutes were drafted in the first year," shot back Henry, as the pitch of his voice rose.

"Mr. Silverman, your client has failed to pay $47,554 of taxes over the past three years, including interest and penalties," Yvonne said softly. A fleeting smile came and left Yvonne's face.

Carl Strovee shouted, "What?" His eyes were blinking wildly.

Jeff knew that the blinking indicated the thinking and feeling process. A high rate of blinking is associated with thoughts that are disturbing or frustrating. Carl was clearly disturbed.

The meeting was not following the normal pattern. Agents

44

are instructed to establish a rapport with the taxpayer and his representative and in a friendly, affable manner to establish the confidence of the taxpayer. They should keep the conversation informal and easy. The objective of such a tactic is to elicit information about the taxpayer's family, gambling, vacations, acquisition of major assets, hobbies, and other expenditures to determine whether the taxpayer is living beyond his reported income.

A friendly approach may encourage the taxpayer and/or representative to answer more honestly since he does not know why the questions are asked. In theory the friendly approach gives the taxpayer a false sense of security and the agent may be able to get information that would not otherwise be revealed. Form 4822 is used by an agent to record the information gathered during the interview.

Yvonne did not respond to Carl's outburst. Agents are trained to ignore taxpayer anger and grumbling and remain polite.

For a moment he was uncomfortable, but Henry calmly responded, "I have prepared Mr. Strovee's tax returns for the past five years. You must be mistaken. Carl could not owe that much money. How did you come up with such a figure?"

With a smile of triumph on her face Yvonne responded, "Our bank deposits analysis indicated that Mr. Strover has not been reporting about 35–40% of his income per year." Yvonne withdrew the Strovee calculations and bank documents from a manila folder on the conference table.

In a combative voice, Henry said, "It's Mr. Strovee, not Strover!" At the same time he looked questioningly toward Carl Strovee. Henry had clearly told Carl *not* to deposit the unreported receipts into his bank account.

In a low voice Carl replied, "I do not believe I owe such a deficiency. My bank records will verify that I have reported all of my income."

Trying to hold back her smile, Yvonne asked, "But what about your mother's bank accounts in Valentine?" Yvonne held up the confirmation letter from the Valentine bank. For a few seconds the only sound in the room was from the overhead fan.

There was a sinking feeling in the bottom of Carl's stomach. Those IRS gumshoes had found his secret Valentine accounts.

From the look on Carl's face, Henry guessed what Carl had been doing. He immediately stood up. "Carl, it is time for us to leave. We need a lawyer," he said acidly.

Carl slowly got up. His eyes were no longer blinking. His thoughts were turned inward. Why had he done such a stupid thing — putting the deposits in the Valentine account.

Yvonne interrupted Carl's thoughts. "I want you to prepare me a statement of net worth for the past five years. Could you get this information to me by next Wednesday?"

Carl nodded.

But Yvonne had still another surprise for Mr. Silverman. Yvonne handed Henry an official piece of paper. It was an IRS summons signed by Jeff Burke.

The summons required Henry Silverman to appear the next Wednesday at the same time and place and to produce his working papers and other records relating to Carl Strovee and to give oral testimony. "Mr. Silverman, would you sign this Certificate of Service of Summons? It merely means that you have received the Summons," Yvonne explained. Henry signed the certificate.

Suddenly Henry Silverman had a headache. He remembered that he had in his possession a copy of the true income of Carl. *Jeez, I should have given those records to Carl before today's meeting. I need to work under an attorney's umbrella of privilege.*

The Fifth Amendment to the Constitution provides that "No person . . . shall be compelled to be a witness against himself." This privilege includes the right to refuse to surrender one's *personal* records which one feels will tend to incriminate him. But this Fifth Amendment privilege does not extend to records of an accountant which might incriminate another taxpayer.

Henry knew that although the summons was issued by an administrative agency, the summons is similar to the investigative-type of grand jury subpoena. Thus, if Henry did not honor the summons, the court could arrest and punish him with a jail sentence or a fine for contempt.

Both Henry and Carl left immediately. Outside Henry tried to explain to Carl that if a taxpayer disagrees with the initial audit by a Revenue Agent, he may protest any deficiency with an Appeals Officer. "Discussions with the Appeals Officer can solve many conflicts. Look, dealings with the IRS are a 'cat-and-mouse' game, with compromises possible at all levels within the IRS and even on the court house steps.

"Where no solution is agreed upon with the IRS, a taxpayer has three appeal choices when a 'notice of deficiency' or '90-day letter' is issued. You can pay the deficiency and after denial of claim for refund, file an action in the District Court, where a jury trial is possible, or Claims Court, which is in Washington, D.C. Likewise, you can refuse to pay the tax and file a petition with the Tax Court — the poor man's court."

Carl broke in, saying, "I should have listened to one of my friends' advice."

"What's that?"

"He said that I should have my tax return prepared by a CPA. The chances of an audit are much higher if a return is personally prepared or is by a non-professional tax preparer."

"I'm a professional!" shot back Henry.

"But you're not a CPA."

Henry just shook his head and replied coldly, "Keep your mouth shut and find a good lawyer." Henry knew that Carl's financial affairs were in the IRS's vise, with the handle slowly being turned. However, Carl was not the only famous person to have trouble with the IRS.

In fact, Carl was in "good" company. Al Capone could only be sent to jail for income tax evasion. While Vice-President,

Agnew pleaded *nolo contendere* to income tax evasion. Representative Adam Clayton Powell was indicted for income tax evasion. Bobby Baker, a protege of Lyndon Johnson, was convicted of evading taxes. And Joe Lewis, the famous "Brown Bomber," had problems with the IRS throughout his fighting career. Remember Jerry Lee Lewis' tax problems.

Even after Jimmy Hoffa disappeared, he was not forgotten by the IRS. The IRS claimed he owed $40,000 of back taxes, and they went after his widow.

After Duke Ellington died in 1974, the IRS claimed that his estate owed $1.4 million for taxes and penalties for 1967–1973. The IRS disallowed big deductions for travel, clothing and other business expenses. Also, the IRS alleged that the musician did not report certain income from television appearances.

Many people do not realize it, but even illegal income is taxable. A "smart" crook should report illegal income, maybe under the category of miscellaneous income.

The IRS never forgets. For example, a skyjacker vanished somewhere between Seattle and Reno in 1971. By 1976, Dan Cooper, the skyjacker, owed the IRS $218,635 in taxes on the money he extorted. The IRS calculated his tax assuming he was alive, single, and never filed a return on the money. He owed $123,090 plus a fifty percent civil fraud penalty because he intended to cheat the government out of his share of the extortion money. Interest at seven percent a year is $34,000, for a total tax burden of $218,635 from the illegal income.

Jeff was in a good mood when he got back to his office and sat down at his desk. In the center of his desk was a plain envelope addressed "To Super Jock." Jeff removed a card from the envelope. On the front was

"This card was designed for a typical,
well-adjusted Normal Human Being."

Inside in black letters was

"But we bought it for you anyway! Get well."

Jeff chuckled as he read the comments written by members of his softball team:

Get Well Soon! *TKM*	You're not normal. *Jim*	I think it may help! *Bud*
Who needs sex? *Hank*	Watch out for the rebound. *Joe*	Join a glee club. *Harold*
Why the shorter steps? *Steve*	Better visit the sporting goods store. *Mike*	Next time move faster. *Jeff*

The team didn't win many softball games, but they had a good sense of humor. Jeff wondered if they had won Monday night. Jeff wrote on his "to do" list to go by the sporting goods store and purchase a "steel jock."

On the way home Jeff was again disappointed. His search of the Flesher garbage dumpster resulted in only one broken mouse trap and a torn sex novel — *See Mary Run.*

CHAPTER 6

In levying taxes and in shearing sheep, it is well to stop
when you get down to the skin.

— Austin O'Malley

Wednesday morning at 8:00 Jeff was again watching the brownstone house. He and another agent were waiting for Rob Fowler to emerge and drive off in his tan Plymouth.

Hank Brown, his companion, was wearily sipping coffee. He was trying to awake for what would be the ensuing chase through Baltimore. Hank's grim humor and his slightly balding head made him a perfect IRS sleuth. Hank was in his early thirties, and he had been with the IRS for ten years. He liked to carry his .357 Colt Python. Hank was divorced with one child who lived with his ex-wife in Alabama. Hank liked to drink beer at a joint near the IRS office, which reminded him of his hometown, Selma.

Hank played first base on Jeff's softball team. He hit a lot of home runs, but he had a short temper. He constantly argued with the umpires.

In the game in which Jeff was hurt, Hank had been thrown out of the ballgame in the second inning. A batter had hit a ground ball to the third baseman. The throw to Hank at first base had pulled him toward home plate. The running batter had brushed Hank's left leg as he passed in the baseline.

Hank got angry. He turned around and threw the softball at the runner. The softball hit the runner in the small of his back. The force of the ball sent the runner spread-eagle along the foul line.

The female base umpire raced over and shouted, "Out, you're out of the game. Get out," she shouted, pointing at Hank. "You're an animal."

"Look, blindy," pointing to his left leg, "he deliberately clipped me."

The umpire pointed toward the dugout, and shouted back with eyes blazing, "You are out of the game!" She turned and walked away. Hank did not follow her.

Hank interrupted Jeff's thoughts. "We should award Rob a CMA certificate — an official member of the Certified Maniac Association."

But today was *the* day. In Jeff's pocket was an official search warrant approved by a U.S. Magistrate. Even if they lost Rob today, they would be back to search his house.

Rob, wearing a blue silk shirt, emerged at 8:21 a.m. with his companion. They entered the tan car and drove off. The tan car stopped at the plumbing outlet, and he gave her a peck on the cheek before she walked into the shop. So far Rob had only run one stoplight.

Out to the rain-slick Beltway the tan car went. Rob was taking the same route he had taken so many times. The traffic was heavy. Hank kept his car close to Rob, not really worrying that they would be spotted. They had their search warrant today.

Rob's driving was a little better today because of the wet conditions. Hank was able to follow him for about eight miles down the Beltway. All of a sudden there were two tan Plymouths ahead. This had happened before. Two or three identical cars would appear ahead of them. They would eventually follow the wrong car.

Today was different. They followed Rob down an exit ramp from the Beltway. He entered a dirty, one-way street. Going the wrong way. Two cars shot past, occupied by startled drivers.

Rob almost hit a light blue station wagon, but it swerved at the last moment. Hank was not so lucky. This same station wagon sideswiped Hank. Grinding shrieks of metal against metal filled the morning air.

Hank shouted, "You jerk!" and sped off after the tan car. The fenders rattled and the wheels shimmied as Hank gunned his Ford. Jeff closed his eyes and let the vibrating valves and rushing wind numb his fears.

Lady Luck had changed today. With a squeaking and groaning engine, Hank and Jeff were able to follow Rob. Rob parked at a moderately expensive apartment complex. He entered one of the apartments. A young girl greeted him at the door in a nightgown.

Jeff and Hank watched the apartment all morning. It was chilly, but the sun was shining. Nothing happened. Suddenly Hank pointed. "There's the third one this morning!" Jeff knew what Hank was talking about. Hank had the habit of counting and pointing out people who were picking their nose in their car. People forget while they are in their cars that other drivers can see what they are doing.

At 12:30 p.m. Hank walked over to the local "greasy spoon" and brought back some Cokes and several hamburgers.

Half-way through his hamburger Hank asked, "Did you ever catch flies with your hands when you were a kid?"

"Catch flies?"

"I got to be the champion on my block. There's a secret to catching flies. You wait until he lands on a flat surface. You then cup your hand like this." Hank cupped his hand in the shape of a U with his fingers together.

"Now you slowly put your hand about two feet in front of the fly — not in back of him. It's important that you are bold and not try to sneak up on him. You grab for him. Now he's going to fly, but if you are fast enough, he'll fly right into your hand."

"What do you do with him?"

"You throw him very hard against a hard surface. That'll

kill him. I wonder if I could patent my hand?" Hank grinned as he admired his hand.

"Do you want my hamburger?"

At about 1:30 p.m. Rob and the young slender girl came out and went swimming in the blue-green-colored apartment pool. There was a fine mist rising from the heated pool. The young girl had on a bikini. Rob had on a wild, multi-colored swimming suit.

Jeff wrote down the address and apartment number. "Why don't we go back and check out his house now? I believe he'll be occupied for a while. Maybe we'll find something in his house that'll blow this clown out of the water."

Hank drove back toward Rob's brownstone and parked about a block from his entrance. "Not a good neighborhood for two white snoopers," Hank exclaimed. They watched the house for a few minutes. Then they walked up and knocked on the door. Several curious blacks walked past them.

No one answered. Jeff picked the lock and they quickly entered. There is no Fifth Amendment prohibition in a tax case against a use of a search warrant in order to obtain incriminating records.

Jeff and Hank systematically searched the house. Jeff was the first one to find anything.

"Hank, here's some slip paper. It's flash paper." Slip paper is the slips upon which the taker of the bets writes down the name of the bettor and the amount of the bet. It's flash paper so that in case of a raid, the slips can be set afire and they will burn rapidly, leaving no evidence.

"They must be involved in a bookmaking operation. That surprises me. Blacks are normally in the numbers racket. Honkies normally control bookmaking operations," Hank responded with a hint of a smile. Hank was from Alabama.

A bookmaking operation is centered around some sporting event, whereas the numbers racket involves the selection of a random number.

Numbers operations use different ways of picking a winner.

The last three digits in the daily "take" at a nearby race track could be the mechanism for picking the winner.

Some numbers rackets use the Federal Reserve Notes to select the winner. The number of Federal Reserve Notes printed per day is published in the next day's paper. The last three digits in the published amount is the winner for the previous day.

Both Jeff and Hank continued to search the house. Jeff heard Hank mumbling something. Jeff walked into the bedroom.

Hank was sitting in a chair in front of Rob's dresser. He was saying, "And this one is for running the stoplight! This one is for going the wrong way on the one-way street! This one is for wrecking my car!"

Hank had found a gross of multi-colored condoms. He was putting a small hole with a pin in each of the condoms. Hank looked up when Jeff entered. "That turkey is certainly not using these on his old lady. He must be shacking up with that young girl. I hope he gets AIDS!"

They found nothing else of significance in the house. The search had been a snipe hunt. A few pieces of paper would hardly convince a hard-nosed judge.

Jeff and Hank drove back to the apartment. Rob's tan car was still parked in front of the apartment house.

They waited. It was not quite as cold as it was earlier. They played several games of "21."

Rob exited from the apartment door around 5:30 p.m. He drove back to the plumbing outlet and picked up his old lady, and they stopped at a local fish joint and ate.

While watching them eat, Jeff said, "You know, she may be running the gambling racket out of the plumbing outlet. Rob may not be a runner. He may just be a gigolo."

They were both quiet for a while as they watched them eat. Finally Hank responded, "I'll find out who owns the plumbing outfit. Can you put a pen register on their phone?" Hank knew that Jeff had a telephone company friend who sometimes did some moonlighting for him.

They followed Rob home and then they went back to IRS headquarters. There was a note on Jeff's desk to call Jake Anderson at his home. Jeff dialed Jake's home number. One of his kids answered the phone. Jake was cutting some firewood.

After a short while, an out-of-breath "Hello" sounded at the other end.

"Hi, Jake, this is Jeff Burke. You're going to have a heart attack cutting wood."

"It will be my wife's fault. She likes to use the fireplace. It lets more heat out of the chimney than it produces. The reason I called is that I have some information concerning Richard Onner."

After a short pause to yell at one of his kids, Jake continued. "My supervisor is on me again."

"What is he hassling you about now?"

"He wants me to forget about Onner."

"Forget about Onner?" Jeff asked in surprise.

"Yeah, he claims our case production has fallen off and doesn't want us getting involved in anything that can't be closed quickly."

"Those damn supervisors. They don't care about quality. All they want are the numbers. . ."

"You are right," replied Jake. "Would you meet me outside the office? I have to be near the British embassy tomorrow. Can you meet me at the north end of the parking lot at the Rock Creek Park around 4:00 p.m.?"

"Sure, see you there."

Jeff then called his friend who was a telephone repairman and asked him to bring a pen register and to meet him in front of the plumbing outlet at 9:00 that evening.

After eating some dinner, Jeff made his nightly unenthusiastic visit to the Flesher dumpster. Tonight was more productive. He found a stained five dollar bill in the pocket of a discarded green shirt.

Jeff arrived at the plumbing outlet five minutes early and parked two blocks away. By the time he had strolled back to the building with his hands thrust deeply into his coat pockets, his friend was waiting with his tool box near the building.

They walked around back and found the lead-in wire for the telephones inside the building. Within a short period of time, a pen register was attached to the appropriate wire.

The device would merely count the number of phone calls received by the phones in the building. A pen register was illegal without a court order. Any evidence gathered from this source could not be used in court. But if the plumbing outlet was receiving a large number of phone calls, this fact would help them decide whether to continue their investigation of Rob and his old lady. Bookies use the phone often in a book-making operation.

Jeff did not mind breaking the law a little bit when he was dealing with organized crime. The major source of revenues for organized crime was from illegal gambling. The second and third sources of revenue were loansharking and narcotics. Jeff hoped he would be able to shut down the gambling racket in Baltimore.

Since 1960 the IRS had worked closely with the Justice Department to stop the menacing tentacles of organized crime. Jeff had been assigned to several Justice Department "strike forces" in past years. Jeff knew the extent to which organized crime had infiltrated legitimate businesses. The Gambino Maria family is reputed to own control of the pizzeria industry in many areas of the East. This family is monopolizing the manufacture of mozzarella cheese. Such information was mind-boggling to the average citizen. Also, organized crime had even penetrated the Federal government; gambling, prostitution and bribery had been found by the FBI in the Interstate Commerce Commission, the Department of Housing and Urban Development, and Congress.

There is a nationwide alliance of at least twenty-four tightly-knit Mafia families which control organized crime in the United States. Their members are reputed to be Italians and Sicilians or of Italian or Sicilian descent. These families are linked together by agreements, and they obey a nine-member commission. This Mafia has infiltrated many legitimate businesses and labor unions. These liaisons give them power over officials at all levels of government.

Most large city gambling is operated or controlled by organized crime members. The numbers racket can best be described as a pyramid:

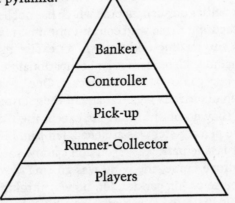

The player is not really a part of the organization, but starts the action by placing a bet with the first member of the organization — the runner or collector.

The runner works at locations that change from time to time, depending upon police operations. The runner may receive as much as twenty-five percent commission on the gross "play" for the day. Further, in some areas the runner may withhold up to ten percent of the winnings as a tip for himself.

Next in line is the pick-up. His function is to collect the day's "play" from the runner and transfer it either to the bank or to a "drop" where other pick-up men leave their day's "play." From the "drop" the money is moved to the bank. These pick-up men may work on a straight salary basis which depends upon the locale or the volume of business.

The controller is next in line. He is the boss. He hires or fires employees, operates the office, and settles disputes between players and runners. His take may be as high as thirty-five percent of the gross from which he pays the runners about twenty-five percent and the pick-up men's salary.

The head master is the banker. He furnishes the capital for the operation and he generally receives an accounting for his profits on a weekly basis. Since he is high up in the organized crime business, his name is protected.

Jeff's job, like the other Special Agents, was to disrupt the illegal gambling by drastically reducing the profits by collecting taxes and penalties on such income which has not been reported and by prosecuting those who commit criminal tax violations. Aside from the income tax, there is an excise tax of 2% on wagering income. Also, there is an occupational tax of $500 on all persons engaged in accepting wagers. One problem is that a large group of citizens regard many of these crimes as minor vices since they do not hurt anyone except the IRS.

Once the pen register was attached, Jeff paid his friend fifty dollars. His last remark was "You don't know me."

As Jeff drove home, the wind was gusting over Baltimore. As he got close to his parking lot, he was thinking about the number of unanswered questions about his case.

CHAPTER 7

In our free enterprise system, the primary goal is to make money. The Intelligence Division has been concerned with how that money was made, what happened to it, and who got what.

— Hank Messick

A person poured nine ounces of methanol mixed with nitromethane and twenty-five percent castor oil into the gas tank of the model airplane. The castor oil is used as a lubricant because it doesn't burn like petroleum oil. The methanol-nitromethane mix is similar to the fuel used in the fast race cars.

The red, white, and blue biplane had a five-foot wingspread and was powered by a six cubic inch displacement Japanese-made engine. The model plane was made of balsa wood, covered with silk. "Snoopy," a white beagle wearing a yellow hat, sat in the cockpit.

The model plane was controlled with a radio transmitter on the ground. The controls on the radio transmitter are basically identical to the controls in an actual airplane. Channels control the throttle, rudder, elevators, and ailerons. Model airplanes may fly as fast as two hundred miles per hour.

Once in the air the plane spun and turned, looped and dipped. In the air the plane took on a different perspective. Although the model plane could only reach a top altitude of three hundred feet, it looked like a full sized airplane flying at three thousand feet.

Buzz-zz-zz. Buzz-zz-zz. Around and around the plane flew. The performance of the plane would have thrilled any of the 280,000 members of the Academy of Model Aeronautics.

*   *   *

Jeff had followed Rob again this morning. He followed him on the Beltway but lost him. He drove over to the apartment and Rob's car was parked there. Around 11:30 a.m. Rob and his girlfriend came outside to swim. Jeff went back to his cluttered office. In the corner on his coat rack was a wrinkled red tie and his temporarily retired Sentry Superstars softball cap.

The morning mail brought the information about Onner's bank deposits from his two Martinsburg's bank accounts. Jeff prepared a bank deposit analysis on Onner. As he had suspected, this analysis did not disclose any unreported income.

Jeff did notice that the bank symbols "EC" appeared twice on the bank statements. This symbol indicates an Exchange Charge for converting foreign currency into U.S. dollars, or a charge for a cable or transmittal costs. Jeff needed to determine the source of such foreign monies in order to determine its taxability.

Jeff knew that some U.S. taxpayers obtain a Canadian bank account which is payable in U.S. dollars. Such a technique circumvents the Supreme Court's ruling that a bank owns the depositor's records, and a bank is required to release such records to the IRS at any time without warrant. For accounts the taxpayer does not wish the IRS to know about, he avoids his U.S. bank account. He can buy money orders from many different places and pay such accounts.

Also, Onner was using the safe deposit boxes regularly. For the three-year period, Onner had entered one or the other box approximately once a week, normally on Monday. This factor may or may not be significant. The Federal Reserve Bank of Boston has estimated that Americans hoard more than $50 billion in cash, with forty percent of this figure in hundred dollar bills. Most hoards are under one thousand dollars.

There was some good news. His supervisor indicated that a U.S. District Court dismissed a couple's claim against Jeff and another Revenue Agent. The couple had asserted that Jeff and the other agent overassessed them due to their personal dislike of them. The judge ordered the couple to pay the legal costs for Jeff and the other agent. "Now there's a good judge," Jeff smiled ruefully, when he heard the news.

Next, Jeff went through the newspaper clippings accumulated by his secretary and administrative aide. They clipped articles from several papers which might indicate lavish spenders or unreported wealth. A lavish wedding party, an individual appearing on a television quiz show, jewelry on the wife of a prominent citizen, a couple embarking on an expensive vacation, a reported theft of a large sum of money, a sale of a valuable piece of property or other items in the local paper may lead to a fraud investigation. Today's clippings were not promising. The clippings of several marriages of well-to-do families and announcements of two store openings were thrown in his special round receptacle.

Jeff made several notes in order to follow up on one item. A private citizen had found ten thousand dollars buried in a vacant lot on the West Side of Baltimore. An internal memo was written to check next year to see if this citizen reported the income. Yes, even money that is found is taxable. Also, Jeff would check with the police in several weeks to see if anyone claimed the money. He would also check on the owner of the vacant lot.

One other item showed some promise. In the obituary column was a notice that Albert D'Estang had died. D'Estang was suspected by many to be a member of organized crime. Jeff filled out Form 4298, Audit Requisition and Information Report, which is used by an agent when he uncovers information or leads relating to estate or gift tax filing requirements. The purpose of the form is to inform district personnel to examine the underground figure. Only with cooperation between Revenue Agents and Estate Tax Examiners will individual income tax returns of an organized crime subject, together with any estate tax return, be subjected to a coordinated in-depth examination. The operation of organized crime was highly vulnerable with the death of a major figure.

Hunches and newspaper reports often lead to conviction. The story is told to young agents about one particular conviction. Apparently a supervisor of a Fraud Squad found things to be slack. The supervisor picked the names of ten pharmacists from the telephone directory and sent out agents at random to audit their returns. One of the taxpayers ended up in a criminal case.

With his paperwork under control and several telephone messages returned, Jeff left his office in order to meet Jake at Rock Creek Park. On the way to the parking lot, Jeff stopped at the "Check This" bulletin board. One bulletin board had been set aside for humorous and sometimes profane letters and responses from taxpayers. Jeff's favorite was a letter in which a taxpayer had sent one turnip, giving the IRS any blood that could be squeezed from the turnip. Still on the bulletin board was a Form 1040 covered with red spots. Typed at the bottom of the form was the following caption:

"I have nothing left. Here is some blood. I hope you are satisfied!"

Aside from the usual obscenities, taxpayers were continually sending in fake forms with such signatures such as Mickey Mouse, Benedict Arnold, Son of Sam, Al Capone, I. M. Ripoff, John Wilkes Booth, and I. No Pay. Often these anonymous jokers included play money.

Jeff had read in the paper several days ago about a university student who filed a lawsuit in defense of his right to scribble comments on the envelopes in which he mailed his monthly utility payment. The student indicated that he included the obscenities on the envelope in order to ridicule, express scorn for and encourage public awareness of the unreasonable, unjust and unfair profit structure of the utility company. Jeff was sure that the IRS received more obscenities than any other organization.

One agent in the Baltimore office had been subjected to

some unusual cruelty by a practical joker last year. For one week an anonymous prankster deluged the agent with visitors and items he did not ask for — a piano, a burial vault, plumbers, carpet installers, an ambulance crew responding to a false report of a heart attack, and a 65th birthday-retirement party. A load of manure was unceremoniously dumped on his driveway. The parade of workers at the agent's home and office included a pest exterminator who said he was told "there was a lot of rats up here on this floor."

Obviously IRS agents are not the most popular people around. One former IRS Commissioner indicated that "on the whole the IRS has taken its lumps stoically, knowing full well that this is the lot of the tax collector. Indeed, the Bible offers cases of tax collectors being stoned to death, so in this light we are not doing too badly. Jesus did befriend Zacchaeus, the chief tax collector, after he climbed a sycamore tree."

During Jeff's second year as an IRS Agent a self-employed truck driver had unleashed his German shepherd and allowed it to attack Jeff. The damage: 26 stitches on Jeff's left arm and 12 stitches on his right leg.

The truck driver was arrested and released on a $2,500 personal recognizance bond. The felonious assault charge carried a maximum penalty of $5,000 and three years in prison. Apparently the judge did not like IRS agents either. The truck driver was fined $1,000 and put on a one-year suspended jail sentence.

Jeff noticed a new addition to the bulletin board today. A taxpayer had sent in a small bag of hair with the following cryptic message:

I am pleased to enclose the hair which I tore from my head while trying to fill out my W-4 Form. Would someone try to simplify this form before I become bald?

Chuckling as he went to the parking lot, Jeff got into his car. Jeff drove towards Washington to meet Jake at Rock Creek Park. The CB chatter was hot and heavy today. Smokey the Bear was out trying to collect his dinner money.

Jeff had bought his CB to break the monotony and alert him to traffic snarls. Radar detectors were illegal in Virginia and D.C., so his Escort was in the trunk. However, today he avoided two "bear bites" by slowing down after being alerted by two anonymous CBers. The first warning was humorous:

"Smile and comb your hair. There's a Smokey in the grass by the airport exit, and he's taking pictures."

Jeff immediately slowed to "double nickels." Jeff's handle was "Super Snooper," compliments of a previous girlfriend.

Both Jake and Jeff drove into the parking lot at Rock Creek Park at about the same time. Jeff walked over to Jake's car and said, "Why don't we walk in the park?" Jake was fidgeting with his pipe.

Once they were walking Jake began talking. "As I mentioned, my supervisor wants me to cool it with Onner. But I did get one more piece of information. Some time ago the Washington office was concerned about the use of secret Swiss bank accounts by U.S. tax evaders. You may remember this caper. But the Swiss banks sent the account holders their bank statements in plain envelopes. Several agents wrote the Swiss banks about opening accounts and noted the postal meter numbers on the replies.

Buzz-zz-zz. Jake paused as he looked at the model plane flying to their left.

"Anyway, the IRS used high-speed copiers at several large post offices to copy fronts of all airmail letters arriving from Switzerland in plain envelopes. Next these letters were checked against the banks' meter numbers. A list of several thousand probable account holders was compiled. I went through the list and found Onner's name. Richard Onner has a Swiss bank account," Jake almost shouted.

They had walked up to a small stream. There was a long pause as Jake filled his pipe and lit it. They turned around and began walking toward the parking lot. Buzz-zz-zz. The plane was still flying.

Jeff seemed reflective. Finally he said, "Well, I prepared a bank deposit analysis on him and he was okay. If he does have a Swiss bank account, he must have a great deal of unreported income. Do you have any theories on how he is getting the money?"

"Nope." Jake frowned slightly. "He is not dealing directly with taxpayers. Could he be screwing around with the computer programs? Maybe he is eliminating taxpayers from the master files for a fee."

An IRS agent dealing with taxpayers was in a better position to extort payoffs than someone like Onner. An agent can subject taxpayers to illegal surveillance and investigation in order to obtain payoffs or blackmail money. There had been situations of illegal payoffs or blackmail by agents. Such situations were, of course, in violation of federal income tax laws.

Jeff thought the model plane was close. He looked to his right in time to see the plane coming directly at them. "Watch out!" he shouted.

At the same time Jeff dove for the shelter of a large rock. Crash! The plane hit Jake on his right side. Jeff heard Jake's agonizing scream. The impact was so forceful that it drove the shaft of the plane through the body's main organs. Then there was a loud explosion.

Jeff was in a long eerie tunnel filled with light. He felt himself leaving his body. Jeff was floating above the park watching the pandemonium unfold below.

He saw two bodies lying on the ground. His body was lying behind a large rock. Jake's distorted body was still. Jake's body was black from an explosion. Blood and methanol nitromethane were flowing freely on the ground. His pipe was broken into two pieces, lying about 15 feet from his lifeless mesh of body and plane.

Two ambulances arrived. Jeff watched his body being placed on a stretcher and slid into the first ambulance. Jake's body was placed into the second ambulance.

Jeff awoke from his nightmare world hearing the sound of a loud siren. At the hospital the doctor in the emergency room decided that Jeff only had a mild concussion. This discovery did not help the ringing in his ears or the soreness in his right shoulder where he had hit the ground.

CHAPTER 8

What always happens — what has happened in every nation that has ever set up a graduated income tax — is that the highest actual rates are paid by the middle class.
                                    — from "The April Game"

Jeff learned that Jake was pronounced dead on arrival at the hospital.

Jeff spent the night in the hospital and was released the next morning. He was lucky. The rock had shielded him from the blast but his ears were still ringing. The dive behind the rock had not helped his prior injury.

The investigating detective came to the hospital Friday. He told Jeff that after the impact of the model plane, there had been an explosion. A plastic explosive device had been taped to the plane. A radio transmitter on the ground had ignited the device.

The detective had been unable to get a description of the operator of the model plane. The operator had disappeared immediately after the explosion. But a strand of blonde hair was found in a crack in a piece of the destroyed model plane.

Jeff had a blank listlessness on Friday and Saturday. He did go to Jake's wake Saturday morning. He stayed only about 20 minutes. It was depressing. What could he say to Jake's wife and his children?

He did see Jake's supervisor at the wake, and asked him to send him a list of Jake's informers. In case of an accident or suspicious death, a group supervisor is allowed to check the informers of an agent. The group supervisor indicated that he would send Jeff a list of these people.

Jeff intended to check out each of these individuals. One of these individuals may have a clue to Jake's killer. Or one of them might be the killer.

While in the hospital Jeff had gone through several Baltimore and Washington newspapers. Jeff noted that there was a regional meeting of the Academy of Model Aeronautics at the Washington Hilton next Friday and Saturday. The person who killed Jake might be attending this meeting.

After lunch on the next Friday, Jeff was at the Hilton. The lobby was filled with people with AMA name tags. Here and there were some Hilton employees with their "We Care" buttons.

Ironically, the lobby was also filled with CPAs. IRS agents and CPAs were natural adversaries. There are more than 300,000 CPAs, most of whom belong to the AICPA. Bob Newhart started out as an accountant, and Milton Mostel (elder brother of Zero Mostel) is a sole practitioner. The chief executive of Chrysler is a CPA. The conservative and secretive society of CPAs was holding their annual convention and vacation in Washington.

Jeff obtained a list of the people who registered for the AMA convention. Even though this was a Northeast regional meeting of the AMA there were a number of individuals from states outside the Northeast.

For a glimpse at his "Special Agent" card with the eagle and the wording "Special Agent, U.S. Treasury, Internal Revenue Service, Intelligence," Jeff easily obtained a free name tag from the lady registering members.

Hi, I'm

Jeff Burke

Academy of Model Aeronautics

A faint smile flickered on her face when he told her that he was checking up on the AICPA group. He asked for her cooperation and silence. Even without looking at the name tags on the people in the hotel, Jeff could tell who were accountants and who were AMA members. The accountants were dressed in their dark, pinstriped suits, and the AMA members were dressed in more casual attire.

Social organizations, non-profit country clubs, and similar social clubs are generally not taxable. Exemption from taxation is granted to such organizations if they are organized and operated for pleasure, recreation and other non-profit purposes. But the net earnings of the organization must not inure to the benefit of any private stockholder or member. Also, the corporate income tax is imposed upon any unrelated business income of exempt organizations. So Jeff could have been legitimately checking on either of the social organizations.

Jeff milled around the hotel lobby for a while and drifted in and out of several lectures on aeronautics on the mezzanine level. Most of the model airplane devotees were glued to their seats, attentive to each word from the speaker's lips.

The largest group was in the Presidential Ballroom. Jeff walked into the room and sat down in the no smoking section under a magnificent chandelier. The foil-colored wallpaper was covered with what looked to be either Christmas wreaths or snowflakes. Along the top of the wall were eagles holding a shield, an olive branch, and an arrow. There were stars around the edges of the ceiling on gold velvet. On the front wall were several large smudge-free bright mirrors.

The podium at the front had Capital Hilton written on it, with a picture of the top of the Capitol. A rangy, rawboned man was behind the podium starting to talk about radio controlled helicopters.

"Remember, airplanes want to fly, helicopters don't."

That's a profound statement, Jeff thought.

"You must do eight different things all at the same time," continued the speaker.

Jeff got up and left. He was tempted to tell the speaker to buy an octopus to fly the helicopter.

Once outside the Presidential Ballroom Jeff thought, "Maybe I should go to some of the CPA's lectures and learn the latest tax avoidance schemes." Feeling at loose ends, Jeff went into the Rogue's Manor, a small lounge inside the hotel. Jeff sat down at a small table and ordered a Bloody Mary. Jeff thought, "How do you find a killer when your only piece of evidence is one strand of hair?"

"Hi, Jeff," came an intriguing voice from the table next to him. "So this is how you miss all of those boring lectures," her voice continued in pleasant tones.

A strawberry blonde encased in a navy suit with a white blouse was smiling at him. She was in her late thirties.

Jeff gulped and responded, "Hello. How are you?" As soon as the words were out, Jeff knew that his response was not very original. He did not recognize the speaker.

"I read your name tag. I was bored myself with the speakers. Hope you don't mind me being so bold. May I join you?"

"Sure," mumbled Jeff. Jeff read her name tag, Deidre Moore, as she moved to his table.

"Are you a model airplane nut?" Jeff asked, smiling.

"Yes, for about four years. I went through the typical housewife vocations: bridge club, African violet club, and macrame and needlework group. I was bored. So I got into the local model airplane club.

"I have a scale model of a World War I Fokker D-7. It cost almost $900. I love to fly it. Watching my plane fly is really an experience rather than a spectator sport. What do you do?"

"I'm a businessman," Jeff lied.

"I'm married," Deidre continued. "My husband is a doctor. A doctor of philosophy, that is. He is a professor. He teaches psychology.

"Professors don't get paid much. He could make more money collecting garbage in New York City or some other major city. Many students spend ten years obtaining degrees after high school and wind up driving taxis.

"Can you imagine an English or Math Ph.D. driving a cab? There are too many Ph.D.s for the available jobs. Why, the other day I read in the paper that a new postmaster at Snook, Texas, makes $24,000 per year. Now Snook has a population of less than 1,000 people. The article indicated that the total receipts from the Snook post office were less than $9,000. Probably one-half of the professors in such disciplines as English, Political Science, and Economics make less than most postmasters with only a high school education."

"That's probably why postage stamps are so high," said Jeff quickly. He could not believe it. Was he being picked up? What should he do, Jeff thought, as he tried to control his anxiety.

There was a moment of silence before Deidre continued. "Most people don't realize it, but many professors work fifty or sixty hours per week. Bill, of course, enjoys his work. He does have flexible hours. But he just works too much.

"I helped him do one interesting experiment dealing with the subconscious. Most of us react to certain symbols without our knowledge. My husband does some experiments in a behavioral lab on campus. There is a machine there which measures the heart's action, brain waves, and perspiration. If he hooked you up to this machine and flashed pictures or signs on a screen, you would react, possibly violently, to certain symbols. This reaction is subconscious.

"A picture of a witch can make an individual react violently. All those machines would go wild. Or a male might react violently if a picture of a woman executive smoking a cigar is flashed on the screen.

"Billy indicates that a great deal of research went into the selection of the ear of corn on a famous package of corn flakes. This image caused mothers to go over and pick up a box of cereal without even knowing why.

"Similar research was conducted with Mr. Clean, the baldheaded fellow, who advertised a laundry product many years ago. Apparently his image caused women to pick up his bottle.

"Do you know what subliminal suggestions are?" Deidre asked as her light blue eyes probed his confused hazel eyes.

As Jeff nodded yes, Deidre answered her own question. "A subliminal suggestion is a message flashed on a screen at a speed too fast for conscious reading. The television industry outlawed subliminal suggestions years ago. You may remember a Columbo episode some years ago dealing with subliminal suggestions.

"My husband used subliminal suggestions to improve the grades of students. He randomly divided each undergraduate class into two groups — a control group and an experimental group.

"At the beginning of each class he showed the experimental group subliminally the message: MY MOMMY AND I ARE ONE."

"Mommy and I are one?" Jeff responded with a puzzled look.

"Yes," she said, removing Jeff's pen from his charcoal grey coat pocket. "It looked like this." She quickly scribbled MOMMY AND I ARE ONE on the cocktail napkin that had formerly been under her drink.

"Do the capital letters mean anything?"

"No, I don't think so. The second section of each group was shown this message." Deidre again scribbled on the napkin PEOPLE ARE WALKING.

"What does that do?" asked Jeff.

"Nothing. PEOPLE ARE WALKING is supposed to be a neutral message. Although both messages were flashed on the screen at high speeds, the messages did register on the unconscious minds of the students.

"Would you believe that the experimental group of students earned significantly higher grades in class than the control group who saw the neutral message? The difference in grades was approximately ten points out of one hundred." Deidre returned the pen.

Jeff was seriously interested in the conversation. "Why did their grades improve?"

71

"Well, at an early age we develop a conflict with our image of our mother — actually, a love/hate relationship," continued Deidre quickly.

"We like our mother because she is the source of all our comfort, nourishment, and security. During this symbiotic stage we develop a sense of oneness with our mother. But mother cannot cuddle us forever. She stops breastfeeding us and fondling us. We resent this lack of attention.

"In self-defense we suppress these two conflicting feelings. The more inner conflict an individual has, the better his grades can be improved by sending a message which reactivates this feeling of oneness.

"The message MOMMY AND I ARE ONE through subliminal stimulation has a comforting effect. It allows an individual to perform better than normal.

"Surprisingly, the message must be shown subliminally. This same message shown *supra*liminally has no effect on the individual. Only when an individual's awareness is bypassed can this message have an effect."

"What's the difference between subliminal and supraliminal?" asked Jeff.

"When it's subliminal it's shown too fast for the eye to be able to recognize the message; but when it's supraliminal, you can read it.

"Remember Son of Sam — the New York killer who prowled the streets during 1977 randomly killing people? He had no knowledge about his mother. Maybe that's why he was hearing voices telling him to kill.

"My husband found that people closer to schizophrenia showed a greater improvement in grades. You know what a schizophrenic is, don't you? That's an individual with a split personality. Such an individual has more inner conflict."

"Probably both the control and experimental groups had grade increases," Jeff said, tasting his drink for the first time since this strange conversation started.

"Placebo is Latin for 'I shall please.' It refers to an inactive substance or procedure used with a patient under the pretense

72

of an effective treatment. A patient receives a pill which may contain only milk sugar. If the patient believes the pill is a powerful drug, it may work.

"Remember laetrile? The drug, which is extracted from apricot pits, was felt by many to be an effective treatment for treating cancer. The government maintained that its only benefit was possible placebo effect.

"Would you believe that the color of a pill may have a placebo effect? Research indicates that red placebos are more effective than blue or green pills when treating arthritis pain. Anyway, the mere fact that the control group of students saw the neutral message might have been reason enough for their grades to improve."

Deidre paused for a moment as if she were turning the page of her lecture notes and sipped at her drink. Jeff glanced at his watch and with some hesitation asked, "Is this your first visit to Washington, D.C.?"

"It has been many years since I've been here. Would you do me a favor? We are only two blocks from the White House. Would you like to take a tour of it? I have two tickets."

"Sure, why not." Jeff was glad to get up. His body had shifted into a position where he was hurting. Besides, Jeff had never toured the White House even though he had been in Washington many times.

The walk to the White House through Lafayette Park was short. There was a brisk wind blowing, so they were thankful that there were only a few people waiting to enter on the side of the White House. They had to pass through a six-foot-tall chain-link fence which had been built in the early nineties. Deidre and Jeff walked slowly along the glass-enclosed colonnade to the ground floor corridor where Jeff saw portraits of Eleanor Roosevelt, Jacqueline Kennedy Onassis, and Lady Bird Johnson. One of the three Regency chandeliers sparkled on a selection of Presidential china displayed in a Sheraton-style bookcase which was made in Baltimore in 1803. On the top shelf, in the center, were plates used by George Washington at Mount Vernon.

Jeff was impressed with the 10-foot portrait of Chester Arthur, the 21st president. Jeff had never heard of him. Jeff saw the white bust of Abraham Lincoln and Christopher Columbus.

Jeff and Deidre spoke very little as they leisurely made their way through the walking tour. Jeff looked into the library on the right of the corridor. The paneling of a soft grey color was broken by built-in bookcases and several paintings of Indians.

The Vermeil Room did not impress Jeff, but the velvet-lined cabinets, silk taffeta draperies, and the colorful English rug made the China Room a sight to see. One of the many tour guides, or maybe they were guards, pointed to the portrait of Mrs. Calvin Coolidge and said, "President Coolidge was scheduled to sit for the artist, Howard Christy, but the President was too preoccupied that day with events concerning the Teapot Dome oil scandal. The president postponed his appointment, and Mrs. Coolidge posed instead."

Next they climbed the stairs to four state reception rooms and the State Dining Room. The Diplomatic reception room had panoramic wallpaper with scenes of the Natural Bridge of Virginia, Niagara Falls, New York Bay, West Point, and Boston Harbor. A tour guide indicated that the Map Room was used by Franklin Roosevelt as a situation room to follow the course of World War II.

The Green Room with its green watered-silk fabric wall and striped beige, green, and coral satin draperies was too green. The multi-colored carpet was very worn. A painting on the far wall looked like some kind of strange, giant insect. The portrait, entitled "The Mosquito Net," was a woman sleeping in bed, covered by a black mosquito net.

Jeff liked the oval Blue Room. A portrait of John Adams hung on the west wall near a beautiful white marble mantel. The blue satin draperies with handmade fringe and gold satin valances and the Bellange bergere armchairs were handsomely offset by the light beige wallpaper with a blue frieze around the top and bottom which was derived from classical motifs.

With only a glance into the Red Room, Jeff walked over to observe the State Dining Room with the gold damask draperies and a large portrait of Abraham Lincoln above a carved white mantel. The family dining room was unimpressive.

Jeff walked down the bright red carpet on Cross Hall toward the North Entrance Hall. He wondered if the portrait of President Truman at the west end of the hall was intentionally separated from the portrait of President Eisenhower at the east end. After glancing at the portrait of Presidents John Kennedy and Ronald Reagan, Jeff walked back downstairs. Deidre was still looking in the Red Room, chatting with one of the guides.

Downstairs Jeff purchased an inexpensive softback copy of *The White House: An Historical Guide*. Deidre was waiting near the doors at the North Entrance by the time Jeff walked back to the front.

"Well, what do you think about the place?" asked Deidre.

"It looks somewhat old and worn, especially some of the carpets. It doesn't fit my image of the home of the most powerful person in the world."

"Did you hear the guide say the place has six floors? President Keeney and his family live on two floors. They *only* have 57 rooms."

"That's bigger than my apartment."

"By the way, did you notice the museum we passed coming down here? It's the museum for the Treasury Building. There's still some time before it closes. Would you like to see it?"

"Sure, why not," Jeff replied. Jeff hoped she did not notice the slight blush on his face. The Treasury Department was his employer.

The Treasury Exhibit Hall was small. Immediately inside the door was a bronzed bulletin board with the names of Treasury Agents killed in the line of duty. There were two numismatic sales counters open. Jeff bought a one and one-half inch pewter disc. Deidre used a coin press and struck a medal showing the White House on the obverse and the Presidential seal on the reverse.

When Deidre passed under the TV screen which showed a picture of her, Jeff noticed her trying to arrange her blonde hair. Next to this TV was a mannequin wearing a Fort Knox guard uniform holding a machine gun.

There was an animated display of sculptors' art, a moonshine still, some U.S. Customs artifacts, and a replica of a 1792 screw coin press. Jeff was looking at a Lienhard transfer and engraving machine when he heard Deidre laugh.

"Jeff, come over here. As a —" she paused — "businessman, you should enjoy this song." She pointed to a piece of paper in a glass display.

It was a song written in the 1920s, entitled "Tax, Tax, Tax":

We are living in the days of the war taxation, Its effect is felt by every occupation. There's a tax on things we drink and a tax on thoughts we think. It's causing lots of trouble and vexation. Such a tax, tax, tax — Quite enough to break our backs on furniture and picture shows, furs and drugs and silken hose. Tax, Tax, Tax. If you fondle your wife and get kisses a plenty you'll pay four cents on all over twenty. Kiss goodbye all your greenbacks. You're paying Tax, Tax, Tax.

"There's a lot of truth in that old song," Jeff said when he finished skimming the words.

"We better get out of here. They're about to close," Deidre said, looking at her petite Rolex watch.

From the Treasury Building they walked down New York Avenue. It was beginning to get dark.

"Would you like to find a cab and go to a restaurant and eat?" Jeff asked.

"Yes! There's an Italian restaurant on the corner on M Street."

Jeff and Deidre engaged in some chit chat in the cab ride to the restaurant and while waiting for the food.

The food was adequate. After the meal they drifted down M Street toward the Hilton.

Across the street from the Hilton, Deidre stopped in front of Archibald's. It was "Washington's 1st Complete Topless Dancing Girls."

"Can you imagine," said Deidre, "only three blocks from the White House." She smiled. "Would you buy me a drink? I've never been in a topless dancing place."

As Jeff opened the door to let Deidre in, he noticed a large sign on the window of the establishment next door: "Quiche." In very small letters underneath was "carryout food."

As they made their way to a table in the dimly lit long room, Jeff noticed a white girl with red hair dancing on a stage in front of a mirror. Jeff noticed that there were smudges and fingerprints on the mirror. The dancer was near the end of her act because she was down to her G-string. Jeff helped Deidre remove her coat and placed it on the back of her chair.

A bar went down the entire left side of the long room. The entire back wall was covered with mirrors. By the time they had gotten their drinks, the girl finished her act. She put on a thin nightgown and became a waitress.

A light-colored black girl got up from a table where she was sitting with a black man who looked like a fullback for the Denver Broncos.

With the song "You Satisfy My Desires" as background, she began her performance. She had a good pair on her chest. When she reached the G-string stage, one of the customers near the stage wrapped a bill, probably $1, around her string.

When Jeff had finished his first beer, he leaned over and whispered, "What do you think about her performance?"

Deidre merely smiled. After a few moments she leaned toward Jeff and took his hand. "One thing I forgot to tell you about the subliminal experiment which I talked about earlier," she whispered. "It is possible to lower the performance of individuals. By using messages such as DESTROY MOTHER, KILL MOTHER, or SHOOT MOTHER, an individual's performance can be decreased. Do you think these messages would decrease your performance?"

Jeff did not respond. He was thinking that a certain softball may have decreased his performance. Was he up to it?

There were three young men sitting at the table next to Jeff. Jeff noticed that the dancer smiled at the table. He heard one of the men say excitedly, "She's smiling at me!"

"No, she's not. She's smiling at me," responded one of the other men.

After a second drink they left. When they got to the busy lobby, there was an awkward pause. "Would you like to get another drink in the bar?"

"No, I would rather talk. Why don't we go to my room."

The hotel room appeared to be recently redecorated. It smelled of perfume. Just like the movies, Deidre excused herself and went to the bathroom to change into something more comfortable. She returned dressed in a black negligee. She had pale red polish on her toenails.

Jeff awoke the next morning. At first he did not know where he was. Then the exciting thoughts of the night before came rushing into his consciousness, increasing his interest again. But Deidre was not there. She had taken his copy of *The White House* and his pen.

A note was on the table with a grapefruit and a Danish pastry on a tray.

Jeff,
    I had to leave early. Thank you.
    Have breakfast on me.

"D"

It was late and Jeff remembered his diet. He ate the grapefruit, drank the orange juice, ignored the coffee and pastry, and left the hotel room.

Jeff hung around the hotel lobby for about an hour but could not find Deidre. He checked the front desk, but she had already checked out. He wrote down her address: 1112 Broad Street, Kent, Ohio, 44242 from the AMA attendance list.

As Jeff left the hotel, he noticed a blonde hair on his coat. "What the heck," Jeff thought, "I'll let the detective check out this strand of hair for the fun of it. I will see how accurate he is in the information he can give me about Deidre." Jeff placed it in a small envelope and put it in his breast pocket.

Buzz—Buzz — Jeff instinctively turned his head toward the sound. His hands were shaking. The noise was merely a telephone in a parked automobile on the street. Someone was trying to reach the occupant, who was missing.

It was a reminder to Jeff that he had to find the model plane operator. Who was he? How could he find him? Even the dreary, drizzly day could not upset his cheerful spirits.

A small article appeared in the Sunday *Washington Post*. Apparently a bellboy had died from food poisoning at the Hilton on Saturday. Jeff did not notice the article in the newspaper.

CHAPTER 9

Proper income tax reform is simple to define: It's closing all your loopholes, while leaving open mine.

— L. A. Mason

Ring-ring-ring.

It was Saturday evening. Commissioner Jimmy Callaway did not expect to have an exciting evening. He and his wife, Betty, were ringing the doorbell of the Cranfords. Harry Cranford was the Press Secretary of the President.

Jane Cranford opened the door. "Hi, Betty. How are you, Jimmy?" Betty and Jane had been close friends for a number of years. Jane was quite attractive, and affluent. She had a long aristocratic nose and her lips were light pink.

"Jimmy, Harry's in the living room."

Jimmy walked into the living room. The card table was already placed in the middle of the room. Today would be one of those infrequent times in which Jimmy would be in a situation in which he felt insecure.

Jimmy did not like to play bridge. In fact, he couldn't play bridge that well. He never had time in college to learn the game.

He was a dummy player. He played so that he would be the dummy hand. The dummy is the player who must expose his hand, and the declarer plays the exposed hand in addition to his own hand.

Jimmy was careful never to introduce a new suit. Jimmy could never keep track of the cards that had been played. He never worried whether the "Jack of Spades" had been played until he lost a trick and his wife would sit very erect and peer fiercely across the table. He tried never to be the declarer.

Let his wife play the hand. She was good! Why not, that was all she did. That and shop and spend money.

"Hello, Jimmy. How are you tonight?" Harry interrupted Jimmy's thoughts.

Harry was a large-framed man over six feet in height. His facial features were sharp. His straight, black hair fell over his forehead, with long descending sideburns. He always wore black-rimmed glasses. Harry was an avid tennis player.

During the Eisenhower era, it was golf. For Nixon it was bowling. Johnson had pulled dogs' ears. Ford had played golf and skied. Carter played tennis and softball. Reagan cut wood and rode horses. The current President carried on the tennis tradition.

Jimmy did not especially like Harry Cranford. Harry was too liberal. As a college student Harry had been an active member of the Americans for Democratic Action. Harry carried this leftward tilt into his current job as Press Secretary.

He was, however, one of the three or four close advisors to the President. For this reason alone Jimmy always kept a civil demeanor while around Harry. Jimmy did know how to smile.

"Oh, pretty good, I suppose," replied Jimmy. Jimmy knew there would be five minutes of social conversation and the wives would be ready for combat.

"Is a whiskey okay?" asked Harry.

"Sure."

True to form, in five minutes they were seated around the table. Betty had won the bid and Jimmy was the dummy hand.

The only advantage that Jimmy had over Harry was that Jimmy could get Harry into a political discussion. Harry would then screw up.

"Harry, did you notice in the *Wall Street Journal* yesterday that the Soviet Union now has a huge superiority over the United States in its total nuclear striking capacity? A recently issued study indicates that Russia has a thirty percent advantage in its arsenal of intercontinental nuclear missiles and bombers."

"Why do you read that right-wing rag? The article probably did not mention overkill. Do you know that Russia could destroy every American with a personal force of 25 tons of TNT?" Harry asked sharply.

"Harry, I'm talking about delivery of destructive force. It does no good if the bombs are sitting on the ground when Russia attacks us. You know Carter killed the B-1 bomber in 1977. Then he had the guts to give away the Panama Canal."

Harry over-trumped his wife. That was an embarrassing mistake. His wife groaned. Harry tried to retrieve the card, but she said mockingly, "A card laid is a card played. Keep your mind on the game, Harry!"

But Harry continued. "Plutonium is the basic material needed to make fission, or the atomic bomb. It is also used as a trigger for the much more powerful thermonuclear bombs. To make a bomb it takes less than ten pounds of pure plutonium. Or about eighteen pounds of plutonium extracted from the spent uranium fuel or approximately twenty-two pounds of plutonium oxide."

"So for that reason Carter tried to cancel the fast-breeder reactor at Oak Ridge, Tennessee," responded Jimmy crisply. "Why the risks associated with the Clinch River reactor are manageable, and the project would turn fission energy into an unlimited resource. We are running out of energy."

"Look, Carter was trying to curb the production of plutonium around the world. Do you realize the exposure of nuclear facilities against dangers of attack, sabotage, and hijacking? Why in the late '70s, one intelligence agency discovered that 8,000 pounds of weapons-grade nuclear material was diverted from a power plant."

Harry paused and threw down a four of spades and then continued. "Jimmy, each year the odds increase for another major core meltdown. Everyone has forgotten the partial meltdown at Three Mile Island and the major catastrophe at Chernobyl. The Russians' mistake will lead to the death of nearly 15,000 people in the Soviet Union and Europe. I'm talking about deaths from leukemia and cancer of the lung, breast, and thyroid. Poor Poland was burned the worst by Chernobyl's fire and radiation fallout. You know they hid other fatal mistakes before Chernobyl."

Harry played his last card. Jimmy's wife made her bid exactly.

As he shuffled the cards Jimmy asked, "So what's the President going to do about SALT III? How much is he going to give away this time? Why doesn't he consider SDI? He never should have banned work on the Star-Wars system when he took office. Smooth-talking Gorbachev really pulled Keeney's pants down. Russia will have a working Star-Wars system in three years. I don't understand how Gorbachev could snow the U.S. press."

"Something has to be done. Layer after layer of new weapons are being piled into the arsenals of both superpowers. As the President said last week, he is determined that the atomic genie will be put back into the bottle so that mankind will not be destroyed. The President believes that a failure to negotiate a realistic agreement may mean the end of organized society on this planet." He ignored the SDI jab.

"By the way, I'm the one who made up that catchy phrase about the genie."

Jimmy could not resist the temptation. He began clapping his hands. His wife kicked him hard on the leg under the table.

Harry must have heard the blow because he smiled sheepishly. They played cards in silence for a long period of time.

The Callaways and Cranfords weren't having outstanding bridge hands. They were having to struggle to make a game. Each couple would get a part score (leg) and the other couple would cut it off. There was one thing neither couple could complain about; one side was not consistently getting all the good cards. There had been no slams.

Jimmy was again the dummy. "Harry, what's the President going to do with the cookie cutter?"

The term "cookie cutter" was the nickname given to the

neutron bomb. President Carter had okayed a limited production of this weapon. But with pressure from anti-nuke forces, Congress had outlawed the weapon just like the banning of bacteriological weapons after World War I. Pressure was now being mounted by the Pentagon to reinstate the weapon into the United States nuclear arsenal.

"I don't know, Jimmy. That's a nasty weapon. This bomb releases a large amount of neutrons which incapacitate and kill most people and animals within minutes. But the victims suffer violent nausea, diarrhea and other unpleasant symptoms before they die. Anyone on the periphery of the target area dies a slow death of convulsions. It destroys the cell structure of anyone in its range — and it is especially devastating to the central nervous system."

"No bomb is perfect," Jimmy answered gruffly. "This bomb is precise and clean. It does not destroy buildings or military equipment. Remove the dead people and the buildings and equipment could be used within a short time. Just think of what it would do to the rat and roach population!"

Harry chuckled and nodded his head. "The bomb does destroy a few square miles of property. You know my position. I'm for total nuclear disarmament."

"But Harry, the Pentagon indicates that the Allies would lose a conventional war with the Soviet Union on the European mainland. The neutron bomb is a defensive weapon. It would stop a Soviet invasion of Western Europe with reduced damage to the besieged cities. Now if there is a Soviet attack, the United States must strike back with conventional nuclear weapons or abandon Europe. As weak as the President is, a neutron bomb could stop an invasion without a nuclear Armageddon. The Soviets could push through the banks of the Rhine in a few hours. Without the neutron bomb the Allies would have no option except to surrender or declare an all-out nuclear war. The Commies would probably choose city-hugging tactics; they won't come in with tanks and artillery. The Western allies could not match the combined resources of the Warsaw Pact forces."

"Total disarmament would decrease the probability of war," Harry shot back as he slammed a card on the table.

Jimmy recognized that Harry was mad so he dropped the discussion. Harry was a "pinko." There was no chance of changing his mind. The President had surrounded himself with the wrong type of advisors. There were other options.

Harry dealt the cards. Jane Cranford began to sit a little more erect in her chair as she picked up each one of her cards. Betty sensed that Jane was probably getting a fantastic hand. Her only hope was that Harry was distracted enough that they would not get a slam.

Harry passed. Betty passed also. Jane bid two spades and gave Harry a withering look that meant you had better do something. Jimmy passed. Harry bid three clubs. Jane immediately bid four nontrump — wanting to know how many aces Harry had. Harry responded six spades. Betty's worst fears were true; Harry and Jane were going to get to slam and from the looks of her hand they were going to make it. Jane bid seven spades without any hesitation. Harry laid down his hand since Jane had introduced spades and Jane looked pleased. She played promptly and methodically. Betty and Jimmy had no hope of setting them. Jane smiled as she pulled in the last trick and then totaled up the score.

Harry was feeling a lot better now, because when Jane had a bad night of cards, things at home were on an uneven keel for a while. He continued his conversation with Jimmy.

"Jimmy, you should forget about defense and clean up your own house. Senator Bentsen said the other day on the Senate floor that the tax code was ready to crumble under its own weight. Too many loopholes, deductions, and credits. He's suggesting a Simpliform. He would substitute a four-line calculation for the present obstacle course on Form 1040."

"Bentsen's off his rocker. Do you want to throw one-third of the accountants and lawyers on the welfare rolls? Remember what happened with the tax law after the Tax Reform Act of 1986? Would you like for me to do away with the charitable contribution deduction? I would have every rabbi, priest, and minister in the country marching on Washington. But maybe Washington needs some religion."

"I don't know, Jimmy. Bentsen indicates that the tax paid by those with incomes of six figures and above does not average more than thirty percent, in spite of a statutory rate of forty percent. He says that sixty billion dollars were retained by individuals and corporations last year because of tax subsidies. He would reduce these subsidies and at the same time introduce a new lower, overall progressive tax rate."

"Fine! Tomorrow I begin this process by advocating the elimination of the political contribution deduction. Ask the President how much money he collects as a result of this particular tax subsidy. Remember we did away with that deduction in 1986, and it came back in 1990."

"Good point, Jimmy. Good point."

"Besides, equity creates complex laws. A blind person receives a larger standard deduction because Congress felt that such a person had a need for this tax subsidy. Congress passed the child care expense credit to help support little children while their mothers work."

"Would you guys stop talking shop?" said Jane in a combative tone.

The rest of the hands were mediocre. Since Jane and Harry's spade slam everything else was pale in comparison. Betty at one time thought her hand might have some possibilities, but she couldn't get any adequate response from Jimmy. She didn't know whether it was because he didn't have a good hand or whether he was afraid he might have to play the hand so he didn't want to show any initiative in introducing new suits. At any rate she figured she had better not take any chances, which was wise, because Jimmy only had six points and that was including distribution. There would have been little hope to make a slam with support like that from your partner.

About eleven thirty Jimmy began yawning and nudging Betty under the table. Betty took the hint and suggested they call it a night. They thanked Jane and Harry for a nice evening even though their cards had not been spectacular.

Jimmy told Harry he would probably be seeing him somewhere around the Hill. He was glad to be going home. It had been a long and frustrating day.

*　　*　　*

On Monday IRS Commissioner Jimmy Callaway reported to the House Ways and Means Committee:

"Recently, I have had the opportunity to conduct a series of visits to a number of our facilities, and to speak to large numbers of IRS employees. I am proud of what I saw. Every day, these individuals perform the tough, complicated, and sometimes dangerous job of making the tax system work. They meet taxpayers face to face to provide assistance, to examine returns, and to collect overdue taxes. They investigate potential FRAUD, so that dishonest citizens are not allowed to pass their share of the tax burden to others.

"It is unfortunate that IRS employees are increasingly becoming the object of taxpayers' frustration with the system. But it is TRAGIC that some of this frustration is resulting in violence. In fiscal year 1993, there were 789 recorded incidents of assaults and threats against IRS employees, an increase of nearly 49% from the previous year. One of our civil enforcement employees was shot and killed doing his job."

CHAPTER 10

To the extent that some people are dishonest or careless in their dealings with the government, the majority is forced to carry a heavier burden.

— John F. Kennedy

"The best type of income is tax-saved dollars — it's not taxable." Henry Silverman was beginning one of his day-long seminars.

"My definition of a loophole is something someone else is doing to save taxes."

He had eight attendees — the typical businessmen and women and wealthy heirs. Each had paid eight hundred dollars to attend. Henry had offered a two hundred dollar discount for this particular seminar.

"In a non-academic book entitled *The Call Girl*, the author indicates that the tax structure created the high-priced call girl. Entertainment of clients and customers is a deductible expense under the income tax laws and a call girl's fee can be treated as a business expense for tax purposes. In effect, the U.S. Treasury frequently pays more than one-half the cost of the entertainment.

"Now gentlemen, if a call girl's fee . . ."

Henry noticed someone vaguely familiar in the back row. "Wait a minute, that's Burke, the IRS agent," Henry thought. "He has a wig on but he can't hide his mustache." He poured himself a glass of water and took a swallow in order to stall for time while he decided what to do. "How did he get in here?

He must have paid the fee. What can I do? Much of my material is about evasion. If I drop the material, I'm dead. If I recommend fraud and evasion, I can be locked up. Is this like the life of an earthworm during a very heavy rain? If the worm stays in the ground, he drowns. If he surfaces, a bird will probably eat him."

Several of the attendees looked around at each other. They were surprised at the long pause in the middle of a sentence.

"Gentlemen, I'm sorry, but we have an IRS agent in the room. It would be unfair to you if I continued this seminar. So I'm going to refund your money. I'll keep you informed of my next seminar. Rest assured that the agent will not learn your names. Thank you."

Henry walked back to Jeff Burke. "Hello, Mr. Burke, can I help you?"

Jeff was stunned. He thought that Silverman might recognize him with the black wig, but he would never have guessed that he would cancel the seminar. At eight times eight hundred dollars, he was giving up sixty-four hundred dollars.

Jeff noticed that the other seven individuals were quickly leaving the room. Jeff had wanted their names. But Silverman was still shaking his hand.

"Er, you didn't have to cancel the seminar. I only wanted to learn the latest tax avoidance techniques," Jeff smiled ruefully.

Controlling his anxiety, Henry responded, "Well, you know how it is. You caught me napping. I don't wish to give away any of my trade secrets. You might retire early and go into competition with me."

By now Jeff was regaining his composure. "Mr. Silverman, on Wednesday I will present you with a summons for a list of individuals who have attended your seminars for the past two years. Also I want a list of the subscribers to your newsletter, 'How to Cheat and Defraud the IRS.'"

"Why Mr. Burke, you know that the courts would not uphold a summons for a fishing expedition."

"We'll see," Jeff responded with little humor in his eyes. Jeff turned and left the room.

*   *   *

Henry was meeting with Carl Strovee and Strovee's lawyer. The meeting with the IRS agent was scheduled for tomorrow. Some kind of strategy had to be developed.

Carl, fidgeting in his chair, had the first question for Ted Abbott, a Harvard lawyer who specialized in taxation. Ted was slim and fortyish, had a receding hairline, and wore round, silver-rimmed glasses. "Should we cooperate with the IRS?"

"Well, I have two rules of thumb. Point one, if a taxpayer has a strong position or evidence that demonstrates a weakness in the government's case, cooperate and produce the requested information. Point two, if your position is weak and you cannot punch holes in the agent's case, avoid him. Don't cooperate.

"A good strategy is to offer the agent any information which he can obtain elsewhere. Thus, you look like you are cooperating. For example, salary information, security transactions, purchases of insurance policies, transactions involving real estate, and bank deposits are items which an agent can obtain with some work. Give it to him since he'll find it anyway."

The attorney paused and then continued. "You told me on the phone that the IRS had found a bank account in your mother's name at Valentine, Nebraska. Is that yours?"

"Yes."

"Did you pay taxes on the money?"

Carl looked over at Henry as he replied. "I thought they were tax-saved dollars."

The attorney slowly shook his head. "Even a fruit cake would give a better answer than that. Remember, now, we have an attorney-client relationship. What you tell me here is confidential and will not be revealed to the IRS or the courts. I am on your side, but I need to know the truth."

Carl did not especially appreciate the term *fruit cake*, but he looked straight at his lawyer and said, "I have been putting about 35 percent of my income into the account. Henry encouraged me to do it. He helped me set up two sets of records."

"Okay, you can't get a reward for cooperating when in fact the evidence appears to the investigating agent that a criminal action is involved. Cooperation will not save you from a conviction. People have gone to jail even though they cooperated with the agent and paid all of the proposed deficiency.

"The deficiency is $47,554," continued the lawyer. "How much money do you have in the Valentine account?"

"About $240,000," replied Carl.

The lawyer again shook his head. "I'll need a substantial retainer, say $30,000. Neither of you is to contact the agent from this point on. I will inform the IRS that all future communication will be conducted through me.

"Mr. Silverman, I want you to attend the conference with me tomorrow with the agents. Don't say anything, however, unless I direct you to. You might tell the agent more than is necessary. It's Henry, isn't it?"

Henry nodded yes.

"Henry, I want you to give Carl all records and relevant documents. Give him your accounting working papers dealing with his tax returns.

"Obviously, Carl, you are *not* to allow any agents to see these records and documents. We will *not* provide them with net worth statements. I've seen too many situations where the net worth increase was calculated on the basis of the taxpayer's own books and records which were given to the agent during the investigative process. I will not cooperate my client to jail. Giving agents net worth statements is like giving your executioner a lethal weapon.

"Even if we hand them your records, they would demand that you submit to a formal question-and-answer session under oath. We don't need that.

"Have you received a large inheritance or other non-taxable income such as insurance proceeds or proceeds from a loan?"

"Nope," responded Carl.

"Is the bank account in your mother's name alone?"

"Yes."

"Did you use her exact name and Social Security number? Did you use an assumed name?"

"I changed an 'e' to an 'r' and used Mary Strover and her real Social Security number."

"Guess we'll use the old standby, a cash hoard. We can try to prove that the bank deposits were in fact accumulated by you and her in years prior to the tax years in question. Have you put monies in the bank account on a regular basis?"

"No, about once a year. I would keep the stash in my home safe and take it to Valentine about once or twice a year when I visited my mother. Mr. Abbott, would you lay it on the line? What is my exposure? I don't quite understand this distinction between a *civil* and *criminal* situation."

"Where should I begin?" Ted looked at Henry. "Have you not told him anything?"

"Nope, I'm not a lawyer."

"That's evident," the attorney replied with intensity in his voice.

He then turned back to Carl. "The IRS has *civil* as well as *criminal* sanctions for violations of tax laws. These civil sanctions are assessed in addition to the tax liability. These civil penalties include a delinquency penalty for failure to file a return or a timely return, the 5% negligence penalty for negligence or intentional disregard of rules and regulations without the intent to defraud, and the 75% fraud penalty on an underpayment on any portion which is due to fraud. The purpose of this 75% fraud penalty is a remedial civil sanction in order to safeguard and protect the government revenue and to reimburse the government for the heavy expense of investigation and loss resulting from a taxpayer's fraud.

"Criminal sanctions provide punishment for offenses and generally involve imprisonment and fines. A person who willfully attempts in any manner to evade or defeat a tax may be guilty of a felony and upon conviction may be fined not more than $100,000 and/or imprisoned not more than five years, together with the costs of prosecution."

"Five years!" Carl almost shouted.

"Yes, and both civil and criminal sanctions may be imposed for the same offense." The attorney paused to allow Carl to appreciate the severity of his situation.

Then the attorney continued in a somber voice. "The burden and measure of proof differs in criminal and civil cases. In a criminal case, the IRS must prove every facet of the offense and show your guilt beyond a reasonable doubt. In case of fraud, the IRS has the burden of establishing your fraud by clear and convincing evidence. You may not be convicted upon mere suspicion or conjecture. Likewise, you should be acquitted if the evidence is equally consistent with innocence as with guilt.

"Now in civil cases," — the attorney paused and cleared his throat — "the IRS's determination of the deficiency is presumptively correct. The burden is placed upon the taxpayer to overcome this presumption. In other words, the taxpayer is guilty and must prove himself innocent in civil cases."

"What must they do to prove I committed a criminal offense?" Carl asked as he slowly rubbed his hands together.

"Three elements are necessary for a criminal offense. Point one: additional tax due and owing. Point two: an attempt in any manner to evade or defeat any tax. Point three: willfulness.

"As to point one, the IRS must establish that, at the time the offense was committed, an additional tax was due and owing. In essence, you must owe more taxes than you reported. But the IRS does not have to prove evasion of the full amount alleged in the indictment. It is sufficient to show that a substantial amount of the tax was evaded, and this proof need not be measured in terms of gross or net income or by any particular percentage of the tax shown to be due and payable." The attorney talked as if he had given this same discussion many times.

"Apparently, the current policy of the IRS is not to authorize assessment of additional taxes and penalties during the time criminal aspects are pending and to preclude discussion or negotiation looking toward settlement of the civil liability.

"Point two. This phrase 'attempt in any manner' does not mean that one whose efforts are unsuccessful cannot commit the crime of willful attempt. The crime is complete when the attempt is made and nothing is added to its criminality by success or consummation. The real character of an offense lies, not in the failure to file a return or in the filing of a false return, but rather in the attempt to evade any tax. The term 'attempt' implies some affirmative action or the commission of some overt act." His phone rang twice, but the attorney ignored it.

"The Supreme Court has given certain illustrations from which acts or conduct the attempt to evade or defeat any tax may be inferred: keeping a double set of books; making false entries, alterations, invoices, or documents; destruction of books and records; concealment of assets or covering up sources of income; and handling of one's affairs to avoid making the records usual in transactions of the kind. Obviously, Mr. Strovee, you fit this pattern.

"Willfulness is an essential element of proof with respect to most criminal violations investigated by special agents. This word 'willful' generally means an act done with a bad purpose; without justifiable excuse; stubbornly, obstinately, perversely. The Supreme Court indicates that this word characterizes an act done without grounds for believing it is lawful or conduct marked by careless disregard whether or not one has the right so to act.

"The most laudable motive is no defense where the act committed is a crime in contemplation of law. For example, you may have intentionally understated your income in order to have sufficient funds to support your mother. Although such motive may be admirable, you have specifically intended to evade payment of your income taxes.

94

"Don't talk to an agent. Don't sign any statements. Remember that, both of you." The attorney turned and looked directly at Henry. "I was involved in a case several years ago in which the court sustained a conviction for tax evasion. It was a close case of willfulness. Even the court indicated that if the taxpayer had not signed a statement which tied down the element of willfulness, the taxpayer would probably have won. But the admission by the taxpayer tied the pieces together into a neat package of tax evasion."

"Suppose I filed some amended returns and payed the deficiency. Would this stop a civil or fraud charge?" interjected Carl.

"No," Ted shot back. "Even a tentative amended return could be considered an admission of guilt with respect to the amount of tax due and fraudulent intent. Before 1953 the IRS had a policy that if a taxpayer voluntarily disclosed before an investigation had begun that he had willfully failed to file a tax return or his filed return was fraudulent, no criminal prosecution would be recommended. The IRS has announced that it will *not* follow a voluntary disclosure policy.

"In a 1954 court case, a taxpayer on the advice of counsel submitted amended returns clearly marked 'tentative.' The returns showed a substantial increase in the tax payable. The returns were never filed and the taxes were not paid. Yet at the criminal trial, the IRS indicated that by submitting these 'tentative' amended returns the taxpayer admitted that more taxes were due and, therefore, the evasion was willful. At the subsequent trial, counsel was unable to argue that a lesser deficiency than that indicated on the tentative amended returns was actually due.

"Remember, in order to impose criminal penalties the IRS must prove you *willfully* attempted to evade or defeat a tax. They must prove your state of mind." The attorney pointed to his head. "They must prove that your state of mind was evil. That you acted in bad faith and deliberately, not accidentally, tried to evade taxes.

"The Supreme Court indicates that 'willfully,' when used in a criminal context, means an act done with a bad purpose, without justifiable excuse." There was a short pause.

"Henry, will you meet me in front of the IRS building at 12:45 p.m?" It was more of a demand than a question. Turning to Carl he said, "Now, don't worry. Go home and drink a couple of beers and watch the tube. I'll call you tomorrow after the meeting. See you. Oh, before I leave, could you write me that retainer check?"

While Carl was writing the check, the lawyer spoke to Henry. "Did they give Carl his *Miranda* warning when you and he met with the Special Agent?"

"No. In fact, they did not even mention that the one agent was a Special Agent. I had to ask for their credentials. When I saw that he was a Special Agent, I tried to get Carl to leave. But he wouldn't."

The lawyer was referring to the *Miranda*-type warning which appears in the Special Agent's manual. According to this manual, a Special Agent is supposed to properly identify himself and show his credentials. He should also state: "As a Special Agent, one of my functions is to investigate the possibility of criminal violations of the Internal Revenue laws and related offenses." He should give the taxpayer a warning against self-incrimination and explain his rights to legal counsel.

Carl made a short detour on the way home. He stopped at a travel agency. He purchased a one-way plane ticket to Omaha under the name of H. Stove for 11:00 a.m. Wednesday. He also reserved a rental car under the same name; his destination was Valentine, Nebraska.

He walked several blocks to another travel agency. Here he purchased a one-way plane ticket to Caracas, Venezuela, under the name J. E. Cajan. Departure time: Thursday 3:00 p.m.

Carl did not realize that Jeff Burke had already called the Valentine bank. He had slapped a "quick" assessment against Carl's account. This procedure is used to assess additional taxes and deficiencies when the statutory period for assessment would otherwise expire before the assessment could be made under normal procedures. Jeff had felt that the collection of tax was endangered.

That evening Henry took the tax records involving Carl over to Carl's apartment. Carl seemed to be in reasonable spirits under the circumstances.

Much later that evening Carl took these tax records along with other personal effects to his self-storage area. He made several trips.

CHAPTER 11

Nothing is easier than the expenditure of public money.
It doesn't appear to belong to anyone. The temptation is
overwhelming to bestow it on somebody.
— Calvin Coolidge

Henry Silverman was waiting in front of the IRS building when Ted Abbott arrived. Henry had gotten a haircut earlier. His tight curly black hair was getting too long for his conservative image.

"Hello, Henry, ready for the inquisition?" joked Ted.

"Sure," came the uneasy response.

Minutes later Ted Abbott introduced himself to Jeff Burke and Yvonne Talbert. He informed the two agents that his client, Carl Strovee, would not attend the meeting. He gave them a copy of a power of attorney signed by Carl.

"My client was unable to get together a net worth statement within such a short period of time," Ted continued. "Aside from the net worth statement, we shall get you a list of bank deposits, his purchases of insurance policies, several transactions in real estate, and his stock brokerage transactions. We do wish to cooperate within limits."

"I'm glad you are going to cooperate, Mr. Abbott," Jeff said. "That's really the best way. But you realize that a taxpayer has ten days to answer our summons.

"Mr. Silverman, did you bring in your working papers and other records regarding Mr. Strovee?" asked Jeff.

"Actually, Mr. Strovee has any applicable working papers and documents with respect to his tax returns. I basically used data that was furnished to me by Carl. Any documents that I used were returned to Carl's office after I finished with them."

"Mr. Silverman, you signed the minutes of Mr. Strovee's corporation involving the Section 1244 stock. Did you prepare these minutes?"

"Yes I did," responded Henry.

"Were the minutes prepared contemporaneously?"

"Sure."

"We have prepared a short statement which indicates that you prepared the minutes and you believe them to be valid. Would you read this and sign it?"

Jeff handed the statement to Henry.

Henry read it and then gave it to Ted. Ted read it.

"Looks okay to me, Henry," said Ted as he handed the statement back to Henry.

Jeff handed a pen to Henry. "Would you sign the statement?"

"No," said Henry.

Jeff did not seem surprised. Next he gave an envelope to Henry. "Here is an administrative summons directing you to produce copies of all tax returns prepared by you for the past three years. If you do not have copies of any returns, please provide us with the names, addresses, and social security numbers of these taxpayers. Also, we want a list of the names and addresses of the subscribers to your newspaper."

Ted watched dumbfounded. The agent did not seem to be after Carl Strovee. They were after Henry. He was being cunningly outmaneuvered. Ted knew that Jeff had just given Henry an open-ended John Doe summons. Although some courts have held these types of summonses invalid, the general rule is that John Doe summonses are enforceable and not unreasonable within the Fourth Amendment.

The John Doe summonses were used frequently in the seventies to uncover incompetent and unscrupulous tax preparers. An agent would submit a standard set of facts to a suspected tax preparer and request that a return be prepared. If the prepared tax return was incorrect, the IRS would issue a summons to the preparer for the names, addresses and social security numbers of the people for whom he had prepared a return.

Ted also recognized that this was a so-called "chain" investigation. The examination of one taxpayer leads to a fraud investigation of another taxpayer having a relationship with the first. For example, while examining one business, an agent may notice that checks payable to a customer were cashed rather than deposited in the payee's bank account or were endorsed over to a third party. A collateral examination may be undertaken on the customer.

Ted noticed that Jeff was again addressing Henry.

"Mr. Silverman, you are in a lot of trouble. I believe it is fair to tell you that we know that the minutes were backdated. The Treasury Department has a program called ink tagging. Most ink manufacturers are participating in this program. These manufacturers change their chemical formulations each year. Each change represents a date prior to which that particular ink did not exist.

"We had the minutes analyzed by our scientists at the Bureau of Alcohol, Tobacco and Firearms. The ink on the minutes was compared with the standard ink samples kept in the library. Your ink matches a library ink that did not exist when the document was dated."

Henry sat in his seat with a defeated look on his face.

Ted had heard of ink sleuths before. Apparently ink tagging aided the prosecutors in the case against former Vice-President Spiro Agnew. An individual had kept a diary of the kickbacks given to Agnew. Scientists were able to verify that all the inks used were available at the time of the entries. Further, the sequence of the entries showed a random pattern consistent with day-to-day work in a diary. Needless to say, in 1973 Agnew pleaded no contest to income tax evasion.

In another court decision a Texas businessman withdrew $15,000 from his company. He claimed that the money was a loan and therefore tax-free. The IRS said the sum was a taxable dividend. The Texan had to prove that he intended to repay the money at the time of the transfer. He produced a promissory note which he claimed to have signed in December of the year he received the money. Two ink experts testified that the ink used to sign the note was not manufactured until a year and a half later. The Texan met his Alamo.

Jeff was not finished with Henry. "Mr. Silverman, we do want the working papers and other records involving Mr. Strovee's tax returns. I hope you are familiar with the facts in the *Couch* decision? I suggest you also peruse the case of *U.S. v. Edmond.*"

Both Henry and Ted were familiar with the *Couch* decision. Here a summons had been served upon an accountant to obtain his working papers with respect to a client. The accountant ignored the summons and surrendered the records to an attorney. The purpose of this transfer was to allow the taxpayer to use his Fifth Amendment right to keep the working papers away from the IRS.

The Supreme Court held that constitutional rights cannot be enlarged by such a transfer. The rights and obligations of the parties became fixed when the summons was served. A transfer of the records can *not* alter these rights and obligations. The attorney had to give the working papers to the IRS.

Henry had never heard of *Edmond*. He merely nodded yes.

Ted realized that he was losing control of the interview. "Excuse me, Mr. Burke, I'm sure you are aware that any evidence obtained by misrepresentation and deception will not be allowed in a court of law."

"What do you mean by deception?"

"You failed to give my client, Carl Strovee, the proper *Miranda* warning when you interviewed him with Mr. Silverman. You used trickery and deceit in order to obtain evidence — the minutes — from my client. You did not tell him he had the right to refuse to answer questions, and that he could obtain legal counsel. Furthermore, today you failed to give these same warnings to Mr. Silverman."

Jeff turned and spoke to Henry. "Mr. Silverman, did you read my credentials when I handed them to you? Did you know that I was a Special Agent?"

"Uh, yes," Henry replied.

Jeff turned to Ted Abbott. "You know that the manual rules are for internal administration and are not constitutionally mandated. Courts have refused to make the *Miranda* warnings fundamental to due process."

"Correction," Ted shot back, "*some* courts have refused to make them fundamental to due process. This whole charade has been a sneaky, deliberate deception to obtain the minutes of the corporation."

"Surely, Mr. Abbott, you remember the *Prudden* decision. The mere failure of an agent to warn a taxpayer that an investigation may result in criminal charges, assuming there are no acts by the agent which materially misrepresent the nature of the inquiry, do not constitute fraud, deceit, or trickery. Do you want me to give you a citation to this case?"

"No, but I have a copy of the *Tweel* decision for you to read. I've underlined some passages pertinent to this situation." The attorney handed Jeff several pages.

Jeff was worried. He should have given the *Miranda* warning. How could he have forgotten? He knew that although investigative subterfuge has long been an indispensable tool of tax law enforcement, since *Tweel* any introduction of an agent must include his actual title. Jeff knew that the lawyer was correct. *Some* courts had held that the failure to give the *Miranda* warning would require suppression of any evidence received. But there had been some erosion of this doctrine during the Reagan era.

The lawyer interrupted Jeff's thoughts. "You are, of course, aware of the exclusion rule. Any evidence obtained illegally by the IRS cannot be used against a taxpayer in any criminal proceeding. The minutes are inadmissible evidence because they were obtained from my client without prescribed warnings or assistance of counsel."

"You are entitled to your opinion, Mr. Abbott, but you are wrong."

"We shall see." The lawyer stood up and said, "Mr. Silverman, I believe it is time for us to leave."

As both Ted and Henry were leaving, Jeff looked directly at Henry and said, "You'll have the materials which we want by next Wednesday, I hope."

"Yeah," Henry replied softly.

Ted was mad as they walked out of the IRS building. "Why didn't you tell me that you had backdated the minutes of the meeting?" he angrily demanded.

Henry shot back, "How did I know those federal snoopers had an ink tagging program? Nothing is sacred anymore. Pretty soon they'll be checking our urine on a weekly basis to determine our weekly expenditures."

"You should know better than to backdate records," the lawyer responded to the outburst.

"What court do you suggest we go to?"

"Well, you should know the rule of thumb. If you have the law in your favor, go to the U.S. Tax Court; if you have the facts in your favor, go to the district court; and if you have neither in your favor, you go to the U.S. Claims Court."

Henry just shook his head.

"Well, we've got two turkeys in the frying pan now — a vanilla one and a chocolate one. I hope you realize that anyone who willfully aids or assists in, counsels or advises the preparation of a document which is false or fraudulent as to any material matter is guilty of a felony. I suggest you read Section 7206 of the Internal Revenue Code. Then you may wish to give me a call. I'll need a substantial retainer — say $15,000."

Under his breath, Henry mumbled, "Forget it." Henry went back to his office and looked up Section 7206. He was guilty of a felony. Upon conviction he could be fined not more than

$100,000, or imprisoned not more than three years, or both, together with the costs of prosecution.

Next Henry found *U.S. v. Edmond*. More bad news. Here a public accountant, who was basically a return-preparer, gave his working papers to his taxpayer-client after receipt of an IRS summons. In court the taxpayer maintained that the working papers were stolen from his automobile, where they were stored. The accountant was found guilty of civil contempt and assessed compensatory damages of $4,000. He avoided a jail sentence only because it was impossible for him to purge himself of the contempt citation by delivering the "stolen" records to the IRS.

Henry checked some material dealing with John Doe summonses. These are third-party summonses that do not name the person with respect to whose liability they are issued. He found that such a summons may be issued only after an ex parte court proceeding in which the IRS establishs that:

1) the summons relates to the investigation of a particular person or ascertainable group or class of persons,
2) there is a reasonable basis for believing that such person, group, or class of persons may have failed to pay income taxes, and
3) the information sought to be obtained from the examination of the records was not readily available from other sources.

So the agents were bluffing here. They would have to bring a lawsuit to get this information.

Henry was nervous when he dialed Carl Strovee's phone number. He couldn't afford a conflict with the IRS. A messy conflict would adversely affect his tax practice, especially his seminars. Who would attend a seminar taught by someone who got caught?

There was no answer. Carl was normally at home.

After trying Carl's number for about two hours, Henry went over to Carl's apartment. No one answered the doorbell.

Henry told the doorman that he was afraid that Carl had had a heart attack.

When the doorman opened Carl's door, Henry was stunned. The apartment was denuded of any of Carl's personal effects. All of his paintings were gone. The safe was open. Henry knew that Carl had left — for good.

For twenty-five dollars, the doorman allowed Henry to look around the apartment. Henry could not find his working papers. He was as good as dead.

CHAPTER 12

> The old American dream of someday becoming a millionaire is largely a pipe dream if the would-be millionaire pays the highest tax rates on ordinary income without taking some steps to minimize taxes.
>
> — Hugh C. Bickford

Last night had been successful for Jeff Burke. His surveillance of the Flesher garbage dumpster had finally paid off. He found one dollar, four aluminum cans, *and* the practice run of the football slips used in the gambling racket in Baltimore. They had printed the slips for the next two weeks and had forgotten to destroy the discarded slips.

Jeff was jubilant when he returned to call Hank Brown, the other Special Agent helping him with the Flesher case. Actually, it was Hank's "jacketed case"; Jeff helped Hank out with the surveillance.

"Hello, Hank; got some good news. Flesher ran off the football slips yesterday and I found the practice run. I have them in an envelope on my desk. Should I send it to the FBI and get the fingerprints lifted?"

"Great! Yes, send them in. Let them know that your prints are on it. I don't want them to lock you up. This case may have more significance than we thought. Guess who is the owner of the plumbing outfit? Ms. Andre Flesher, the *wife* of B.W. Flesher. She works there several times a week, but draws a $62,000 salary. Probably unreasonable compensation."

"Super! We'll disallow part of her salary. I better check on the pen register. I'll get that off before we blow the case."

"You're right. Get that off fast!"

"I'll call my man and get him to take it off tonight. What do we do now?"

"I'm going to watch the plumbing shop this afternoon and tomorrow. I'll photograph anyone who enters or leaves the place. I believe their gambling operation is in the back. I've been inside — bought some washers for my leaking spigots. Would you believe I fixed two last night? Maybe I could disguise myself as a plumber and infiltrate the organization."

"You could probably make more money. A plumber is paid well. But you'll have to join a union," joked Jeff.

Hank liked to joke himself but resented anyone else who followed through with a joke. "Anyway," he broke in, "there is a door which leads to the back room. The front room seems very small compared to the length of the building. We probably should begin to make plans for raiding the plumbing shop. Should we raid the porno shop and the printing shop also?"

"I don't know," replied Jeff. "Let me think about it awhile. I'll call you tomorrow and let you know the results of the pen register."

After hanging up Jeff called his telephone man and instructed him to remove the pen register at the plumbing outlet. Jeff asked his contact to call him back in the morning and let him know the number of outgoing calls.

Jeff took the discarded football cards and wrote his initials and date on the back of them with his anthracene pencil. He did this so that he could later testify that they were the cards he found. Anthracene is a substance that can be obtained either in powder form or pencil form. It is invisible, but gives off a brilliant fluorescence when exposed to ultraviolet light. It can be placed on documents or other objects that a Special Agent might want to identify later.

He then made a photostatic copy of the cards and put them in a large, brown envelope, writing a description of the contents on the face of the envelope. He then sent the envelope to the FBI fingerprinting division.

Jeff began jotting down some notes. He drew a diagram of B.W. Flesher's known business associations.

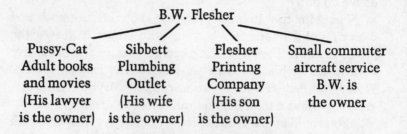

B.W. Flesher

Pussy-Cat	Sibbett	Flesher	Small commuter
Adult books	Plumbing	Printing	aircraft service
and movies	Outlet	Company	B.W. is
(His lawyer	(His wife	(His son	the owner
is the owner)	is the owner)	is the owner)	

The businesses were called brother-sister corporations in tax jargon. B.W. Flesher had all the trademarks of an organized crime member. Or he was a front for someone else. The plumbing outlet was owned by his wife; it was probably a front for gambling.

His fourteen-year-old son was the owner of the printing company. It was a Subchapter S corporation. It was probably a legitimate business except that it probably printed the pornographic books. Nothing wrong with a minor child owning an S corporation. Good tax planning, thought Jeff. An S corporation is taxed like a partnership.

Flesher's lawyer was apparently the "front" or "nominee" owner of the pornographic business. Well-known criminals or underworld figures often place their business operations in the name of their lawyer in order to lend an aura of respectability to the business. Trusted girlfriends or wives have been known to hide assets for racketeers.

Retail adult book stores are generally *not* directly owned by members of organized crime. Although the porno business itself is legal, investigative experience indicates that large amounts of income are never reported for tax purposes.

The bookstore is the largest and most profitable outlet of pornography. Here sex-oriented books, magazines, photography, "peep shows," films and other erotic items are displayed and sold. Illegal hardcore pornography material is often sold "under the counter" for regular customers who are not suspected of being the "fuzz."

Sexually-oriented manuscripts are purchased from individuals at nominal prices. These manuscripts are then sent to a printing establishment for volume printing and the books are later sold to related or controlled corporations. These corporations may be shell corporations in order to provide legal insulation. The books are then distributed to local retail stores to be sold to the general public. The printing company may never receive payment for the books.

The small commuter aircraft company might be involved in narcotics. The planes may be used to smuggle drugs into the country. The narcotics business is organized like a legitimate importing-wholesaling-retailing business. Only organized crime could provide the large amount of funds and the international connections necessary for a long-term cocaine distribution system.

Then again, Jeff thought, the aircraft business might be legitimate. A prominent figure in organized crime may not have a legitimate source of funds. Often his only means of support is from income realized through illegal activities. Thus, in order to be able to prove how he supports himself and his family, the individual has to have a source of legal income which he reports for income tax purposes. He must find a business which will put him on the payroll and issue him a regular payroll check. Sometimes these payroll payments are returned to the business in cash and diverted.

Flesher's wife was receiving a large salary for the performance of few services for the plumbing company. Mr. Flesher may be getting a large salary from the aircraft company, Jeff hypothesized.

A stab of doubt erupted inside Jeff. Maybe he and Hank were all wrong. Maybe all these businesses were legitimate. Maybe the businesses were operating labor black markets. Maybe . . .

During the Carter administration, a combination of high

inflation and tax increases imposed a heavy tax burden on individual businesses. Labor unions continued to increase in power and United States goods became too high priced to compete with foreign goods.

But Ayn Rand, author and conservative philosopher, had been wrong. In her classic book, *Atlas Shrugged*, her heroes, producers and workers, just stopped working because of the oppressive governmental regulations and high income taxes. When all the producers "retired," the world collapsed.

Rather than retiring, the producers/workers went underground. Many Americans adopted the Latin approach to the problem of the disappearing value of the dollar. A network of unofficial jobs was created in a secret economy. This clandestine industry became known as the labor black market.

About ten million individuals worked part time or full time at jobs that did not officially exist. Entire families worked at home in the basement or in a hidden room making towels, shoes, furniture, and other necessities. Barbers worked after hours doing electrical or plumbing chores. Policemen worked after hours as carpenters. There were rumors that some Southern states were tacitly encouraging the labor black market.

Why? Wages at these unofficial jobs were substandard. But with no tax or social security payments, these low salaries might be higher than the counterpart salary with a tax rate as high as forty-five percent.

Pro-union laws do not allow employers to fire inefficient or unneeded employees. Soaring fringe benefit payments and high official wages resulted in runaway inflation. Right-to-work laws were outlawed. The government merely ignored the continued deterioration in the U.S. balance of trade.

Americans adopted the sport of fiddling. This game of fiddling is slang for cheating; tax evasion became popular. The short-lived reduction in individual tax rates in 1986 did not stop fiddling. Plumbers, carpenters, and other home-repair specialists began to quote two prices for a repair job; one price for payment by check and a lower price for a cash payment. The cash payment could easily be shielded from the tax collector. Even salaried employees began to pad their expense accounts, often with the tacit approval of their employers. This mechanism allowed the employees to receive tax-free income. The high tax burden and the price increases outstripping the wage increases were the prime causes of the new nation of fiddlers.

In the early nineties the Republican party had disappeared like the Federalists and Whigs. The new era of a one-party system ushered in new problems such as corruption and bribery. It was not uncommon to have only one slate of candidates to vote for on an election day. Jeff was a member of the Democratic party only because otherwise he could not have a government job. There were now only closet Republicans or Independents. Deviating from *the* Democratic party was dangerous to one's advancement and health.

Part of the United States' problem had been the slow growth in productivity and output since the early 1960s. Even poor Great Britain had experienced more per capita growth than the United States. The low two percent increase in real output per employed individual had been due to resources being applied to government and consumption and not enough resources devoted to United States capital formation. Capital formation is what makes growth possible.

Some economists believe that the multiple taxation of income which is saved and invested has caused a fundamental bias against capital formation. Income that is saved is taxed at higher rates than income used for consumption. Why? Income spent on consumer goods is taxed only once, whereas a second tax must be paid on dividends, interest, and gains that result from investing or saving income. Quite naturally United States individuals save and invest less. The elimination of the favorable capital gain rates during the Reagan administration only compounded the problem.

Maybe, Jeff thought, we'll find out if Flesher is a crook when we raid his places.

CHAPTER 13

Where there is an income tax, the just man will pay more and the unjust less on the same amount of income.

— Plato

Jeff noticed the short item in the paper himself.

Two Baltimore police officials found $77,240 in the back of a van stopped for drunk driving arrest and took the funds into custody for "safekeeping."

According to the local press, the car was driven by Charles Z. Samson, and the money in $5, $20 and $100 bills was banded into $1000 stacks and stuffed in a brown paper bag under the vehicle's back seat.

Samson denied knowledge of the money and told officers the van belonged to the company for whom he worked.

Jeff called the police department and found that the van was owned by Stibbett Plumbing Outlet. What a break! This probably was money being transferred in Flesher's gambling racket.

Jeff called Hank Brown and gave him the details. Hank prepared a quick assessment and seized the money. Since Charles Samson had previously been arrested for allegedly smuggling marijuana and cocaine, Hank seized his home, his Chevrolet pickup, and his bank account. To rub it in, Hank placed a lien on the $5,000 bond that an anonymous friend posted for his release from police custody.

In addition to seizures for tax purposes, the IRS can seize assets related to the sale or transfer of illegal narcotics. This includes items used to transport (i.e., cars, boats, planes) and items bought with illegal drug proceeds (i.e., ranches, houses, businesses). It is through this seizure process that the IRS gets a lot of cars for special agents to drive.

Hank informed Mr. Samson that he owed $87,500 in taxes, payable immediately, on income earned to that point. Hank told Jeff that he wanted to be rough on Mr. Samson in the hopes that he would confess that he was a pick-up man for Mr. Flesher.

It was not uncommon for seizures and assessments to sometimes far exceed apparent tax liability. The Nixon administration before Watergate had used the little-known tax law that provides for quick assessment and seizure of tax from people who appear to be about to flee very effectively in a crusade against illicit drug dealers.

Operating in ninety metropolitan areas and over a two-and-a-half-year period, over $27 million was seized by the IRS and an additional $101 million was assessed against 3,500 drug suspects.

The seizure law is more than a half-century old. The law is vague and places few restrictions upon the IRS. The language of the law leaves the courts with little cause for intervention.

Local police departments often work closely with IRS agents. If the police arrest someone and the person has a sizeable amount of money, the arresting officer may immediately call the IRS. Where there are indications that the person is dealing in drugs, gambling, or other illegal activities, the agent will make a large tax assessment and grab the individual's money or property in order to cover the assessment. The agent may seize the assets even before making the formal assessment.

Jeff recalled one episode while he was working in the Miami office. Apparently Sharon Mills, a former National Airlines stewardess, was arrested for speeding in northern Miami. Rather than writing a speeding ticket, the plainclothesmen took her to the police station. Instead of being policemen, they were actually narcotics agents, and they searched her purse. They found $4,420 in cash, a small bottle containing four pills, and a .38 Colt revolver.

She was charged with speeding, carrying a concealed weapon, and possession of drugs. The IRS seized her money, several rings, and other jewelry she was wearing. The IRS informed Ms. Mills that she owed $25,449 in back taxes and seized her safe deposit box at her bank.

Apparently Ms. Mills, a divorcee, lived with George Craver, who was alleged in court to be a major seller and smuggler of marijuana and cocaine. Craver had never been charged with these crimes and denied dealing drugs.

In court an IRS agent indicated that the $25,449 tax assessment was the tax on an estimated commission Ms. Mills allegedly received for helping Craver and others sell cocaine. In further testimony the agent admitted that neither the police or the IRS had any evidence that Ms. Mills participated in the scheme or derived any income from it. They could only prove that Ms. Mills lived with George Craver.

The police charges were dropped against Ms. Mills. She was found innocent of speeding. The pills in her purse were prescribed by a doctor, and she carried the gun legally. There was no known evidence that the $4,420 came from an illicit source.

When Jeff left Miami, the IRS still had the money, the safe-deposit box, and the $25,449 assessment was in effect. Reason: Assessment and collection of tax may be restrained by the courts only when 1) it was clear that under no circumstances could the IRS ultimately prevail, *and* 2) the taxpayer would suffer no irreparable injury for which there is no adequate remedy under law.

Hank called Jeff later in the afternoon. "Jeff, we are going to raid the plumbing and printing shop tomorrow morning."

Jeff asked, "Do we have probable cause?" Jeff knew that a warrant must be based upon probable cause in order to be valid. This illusive concept of probable cause consists of facts or circumstances which would lead a reasonably cautious and prudent person to believe that

1) the person to be arrested is committing a crime or has committed a felony, or
2) the property subject to seizure is on the premises to be searched and an offense involving it has been or is being committed.

"The fact that a large sum of money was found in the plumbing truck and the discarded practice run of the gambling tickets in the outside garbage bin should be enough evidence for probable cause," Hank reasoned.

But Jeff asked, "Was the garbage bin evidence obtained in violation of constitutional provisions and therefore not permissible in a later trial?"

"No, the evidence from the garbage bin is okay," answered Hank. "When an individual throws records in a trash can, the person has abandoned the records and cannot claim that you violated his rights under the Fourth Amendment."

"You're probably right," agreed Jeff.

"We will meet at eight o'clock in the morning for instructions. There will be eight of us in the search party. Will you be able to help us?"

"Sure."

At eight o'clock Hank addressed the seven assembled people. Hank was the raid leader. He had organized the search party and he was charged with the responsibility of conducting the search.

"Good morning. I decided to raid Flesher before they move their operations. With the police finding the $77,000 in the plumbing truck and us slapping liens on the truck and the money, they may decide to move out. I believe they are

115

operating a gambling racket in the plumbing outlet. Also, I believe they store wagering paraphernalia in both the plumbing and printing shop.

"Here is a copy of the search warrant. The warrant is based upon information which I provided Magistrate Howard yesterday. He reviewed my affidavit, placed me under oath, and I signed the affidavit. He issued the warrant, which is good for ten days. But I wish to hit as soon as possible.

"The remainder of the raid kit you have contains the normal items. Let me review them since this is the first raid for Jane Henderson. Good luck, Jane." Hank motioned to a smiling Jane sitting on his right.

"There's an arrest warrant. Please take a couple of minutes to read my memo setting forth the plan for the raid, responsibilities of each of you, and a description of the suspected violators. There is a detailed map showing the location and approximate interior layout of both the plumbing and printing shops. You have masking tape to seal entry and discharge chambers of any gaming devices; money wrappers, pencils, writing pads, paper sacks, and a hand stapler are included.

"You have the following forms:

"Seized property notice and identification tags;
Inventory record of seized vessels, vehicles,
 and aircrafts;
Special monies reports;
Appraisement list for seized personal property;
Seized property report;
Affidavits; and
Summons."

Jeff quickly read through the memo explaining the plan of the raid. He noticed that he would go with Hank, Jane, the greenhorn, and a fourth agent to the plumbing outlet. He and Hank would enter the front door. Jane and the other agent would cover the back exit. They were to use subterfuge to gain entrance to the back room.

"Are there any questions?" Hank was speaking again. Seeing there were no questions, Hank continued. "We have CB radios in our cars. We will try to enter both places at the same time. I will call you on Channel 38 at 9:59. When I give the signal 'cantaloupe,' go to your designated entry point and enter."

Jeff and the three agents parked near the plumbing outlet at 9:45. Hank said, "Okay, let's set our watches. I have 9:45. Frank, you and Jane go to the corner. When you see us get out, go directly to the back door. Do not try to enter until exactly 10:00."

At 9:57 Jeff called the other mobile unit and gave the speaker to Hank. At 9:59 Hank spoke firmly the word "cantaloupe" twice into the speaker. "Did you copy?"

"10-4" was the response.

Jeff and Hank put on their Special Agent badges and walked briskly toward the plumbing outlet. Once inside the business Hank walked up to the counter, pointed to his Special Agent badge, and showed his credentials. As Jeff walked behind the counter to the door leading to the back room he saw the employee's hand reach under the counter and push a button.

Hank identified himself and began to read the search warrant to the employee.

The door was locked. Jeff knocked on the door. "We are federal agents with a search warrant. Open up immediately," he shouted.

Jeff waited a reasonable amount of time — about four seconds. He knocked again. "Open up the door. I'm a federal agent with a search warrant," Jeff roared. After several seconds Jeff stepped back and then smashed his shoulder into the door; it didn't open. He hit it again; his shoulder was hurting. The door didn't open. He then stuck a crowbar near the lock of the door and firmly yanked on it. There was a sharp, cracking sound. Jeff crashed into the door again. It flew open.

Jeff shouted, "Come on, Frank!" Jeff saw several employees shoving reports and paper into two shredding machines. Still other people were throwing papers into a fire and washing papers in a sink.

Hank came in behind Jeff, pushing the outside employee onto the floor. He shouted, "Stop that, you are under arrest. There's a federal law against the destruction of evidence."

Frank and the other agent could not get in the back door. Jeff ran to the back door and unlocked it. When he turned around he saw that the employees were still shredding and burning the evidence.

Jeff ran toward the fire since Hank was heading for the shredders. With his gun still drawn, Jeff shoved two people away from the fire. The paper shredders became silent as Hank pulled the plugs.

The greenhorn agent turned off the water. Apparently the records were water soluble. Jeff noticed one employee putting his hand inside a drawer at his desk. Jeff turned and pointed his gun directly at the bald head of the man and said firmly, "Withdraw that hand very slowly or you are a dead man."

The man was so surprised and frightened that he actually fell backward in his chair.

Jeff moved to the desk drawer expecting to see a pistol. Instead he saw a buzzer inside the desk drawer. Jeff turned toward the man on the floor and asked, "What's the buzzer for?"

The man merely shook his head. Jeff walked over and raised his gun as if to strike the man. The man covered his head with his arms and began shouting, "Don't hit me! Please don't hit me!"

Jeff didn't. He knew that a Special Agent can use only that degree of force necessary to ensure compliance with the order of arrest. Use of excessive force could subject him to lawsuits and disciplinary action. A gun may be drawn from a holster only if an agent's life or that of a fellow law enforcement officer is in danger.

But the man would not tell what was the purpose of the buzzer.

They had hit the jackpot, however. There was a row of about twenty telephones used in the bookmaking racket. The employees were unable to destroy all of the papers and records, which could be used in a later trial. About one-half of the large room was filled with coin-operated gaming devices and other gambling paraphernalia.

Two agents took all of the employees to the front of the room and began the process of fingerprinting all of them. Each individual was advised of his or her constitutional rights. Ms. Andre Flesher was not working, but Rob's old lady was among the employees caught. "Too bad," thought Jeff, "Rob may have to go to work."

Jeff and Hank began the tedious search of the entire establishment. All articles which could be of evidentiary value were marked with anthracene pencils for identification. The markings did not injure the evidence itself, yet were not subject to obliteration. The markings denoted which agent found the item, the date, time, and exact spot where it was located. They made photographs of the back room and the paraphernalia and the property. Photographs would make it easier to refresh their memories at the time of the trial.

Once the tagging was completed, they brought the person who they thought was in charge of the operation into the back room. They made an inventory of all the property they were going to seize in the presence of the man. Hank had the man sign a copy of the warrant and a signed copy of the inventory of the seized property.

They closed down the plumbing outlet. They padlocked the doors. They placed the following sign with bright red letters on both the front and back doors: "WARNING: United States Government Seizure." They seized the four plumbing trucks in the back lot.

It had been a good day. Enough records were found to estimate the volume of bookmaking activity that had occurred for the past several years. The seized betting slips and other documents would be excellent evidence to impose the wagering excise tax against the owner.

As expected, there were only three days of records. Records are destroyed after three days. But they would be able to determine the gross volume per day. If they could place Flesher in

119

business for three years, they would be able to extrapolate backwards to calculate the 10% excise tax on the gross daily receipts.

There is, of course, a wagering excise tax on the "take" of anyone in the business of accepting wagers. Then, of course, there were the corporate income taxes owed on the income from the entire operation.

They would be able to project the average daily receipts from the seized records over the time Flesher had been in operation. Jeff knew that courts will generally accept such projections by the IRS unless the taxpayer can prove otherwise. As one court indicated:

> It is immaterial whether the IRS proceeded upon the wrong theory in determining the deficiency. The taxpayer has the burden of showing that the assessment is wrong upon proper theory.

The other four agents found some gambling paraphernalia and a storage of pornographic books and movies at the printing shop. Hank joked that the agents would have a good time sorting through the seized materials making sure it was pornographic. "How else can a determination be made that the books and movies are 'porno' except by reviewing a fair sample of the material?"

Hank indicated that he would begin a surveillance of the Pussy-cat bookstore and the commuter aircraft service. "When I have probable cause for a raid, I'll be in touch."

CHAPTER 14

There's nothing that says a man has to take a toll bridge across a river when there's a free bridge nearby. [Referring to tax avoidance.]

— Senator Pat Harrison

Henry Silverman had called Jeff the previous evening. Henry was obviously scared. He asked Jeff for immunity. Henry was willing to testify against Carl Strovee. But Henry made the mistake of telling Jeff that Carl had left town.

At first Jeff would not bite. Suddenly Henry said, "I have some information about an employee of the IRS. For immunity, I'll give you the full details of this individual's illegal activities."

Jeff became more cooperative. "I'll give you a tentative promise of immunity *if* the IRS employee is significant *and* you can provide convincing evidence of wrongdoing."

"Look, Jeff, the information is quite valuable." Of course, Jeff knew that an agent had no authority to make a personal promise of immunity. Even if the promise is made, it would not be binding by the IRS. Someone higher up in the organization must provide the binding commitment.

"Okay, Henry, I will come down to the jail this afternoon and talk about it."

In the late afternoon paper, a short article appeared:

Henry Silverman, author of a newsletter entitled "How to Cheat and Defraud the IRS," was held on a $120,000 bond Tuesday after his arrest on an indictment alleging a violation of federal income tax laws. Silverman, who writes under the pen name I.M. Clever, was indicted and was arrested by IRS intelligence division agents. Silverman appeared before U.S. Magistrate Blane Hunter. The indictment accused Silverman of knowingly preparing false corporate minutes in connection with a corporate tax matter.

Jeff talked to Henry around 4:30 at the county jail. Henry's information *was* valuable. He knew Richard Onner.

"Richard Onner attended one of my seminars under an assumed name. He seemed to be interested in how to embezzle money with the use of a computer," Henry related his information to Jeff.

"After the seminar he took me to dinner. He indicated that he worked for a large company which received a large amount of cash through the mail. I referred him to an article which appeared in the *Journal of Accountancy* about computer frauds. I figured he was lying about his employer.

"Several weeks went by and he called me again. At least he had his secretary call me. She gave me his name and city. We had lunch. He wanted my advice about how to set up a system whereby a claims reviewer could prepare false claims payable to friends. He wanted the computer to pay the claims automatically.

"He paid me two hundred dollars for my time," Henry continued. "Several days later I called his home number in Martinsburg. His girlfriend answered the phone. She gave me his office number. A simple call to his office phone gave me his employer — the IRS. I figure he's ripping off some bread. I'm willing to testify about my meetings with him if you'll get me off the hook. How about it?"

"I can't promise anything, Henry, but I'll try to help you. Keep cool."

When Jeff returned to his office he received a frightening

telephone call. He was not prepared for the call. Detective Garrison was on the other end.

"You found her," the voice almost shouted.

"Found whom?" asked a puzzled Jeff.

"You found the killer. The hair which you gave me belonged to the killer. Who is she?"

Jeff was silent for a moment. He had slept with her all night. Why had she not tried to kill him? Maybe she was merely after Jake. But why would she take such a chance and pick him up for a one night stand?

"Hello! Are you still there?" the voice on the other end of the line broke his concentration. "Who is she?"

"Uh, Deidre Moore," Jeff replied. "You will not believe this, but I picked her up at the Hilton the other day when I was checking out the model aeronautics convention. I stayed with her the entire night," Jeff admitted.

"Boy, you picked a fine bedfellow. We used an Aggie nuclear hair analysis. Do you know what an Aggie is? That's an alumnus of Texas A&M University. There must be a thousand Aggie jokes. Did you hear the one about the Aggie who invented an ejection seat for a helicopter? That's the joke.

"Anyway, at A&M there's a nuclear hair analyzer. This device analyzes thirty or more characteristics in each strand of hair from a human. A conventional microscope can provide on an average only seven identifiable characteristics such as color and texture. In fact, hair tests are preferable to urinalysis for detecting drug use. A hair will show the degree to which a person is a chemical abuser.

"Neutron activation analysis makes many elements in the hair radioactive. Each element that is irradiated produces a distinct signal which can be monitored and recorded. A strand of hair is *almost* as good as a fingerprint. The chance of reproduction of the same combination in another person's hair is one in six million. This is called the likelihood ratio that the hair on the model airplane matches the hair which you gave me."

Garrison took a deep breath and continued. "There was, of course, surface contamination from the explosion. So both hairs were washed and analyzed. The great thing about forensic activation analysis is that the wash solution can be retained and studied separately from the clean hairs. This technique does not destroy the item analyzed. The two hairs can be preserved for use in the courtroom or for further tests."

Garrison chuckled. "My Aggie scientist indicates that the tests showed that Napoleon had ingested a significant amount of arsenic twice during his life, but not enough to kill him. He indicates that the trace elements are significantly different between male and female hair. This allows identification of the sex of the supplier of unknown hair at least ninety percent of the time.

"The murderer of your friend was a woman. The hair which you gave me is quite similar to the hair found on the plane. In all likelihood they are the same person. She's a strawberry blonde who uses a rinse to hide the gray hairs. She's in her forties. She has lived around steel mills — maybe she's around Pittsburgh or Gary, Indiana. Good diet, so she is middle or upper class.

"Where can we find her? Where does she live?" the detective asked abruptly.

"I don't know. Wait a minute. Her registration form indicated that she was from Kent, Ohio. She registered for the Academy of Model Aeronautics Convention held at the Hilton Hotel two weeks ago."

"The hair does not provide absolute identification. But if we can find her workroom where she built the model plane, we can match the pieces of the exploded plane with material in her workshop. In another courtroom situation a man was convicted of murdering a former girlfriend by sending a bomb through the mail which exploded upon opening. With reasonable scientific certainty the prosecution was able to show that the particles from the exploded bomb matched materials found in his workshop."

"Look," Jeff said, "I'll check Kent, Ohio, and will be back in touch. I'll also try to get the signed registration form."

There was a dull click at the other end of the line.

Jeff was curious so he went to the IRS library and found the Kent, Ohio, phone book. He made a list of the various Moores listed as well as the number for Kent State University. There were five Moores, so he went back to his office and called each of the numbers. He was able to call four of the numbers, but no one by the name of Deidre lived at any of the four numbers. Jeff then called information at Kent State and got the telephone number of the Psychology Department. There was no Professor Moore on the Psychology faculty.

"So she lied to me," Jeff thought. He decided to try a different tack altogether. Jeff then called Martinsburg and asked for the names, addresses, and a copy of the tax returns of all taxpayers with the last name of Moore listing themselves as a professor or educator. The computer could do this chore in a short period of time.

As easy as it was to get tax returns, it was surprising that more tax returns were not "leaked to the press." Nixon's tax return was leaked by a dissatisfied IRS employee. Yet, known unlawful disclosures of private citizens' tax returns have been relatively infrequent. The guilty party could go to prison.

The small number of tax disclosures was not due to the lack of opportunity, however. The IRS relies very heavily on the integrity of its employees rather than on strict enforcement of security measures. The law requires the IRS and other federal agencies to protect the confidentiality of the taxpayer's data. But Jeff knew that security weaknesses were numerous. Under the computerized data retrieval system more than 48,000 authorized users had instantaneous access to most taxpayers' records.

The IRS was powerful and intimidating. A massive computer system makes America's income tax returns available on thousands of terminals in IRS offices. Costing one billion dollars, the computer system provided forty-eight thousand

IRS employees with access to the tax returns through nine thousand terminals scattered throughout the country. IRS employees were able to obtain any tax returns for the past five years for any taxpayer in any of the ten regional computer centers. Big Brother was watching taxpayers.

Jeff left a note for his secretary to pull any information from the IRS computer files about Deidre Moore. It was a long shot. He also asked for any clippings about any research on subliminal suggestion.

Jeff had made plans to drive out to a Safe House on the outskirts of Baltimore. Several of Jake's informers were staying at the "Safe House." So far Jeff had been unable to learn anything of value from Jake's informers which might lead to the reason for his death or the identity of his killer. Jeff could now inquire about an educated, strawberry blonde hit woman.

As he was driving to the "Safe House," he remembered his conversation with Henry Silverman. He had forgotten all about Henry after the phone call concerning Deidre Moore. He wondered how valid the information was that Silverman had given him. Silverman had made some serious mistakes, but he was not stupid and didn't forget names or faces. If Richard Onner had been at one of his seminars, Silverman would have remembered. At this point in time, he didn't think Silverman would be doing any more lying. He just wanted to get out of his present situation if at all possible. Jeff made a mental note to check out Silverman's story at the first opportunity.

For now it was back to the task at hand. He surely hoped that he could get some information at the Safe House. A Safe House is a hideout for defectors, spies, and informers. An individual may need protection or may be in the process of obtaining a new identity. In the sixties this Safe House had been operated by the CIA under the code name "Operation Midnight Climax." It had been used in mind control experiments. Drug-addicted prostitutes were kept as one-hundred-dollar-a-day informers. They slipped LSD and other drugs to unknowing customers while CIA observers recorded what happened.

The Safe House was now used for more legal purposes. Although still operating as a brothel, it was a front for various agencies of the government. It came under the Federal Witness Protection Program (FWPP) and was operated by the U.S. Marshal's Service. An individual could be "hidden" at the brothel for a temporary period of time. Or an informer of organized crime might find the Safe House a temporary home before fading away into obscurity or at least trying to disappear permanently.

Neither of his informers could provide Jeff with any leads with respect to Jake's death. Further, no one was aware of a professional hit woman fitting the description Jeff had.

The trip had been a total waste. The old, two-story home reminded him of the stress seminars he had attended in Chicago as a young agent. The IRS operated the secret school for undercover Special Agents. They tested them with liquor and women in order to determine if they could resist disclosing their identities. The program had been billed as "stress seminars" for reimbursement purposes.

Buzz — Buzz — Buzz ——

Jeff ducked when he heard the sound. It was only a bee. Yet cold sweat rolled down his back. Could he never get the sound of that destructive airplane out of his mind?

CHAPTER 15

If taxes are the price we pay for a civilized society, let us be sure they are collected in a civil manner.

— Rep. Robin Tallon

"There are similarities between rare coin investing and the over-the-counter stock market. Rare coins on the wholesale market are sold on a bid-and-ask system, similar to the over-the-counter market. Several publications provide a weekly service of providing the bid-and-ask prices of the many coins available to a numismatist. Many weekly or monthly newspapers, magazines, and newsletters extol the virtues of collecting rare coins." Jack Rosenbaum was giving his standard speech at a Los Angeles coin club.

"A numismatist is a coin or paper money collector. Aside from the many types of coins and dates, a numismatist must worry about a maze of double-die varieties, overdates, mint errors, three-legged buffalos, and many other subtle differences. Coin collecting involves an art which has been practiced for almost two centuries.

"The name Rosenbaum has become synonymous with coin collecting and investing. Rosenbaum, Inc., is the major enterprise in the rare coin business. Rosenbaum is one of a diminishing breed of businesses — the family-owned enterprise."

Of course, Jack Rosenbaum did not include the following facts in his standard speech.

In the mid-'70s Rosenbaum was one of several large companies in the mail-order coin business. At the end of the '70s the rare coin industry went into a severe bear market similar to the 1954–64 coin bull market. Many of the mom-and-pop small retail dealers went out of business. But the coin slump was a blessing in disguise for Rosenbaum, Inc. The youthful president, Jack Rosenbaum, bought out many of these small retail dealers. His father had established the parent coin company many years earlier in Phoenix.

After the coin slump Rosenbaum controlled more than 1,500 small retail rare coin outlets. Much of the coin inventory had been bought at reduced prices during the middle of the bear market.

Slightly portly, Jack Rosenbaum was characteristically dressed in a brown double-breasted suit. He wore a full black mustache and had neatly parted wavy hair. When not lecturing, however, Jack Rosenbaum ran a tight shop; he told precious little about the business. His taciturnity took second-seat only to his fanatic obsession with profit-making. Employees indicated that Jack Rosenbaum was so tightfisted that he rummaged through employees' desks looking for excessive stockpiles of paper clips and pencils.

Rosenbaum, Inc., had two basic operations. The many investors were sold coins through the mail-order business located in Phoenix, Arizona. An investor is an individual who purchases a rare coin for the future price increase. He is in the coin market for a profit. An investor generally buys coin rolls or type coins. A type coin is the key coin that is needed in a collection which is composed of one of each coin in a given series.

Rosenbaum, Inc., sold rare coins through the mail like Cal Worthington sells used cars in Los Angeles. The coin prices are high. Once an investor buys the coin, it's at least five years before the person can sell the coin at his purchased price. "Buy them cheap, sell them high, turn that inventory over," was Jack Rosenbaum's philosophy. It worked with heavy advertising.

Rosenbaum, Inc., in essence, was in the business of selling rare coin portfolios. Sales were stimulated by advertising in such media as airline magazines, journals used in the medical profession and other similar outlets. Thus, its typical customers were those who responded to its sales pitch. These customers had little knowledge of the rare coin market.

Upon a showing of interest by a customer, Rosenbaum mailed to the customer an elaborate advertising brochure which contained a description of the procedures involved in choosing the rare coins. The advertising brochure sent to the customers consistently described the rare coins as an investment. There were comparisons of gains in the stock market with returns from rare coins. Analysis of coin appreciation and similar investment information were provided.

Jack continued his smooth talk. "If purchased with care along with some good luck, a rare coin can earn an investor a significant return on investment. Over the past nine years rare coins had an annual rate of appreciation of approximately 13%. Only antiques and paintings by old masters have outperformed rare coins." Jack did not tell the group that an investor who purchased coins from Rosenbaum paid a significant mark-up above retail.

Lifting up a red book, Jack said, "The retail price of coins can be found yearly in the numismatist's bible — the *Red Book*. This book has sold more copies than any other book except the Bible. Weekly or monthly retail price lists can be found in the various numismatic publications such as *Coin World* and *Numismatic News*." Jack omitted from his prepared speech that a rare coin buyer cannot sell his coin to a dealer at retail. The only way a buyer can sell at retail is through an auction. If sold at an auction, however, the buyer must pay a commission as high as 20%.

Dealers often speak about the possibility of a buyer selling his coins over the teletype system. Hundreds of dealers are connected to each other by teletype machines in their establishments. If the buyer uses the teletype, he must pay the dealer a fee.

Jack's slick investment brochures did not include a mention of "gray sheets." The wholesale price of rare coins is found in the "gray sheets" where both a bid and ask price are given for a particular coin. A dealer will try to pay as little as possible to a buyer when he tries to sell his coin. The most a buyer can receive is a 10 to 20% discount from the wholesale price.

Jack Rosenbaum's voice rose as he said that "the value of a rare coin depends to a certain extent upon the number of coins issued by the government in that particular series. In general, the fewer coins issued of a particular series, the more valuable the coin might be."

The condition of the coin is a very important factor in a coin's value. There are a number of grading systems, but the most common is the *Red Book* grading system:

	Grade	Description
PF.	Proof	Coin with a mirrorlike surface, specially struck for coin collectors.
UNC.	Uncirculated	New. Regular mint striking, but never placed in circulation.
EX. FINE	Extremely fine	Slightly circulated, with some luster but faint evidences of wear.
V. FINE	Very fine	Shows enough wear on high spots to be noticeable. Still retains enough luster to be desirable.
F.	Fine	Obviously a circulated coin, but little wear. Mint luster gone. All letters and mottos clear.
V.G.	Very good	Features clear and bold. Better than good, but not quite fine.
G.	Good	All of design, every feature, and legend must be plain, and date clear.
FAIR	Fair	Coin has sufficient design and letters to be easily identified. Excessive wear.

Jack did not mention the problem with grading. The condition of a coin is in the eyes of the beholder. When a dealer sells a coin he will often overgrade the coin in order to get a higher price for the coin. But when a person tries to sell the same coin to the dealer, the dealer will undergrade the coin. The dealer will try to steal it from him.

Then, of course, there are counterfeit coins. When one coin can sell for more than $400,000, naturally there will be counterfeiters.

There are also "whizzers." A machine is used to brush the coin in order to simulate mint condition. In other words, an almost uncirculated coin may be whizzed in order to make it look like an uncirculated coin. An uncirculated coin may sell for as much as 60% more than an almost uncirculated coin.

Rosenbaum, Inc., did not have to resort to counterfeit or whizzed coins. They used a technique called "sliding." The company would purchase an almost uncirculated coin and sell it to a customer under the uncirculated condition. Since most of their customers were not coin collectors, many years might go by before the buyer found out that he had been taken. He has bought a "slider," which is worth significantly less than an uncirculated coin. An uncirculated coin is one that has never been placed in circulation. It has luster and has no evidence of wear. A favorite strategy is to place three or four sliders in a roll of coins sold to an investor. The coin roll may be kept many years and exchange hands many times before those "sliders" are found. Many buyers look only at several coins at both ends of the roll before purchasing the roll of coins. Besides, a microscope is needed to accurately ascertain whether a coin is uncirculated.

"Rosenbaum, Inc., has not forgotten about the coin collector. Coin collectors are serviced by our more than 1,500 retail outlets throughout the U.S. They are in small and large cities, from Maine to California, from Michigan to Florida. Rare coins, mint sets, gold coins, silver dollars, coin rolls, commemorative coins, and many other numismatic items are sold from these small shops. Our buyers are school children, businessmen, priests, salesmen, carpenters, or any of the more than 12 million individuals who are devoted to this fine 'cultural hobby.'"

Obviously Jack did not speak about his inventory problem. Since the inventory turnover was slow, the coins were priced high in the retail outlets. Jack Rosenbaum checked on the small outlets regularly. Either he or two trusted employees visited the shops unannounced. It was not uncommon for an unkempt Jack Rosenbaum, possibly with a wig or sunglasses, to ring the security bell and then enter a shop to browse around. He would check the security system, cleanliness of the shop, friendliness of the employees, displays of the coin merchandise, and the advertisements in the local papers or telephone book. Obviously their published monthly magazine entitled "The Best Investment: Rare Coins!" had to be prominently displayed. Jack was quite proud of this publication. He personally wrote a "Dear Collector" letter for each issue. Well, he signed the letter; it was written by the editor of the magazine. That's what the editor was paid to do.

As a younger man Jack had published. He was, in fact, a lifetime member of the Numismatic Literary Guild. The organization's claim to fame is its yearly award of an old beat-up typewriter to one of its members.

Jack was admitted to the Guild for research he did on the origin of the word "Dixie," the nickname of the South. The Citizens' Bank of Louisiana in New Orleans issued a $10 note before the Civil War. These tenspots with the French word "DIX" (meaning ten) on its reverse became widely circulated in the South. In 1859 a composer by the name of Dan D. Emmett wrote a song which began, "I wish I wuz in de land of the dixes." The song became a hit, and the word dixes became corrupted to "dixie." Thus, a numismatic term gave the South its nickname.

All Rosenbaum shops also had a red, white, and blue sign indicating that an individual should "Buy the Book Before the Coin." Under another sign were free pamphlets entitled "Ask Us About Coins in IRS-approved IRA Plans." Many retirement programs were now purchasing gold and silver Eagle coins rather than securities.

Often the shop employee did not know that he had been visited. If anything was out of order or something needed attention, he would receive a telephone call the next day, followed by a letter outlining the demerits. Demerits meant a reduction in the shop employee's profit sharing plan at the end of the year. These unannounced visits were very effective. They kept the employees constantly on their toes.

Jack developed a system to eliminate skimming by shop employees. At least once a year shop employees had to take a lie detector test. Among other questions, shop employees were asked:

1) Did you steal any coins from the shop this year?
2) Did you receive any kick-backs from customers for selling coins at a discount or buying a coin for too much?
3) Did you skim off any of the profits of the coin shop this year?

Infrequently, an employee was fired because he flunked the lie detector test. The number of "flunks" was listed prominently in the corporate newsletter which went to each coin shop employee.

Whether a customer was purchasing coins from a coin shop or through the mail from Phoenix, the customer had a choice of payment. The customer could pay the full amount, naturally, and he received his overpriced coin. Or the customer could purchase the numismatic items under an installment plan. Payments for the coin or coins could be spread out over a number of months. The buyer received the coins only when he had paid all installments. Rosenbaum, Inc., had been the harbinger of the installment method in the coin industry.

Jack continued his sermon. "I am a former-President of the American Numismatic Association. This non-profit organization has the distinction of being one of the few organizations operating under a Federal Charter. The charter was signed by William H. Taft on May 9, 1912. Membership is open to any person 11 years of age or older. The organization provides a numismatic library in its Colorado Springs headquarters, presents awards and prizes, and provides a service of authenticity of numismatic materials submitted by anyone.

"While I was President of ANA, I led a campaign against the Treasury Department and the Bureau of the Mint. I campaigned with the slogan: 'The little man's friend.' My campaign was against the Treasury Department charging so much for the proof and mint sets which are sold each year.

"A proof set includes one of each type of coin minted during a particular year. The coins are made from carefully selected coin blanks that have been highly polished before being fed into the presses. The coins are hand-fed to a slow-moving press, and each coin is struck twice. The smooth, brilliant, mirror-like reflective surface makes the coin worth much more than even an uncirculated coin.

"A mint set has one coin of each denomination produced by a particular mint in a given year. A mint set has uncirculated coins, but they are not proof-like.

"The Tax Reform Act of 1986 caused an adverse effect upon many tax shelters such as oil and gas, real estate, and movies. These changes encouraged me to diversify. I created a publishing house."

Jack did not mention that he owned "The Factory."

Like a pied piper, Jack found a number of followers that evening. "Let the buyer beware" was forgotten by the assembled group. There were no tough or embarrassing questions from the audience.

CHAPTER 16

An income tax form is like a laundry list—either way you lose your shirt.

— Fred Allen

Richard Onner had one major flaw which he guarded vigorously. He was tall, slim, and handsome. He did not fit the image of a computer operator. In fact, he was the perfect image of the old-fashioned, straight-arrow G-man. He should have been a Special Agent or an FBI agent. He was a good computer operator. But he was a "fanaholic." Since high school Richard could not sleep unless a fan was running. He needed the constant hum of the fan to drown out any extraneous noise. He told his girlfriends that the fan helped the air conditioner. He said that the circulating air was good for his body and for his sex life. Even when he traveled Richard carried a small but noisy fan in his suitcase.

Onner entered the Rosenbaum Coin and Stamp Shop on Saturday morning. The small business was located on Main Street in Martinsburg. There were several teenagers in the shop. Two boys were looking at the inexpensive coins in the two for $1.00 box. A girl wearing braces on her teeth was thumbing through a United States stamp collection.

Onner merely browsed through the shop looking at the various coins in the finger-smudged glass counters. After the buzzer on the door indicated that the last teenager had left, Onner asked, "May I see this 1916 Standing Liberty Quarter?"

"Sure, it's a nice one. It's not often you can find an uncirculated 1916 Quarter," responded the smiling shop manager.

Onner knew that the Liberty standing motif had been the victim of censorship. In 1916 the design of the quarter was changed. The new, controversial obverse side of the coin featured Liberty in the form of a goddess who was draped in a sheer gown. The goddess was holding a protective shield in one hand and an olive branch in the other. She was standing at the gate of a parapet. The goddess Liberty, "Heaven Forbid," was shown with her bosom undraped and visible.

This classical pose was short-lived. There was a tremendous public outcry, especially by a number of women's groups. The goddess of Liberty was redesigned midway through 1917. In order to protect the goddess from onlookers, she wore a heavy vest of armor from 1917 until the coin was discontinued in 1930.

Onner noticed the abbreviation Unc. and Type 1 written on the coin holder. On the back of the coin holder were the following symbols: ⌐ ⌐ L ☐ XX. Richard knew the code; the cost of the coin to the dealer was $1,375. The dealer was using a tic-tac-toe code, with one in the top left-hand corner and nine in the bottom right-hand column. An X stood for a zero.

1	4	7
2	5	8
3	6	9

Thus, the symbol ⌐ was one; ⌐ was three; L was seven; ☐ was 5; and XX was 00.

"I'll take it. I want a written guarantee that the coin is genuine. How much?"

"That'll be $950." The shop manager handed Onner a receipt which contained the following description: 1916 S.L. 25¢, XF, $950. The shop manager also handed Onner the standard guarantee form. He had signed and dated the guarantee and included the description of the coin.

When Onner returned home, he put the coin in a small wall safe behind a false receptacle. Above the wall receptacle was a picture of himself hang gliding. He then picked up the copy of *Coin World* on a coffee table and turned to the "U.S. Trends" section. He saw under the UNC column that the 1916 25¢ was worth $1,600. In XF condition the coin was worth $975. Onner smiled, "Not bad for one day's work."

Jeff had called in sick Friday. He called from Martinsburg. He had observed Onner all day Friday. He had followed Onner all day Saturday.

It had been necessary for Jeff to call in sick. His group manager had told him to leave the Onner case alone. Another agent was in charge of the investigation. When Jeff asked who, his supervisor said he did not know. Jeff was determined to catch Onner *and* Jake's murderer. A gut feeling told him that there was *some* connection between the two.

On Sunday when he got back to Baltimore, he looked up Rosenbaum in the phone book. Sure enough, there was a Rosenbaum's Rare Coins listed in the yellow pages. There might be a chain of these coin shops.

After lunch on Sunday he went to his office. He spent five hours in the library looking through telephone books. He looked in the cities where a major university was located. He looked for the name Deidre Moore. Maybe Deidre was a professor herself. He had no luck.

Jeff looked in the various Who's Who reference books. Nothing!

Shifting his attention to Rosenbaum, Inc., he checked *Standard and Poor's Register*:

Rosenbaum, Inc.
(Subs. Rosenbaum Press)
1010 West Indian School Road
Phoenix, Arizona 85026
602-964-3730

*Pres. Jack Rosenbaum
V-P and Secy. Harriet Coupland
V-P and Treas. Harry Fein

*Also Director, Other Directors
Faye Rosenbaum
Jack Rosenbaum, Jr.

Accts. Peat, Andersen & Ernst, Co.
Sales Range $120 mil. Employees 127
Products: Rare coins, stamps, books
S.I.C. 3611

He checked the *Directory of Inter-Corporate Ownership*. More than fifteen hundred small coin and stamp retail outlets were controlled by Rosenbaum, Inc. Strangely, an ammunition plant located in Wickenburg, Arizona, was wholly owned by Rosenbaum, Inc.

Next, Jeff went to the computer console and retrieved the past three corporate income tax returns of Rosenbaum Coin and Stamp Shop in Martinsburg. For the past year the corporation showed a small profit which was offset by net operating loss carryovers, resulting in a refund of $28,600. For the other two years the corporation showed net operating losses of $62,550 and $42,620. "That's fairly large for such a small business," thought Jeff.

Excitedly, he began retrieving each of the tax returns of the other coin outlets on the console. A pattern began to emerge. Most of the outlets showed losses. If they did not show a loss, the profit was minimal.

Also, a number of the shops had been purchased in recent years. Before the coin shops were purchased by Rosenbaum, they normally showed a significant net income. Yet the year after they were purchased, the purchased businesses would show a loss.

After looking at about two hundred coin outlets' tax returns, Jeff's eyes felt like they were falling out of their sockets. He took another bite of his Mars bar, and then he retrieved the tax return of the main headquarters in Phoenix. It was a consolidated tax return. The wholesale business showed a tremendous net income. One hundred and twenty million dollars gross profit, with a sixty-two million dollar net profit. But this net profit was offset on the consolidated tax return by the net operating losses of the various retail outlets. After all adjustments, the wholesale business showed a refund of one hundred and sixty-two thousand dollars.

"Wait a minute," Jeff shouted to himself. He immediately retrieved the tax return of the Martinsburg coin outlet. How can the Martinsburg shop have a net operating loss and receive a tax refund if the wholesale parent company is filing a consolidated tax return? Like a thunderbolt, the answer came to him. He almost shouted, "They can't do both! When a group of affiliated corporations files a consolidated tax return, the parent corporation files the return and receives any refund — not the individual businesses."

Jeff excitedly made some calculations on a piece of paper:

Parent company (.40 × $62M)	$ 24.8M
Subsidiaries (1507 × Average refund of $120,000)	180.8
	$204.6

"Wow! This company is ripping off more than two hundred million dollars a year from the government!" Jeff whispered to himself. "They're sending in double tax returns. Each outlet sends in a separate return and receives a refund. The parent corporation files a consolidated tax return and receives a refund. The parent corporation files a consolidated tax return and turns its sixty-two million dollars taxable income into a refund of one hundred and sixty-two thousand dollars."

Next Jeff checked to see if the corporations had been audited in the past. None of the retail outlets had been audited in two out of three years. The wholesale business in Phoenix had been audited in two out of the three years. Both years the supervising agent had been Tony Blake.

Why hadn't the retail outlet been audited? Why hadn't the Martinsburg's computer system caught this double counting of losses? It had to be Onner. Somehow he was short-circuiting the internal controls system.

Onner was circumventing the IRS's fail-safe system. Any refund greater than $200,000 must be approved by the Joint Committee on Taxation, a Congressional committee. This was the same committee which produced a 1974 study showing that the then President Nixon had underpaid his taxes from 1969 to 1972 by $476,431. Someone had set up a system whereby the numerous retail outlets received refunds each year of less than $200,000, but the total refunds for the businesses were a staggering two hundred million dollars.

Each District Office thought that the individual coin shop was being audited with the consolidated parent. Apparently this agent Tony Blake was either stupid or a crook.

Jeff got up from the computer console and walked around both tense and excited. Jeff wanted to think a minute. He walked over to the window to check his car. There was little traffic tonight.

Jeff looked through the window. He had parked his dirty car on the street under a light. Someone was in the back seat of his car!

Jeff pounded on the window. "Get out of my car!" he screamed. But no one could hear. He was on the fifth floor. He turned and ran to the elevator. Important seconds flew by. It took him about three minutes to get to the front door. He drew his gun as he raced to his car, his adrenalin flowing. Why would a hot dog break into his car? He had locked it and had left nothing in the car.

No one was there. He looked around. No one. His car doors were still locked. He unlocked the left door and looked in the back seat. Nothing unusual.

Then he saw a small wire leading to the edge of the door frame. There was something black under the front seat. Jeff remembered the model airplane. He turned and ran with all his might. He dove behind another car.

There was a loud explosion. Pieces from his car were falling around him. His car was on fire. *His* only car.

Suddenly Jeff knew. A maniac had killed Jake and was now trying to kill him. It had to involve the investigation of Onner. Jeff was shaking when he stood up from his protective spot. He had cheated fate twice. What had caused him to walk to the window at that particular moment? He was still carrying the uneaten portion of the candy bar. He threw it in the street next to a part of his fender.

He slowly walked over to an unlit phone booth. The telephone cord had been severed. Typical of Baltimore's telephone system. Jeff cursed.

Twenty minutes later, after calling the police from his office, Jeff gave a description of the drama to the Baltimore police. The fire was still smoldering. A crowd had gathered. The police had theorized that the bomb had been timed to explode about fifteen seconds after the left door was opened.

Jeff asked the policemen to save any remaining pieces of the explosive device. He suggested they call Detective Garrison in Washington, D.C., in order to coordinate the investigation. He indicated that Jake's death and this bombing were related.

Jeff went home and called Detective Garrison. He related the evening's events, giving the detective the name of the Baltimore policeman who investigated the explosion.

The detective indicated that there was no Deidre Moore living in Kent, Ohio. In fact, no one by the name of Deidre Moore owned an automobile in the United States. He had checked each state looking for an automobile owner by such a name. Jeff told the detective about the possible connection between the bombings and Onner.

Early Monday morning Jeff called Jake's supervisor and asked him who was in charge of the Onner investigation. "I don't know," was the response. "What investigation?"

Jeff explained his suspicions about Onner and Rosenbaum, Inc. "Since this involves a federal employee and my friend Jake was killed, can I help your task force find the guilty parties?"

"Okay," was the simple answer.

CHAPTER 17

A taxpayer is someone who doesn't have to take a civil service examination to work for the government.

— Anonymous

On his morning flight to Phoenix Jeff tried to estimate the minimum number of IRS employees who had to be involved in this conspiracy. Jeff knew there were dishonest IRS employees. He himself had padded his expense account. A mail clerk in an IRS center of South Carolina stole 300 IRS returns in 1987. His intentions were to cash the checks, but he was arrested by police searching for a man who robbed a Pizza Hut.

The "Whiskey Ring" prosecutions had revealed corruption in the Bureau of Internal Revenue. An Assistant Treasurer of the United States resigned after revealing that he used inside knowledge of his office to gamble for profit on the gold exchange. A deputy collector in Newark, New Jersey, organized a sideline business of selling the names of New Jersey taxpayers for three cents each to a New York business dealing in mailing lists. Even former President Rutherford B. Hayes indicated in his diary that he forgot to file tax returns in 1868 and 1869. But nothing compared to this rip-off.

Jeff decided that Onner was involved, that the auditing revenue agent, Tony Blake in Phoenix, was involved, and probably the agent's group supervisor. The group supervisor assigns the taxpayers to the various agents and double-checks the finished products. "Yes, a minimum of three employees could pull off such a caper," Jeff decided. But more people could be involved. Whom could he trust in Phoenix?

As the big plane made its approach and descended blindly through the white clouds, Jeff saw that Phoenix was bordered by mountains on the north and south and small ranges could be seen in the distance to the west and east. What amazed him was the stark contrast of the countryside around Phoenix. Immediately around Phoenix was lush emerald green landscape from the irrigated farmland. As if someone had taken a giant knife and cut a circle around Phoenix, outside this circle began the brown, unimpressive desert.

"To your left, folks, you can see the Camelback mountain, a famous landmark in Phoenix." Jeff was not impressed by the information furnished by the pilot. To Jeff, the Camelbacks were just little hills. How could anyone get excited about two little lumps?

Soon after the plane landed on the west runway of the Sky Harbor airport, Jeff went downstairs to retrieve his one suitcase. Passengers were already pushing and shoving around the silver luggage carrier. It reminded Jeff of pigs on a farm lined up to get the slop from the trough. Jeff was tempted to tell one big, fat lady to get out of his way. But he held his temper.

Next Jeff rented a compact car and drove north on Freeway 10 and turned left on West Indian School Road. It was hot and dry. Typical desert weather. He noticed the palm trees and the stately cottonwood trees.

Rosenbaum, Inc., was located in a massive, stark white brick building. A brightly painted sign indicated that this fortress was the headquarters of the "Largest Rare Coin Company in the World." The building had no windows — solid brick. Jeff wondered if a bazooka could pierce the fortified building.

After leaving his blue car in a nearby parking lot, Jeff walked to the entrance to the building. He noticed a metal grille which could be slid in front of the door at night. A stately cactus seemed to guard the entrance.

Inside the door Jeff found himself in a small room. A recep-

145

tionist sat behind a bullet-proof glass wall. There was a television camera focused on Jeff.

"Hello there," came the receptionist's voice over a speaker. "May I help you?"

"Yes, I would like to purchase some rare coins."

"Sir, we do not sell rare coins here. This is our mail order outlet. We do, however, have a retail store at 1711 Main Street. I'm sure that they have whatever you might need."

"Okay, I'll go there."

"That's 1711 Main Street," came the sweet voice over the speaker as Jeff turned and walked to the door.

Jeff checked into a motel and called Rosenbaum, Inc.

"Hello, Rosenbaum Company."

"I'm Jeff Burke. I have a manuscript dealing with coin collecting. Could I speak to someone in your publishing department?"

"Just a moment."

Country music came over the telephone. Jeff hated to be put on hold. He began to exercise his fingers. First his left hand, then his right hand. He switched to rotating his head, exercising his neck muscles.

The music abruptly stopped. "Hello, I'm Miss Calhoun. So you have a manuscript. What's it about?"

"Silver dollars."

"Mr. Carter is not here today. Could you bring a copy of the manuscript to our office tomorrow at 10:30 a.m.? 1010 West Indian School Road. Ask for Mr. Carter at the door."

"Sure, I'll be there."

Jeff then called the IRS office in Phoenix and asked for Tony Blake.

"Hello, this is Tony Blake."

"I'm an accountant for a racketeer in Phoenix involved in vending machines and garbage collection. I'm in trouble and believe I may be eliminated. Could I talk to you about a deal? I could meet you in the lobby of the Ramada Inn on Indian School Road at nine o'clock tonight. Will you come?"

"I'm not a Special Agent."

"That's okay. I know you, but you don't know me. Please come alone. I'll talk to a Special Agent at another time. Bring in a milkshake cup from McDonalds in order for me to recognize you."

"I don't know."

"Please!"

"Okay. I'll be there at eight thirty. Is that all right?"

"Yes."

Next Jeff looked for Wickenburg on the map provided by the rental car agency. Route 89 North would take him to the ammunition plant owned by Rosenbaum.

The scenery on the way to Wickenburg was beautiful. There were short cacti and tall cacti. He saw a Saguaro. He had read on the plane that a Saguaro cactus takes two hundred years to reach maturity.

This was Jeff's first trip to Arizona. He still remembered the television commercial about giving your sinuses a rest in Arizona. He drove through Surprise: population 277. What a strange name for a town.

Near Morrison the terrain became hilly and the road began to wind. For some distance the road followed the Hassayampa River. He noticed a big bird climbing majestically in the sun-drenched air. There was tall Galleta grass along the right-hand side of the road.

In Wickenburg, population 2,744, Jeff stopped at one of the two service stations and inquired about the location of the ammunition plant.

A darkly tanned attendant wearing cowboy boots was responsive to Jeff's inquiry. "Take Route 60/70 West for about two miles; there's a small road to the left. When you see a small airport, you've passed the road. Take the country road for about four miles toward Vulture Mine. Cut left on the first side road. Go about five miles. It's near Vulture Peak. Need any gas?"

"Fill it up."

Jeff found the small road. Boy, would he hate to get stranded in this place. Unconsciously as he turned onto the road he looked in his rear view mirror to see if anyone was following him. He half expected to see Deidre Moore chasing after him.

Jeff was glad he had his .38 revolver strapped on. Although an agent has the right to carry a weapon while on duty, Jeff hardly ever wore his pistol. But this Deidre Moore affair was making him jumpy.

The strapped weapon near his armpit jogged his memory of the "Cowboy." "Cowboy" had been the nickname of an agent from Texas who had been assigned to the Baltimore office several years ago. He received his nickname from the fact that he always wore his weapon on his side-hip in a holster like a cowboy.

One day during the Christmas holidays Cowboy was shopping with his wife in Baltimore. A young hood tried to rob him on the street with a knife. Cowboy drew his revolver to defend himself. Somehow the robber took the pistol away from Cowboy and shot him with his own gun. Cowboy died.

The Baltimore office would not forget this episode. Some of the agents began to refer to the deceased Cowboy as "quick-draw."

Far ahead on the left side of the road was apparently Vulture Peak. A fairly large mountain for the desert scenery. A huge tumbleweed rolling in front of him brought his attention back to the rough road. Shortly before Jeff reached Vulture Peak, he turned left onto a gravel road. His compact car began to strain as the elevation increased. The landscape was covered with small bushes, with gullies here and there.

Ahead was a small sign: "Rosenbaum Ammunition. No Admittance." The plant was surrounded by a tall metal fence. About every fifty feet on the fence was a sign that said "Danger: No Admittance."

Jeff drove up to the guard house. "Hi, I'm a reporter from the *Phoenix News*. We are doing a story on the ammunition plant and its impact on Arizona's economy. Could I take a tour of the plant?"

"Sorry, no one's admitted. We don't give tours," was the rough reply from the heavy-set guard.

"What's your name? Do you realize I can write either a favorable or an unfavorable article about your employer?"

"Look, mister, do you see that sign? It means no admittance. Turn your car around and don't come back here unless you have a signed letter from the plant supervisor."

"Who is he?"

"Call and find out," was the curt response.

Jeff turned the car around and left. He did not want to argue with a moron guard holding a weapon.

Once back in Wickenburg Jeff stopped at Harvey's Diner. Jeff sat down at the counter and ordered some chili. It was a spiced stew of ground beef and minced chilies — diarrhea food, for sure.

After some casual conversation with Harvey, the owner, Jeff asked, "What do they do at the plant near Vulture Peak?"

"You're new here, huh? Are you a Yankee?"

"Yes, just driving through."

"They make ammunition."

"Why is it just stuck out there in the desert?"

Harvey looked at Jeff as if he were dumb. "Do you realize what would happen if the place were to catch on fire? They also make some bombs. They made a lot of bombs during the Vietnam war. Rumor was that they were going to make the neutron bomb here, but Peanut Carter killed that. I have some land near Vulture Peak. I would be rich now if they had been able to make the neutron bomb here. Do you want to look for some gold? For ten dollars I'll let you look for gold on my land."

Harvey reached behind the counter and showed Jeff a rock. "See that? That's a gold nugget from my land. I'll rent you a gold detector. It will detect a single speck of gold no larger than a pinhead.

"I also have a dowsing detector. It's a directional locator. The early Spanish settlers used dowsing instruments to locate gold and silver deposits in Mexico. Our boys used this triangulation method to find V.C. land mines in Vietnam.

"Henry Wickenburg discovered gold at Vulture Mine in 1863. This town grew as a gold mining camp. The mine produced millions of dollars of gold. But Henry Wickenburg died a pauper; he killed himself.

"How about it? Do you want to look for some gold?"

"No, I don't have time. Where's your bathroom?"

*　　*　　*

Jeff was more interested in silver — silver dollars, that is. Jeff had watched Tony Blake arrive at the Ramada Inn the night before with a milkshake cup. Jeff had not approached him but had observed him at a distance. After about forty-five minutes Tony Blake had left, a little angry.

At ten-thirty Jeff arrived at the entrance of Rosenbaum, Inc. He entered the small room separated by a glass wall from the receptionist.

"Hello, I'm here to see Mr. Carter about writing a book. I'm Jeff Burke."

"Just a moment."

The receptionist called someone on her phone. After a few brief remarks which Jeff could not hear, she looked up and pressed a button which caused a buzzing sound in the glass wall.

"You may come in, Mr. Burke. Go through the door and turn left. Follow the wall to the door on the left labeled Publications. Mr. Carter is in a conference now, but he should be out in a moment."

Inside was a very large room with many employees. Around the outside of the room were a number of small offices. The front of each office was enclosed by glass except for a wooden door leading into each office.

Jeff immediately noticed that many of the employees had weapons on their desks. Not your ordinary paperweight! A pistol here, a rifle there, next was a pump shotgun. There were several gun racks on the walls with weapons. "Good grief," Jeff thought, "this place must be Fort Knox."

150

Jeff followed the wall for a while, but turned right before reaching the door marked Publications. He walked past about thirty people in what looked like enlarged telephone booths. Each person seemed to be talking to a customer, trying to get a sale. One was talking about a gold coin, another about a "key" coin. A young woman was talking about the explosive investment potential of rare coins.

Ahead was an office not enclosed by a glass front. On the door in large letters was

Jack Rosenbaum
President

A secretary sat near the entrance of the door. Jeff approached the busy lady and said, "I would like to speak to Mr. Rosenbaum." Jeff had not planned to act as an agent here. He merely wanted to look around. But at this moment Jeff decided that he wanted to try to get inside the ammunition factory.

She looked up, surprised, and asked, "Do you have an appointment?"

"No, but I believe Mr. Rosenbaum will speak to me." Jeff showed her his "Special Agent, Treasury Department" card.

Without hesitation the secretary dialed two numbers and said, "Mr. Rosenbaum, there is an IRS agent out here who wishes to speak to you."

In several seconds a tall, portly man with a precisely trimmed black mustache bounced out of the door smiling. But as soon as he saw Jeff his smile disappeared.

"Uh, hello. What can I do for you?"

Jeff decided that Jack Rosenbaum had expected to see Tony Blake. "Oh, nothing important. Tony Blake just asked me to drop by and say hello. He wants me to go over your tax records of the ammunition plant."

"Won't you come in," Jack said as he pointed toward his door. "Could I see your identification? You know we can't be too careful with as many robberies as there are in Phoenix."

Jeff handed Jack his credentials. Jack studied them for a few moments and gave them back to Jeff.

Before Jeff went into the office another gentleman exited and walked towards the front entrance.

Jeff entered the spacious office and Rosenbaum motioned for Jeff to sit down at a small table on the front side of Jack Rosenbaum's mammoth oak desk. Jeff noticed that a Remington shotgun and a bolt-action Remington rifle with a leather sling rested within easy reach of Jack's chair behind his desk.

On Jack's desk was a picture of an attractive lady and two boys. On one wall was a framed dollar bill with the caption, "My first dollar," followed by the signature, Jack Rosenbaum. Also on the wall was a sign:

Impossible is a word to be found only in the dictionary of fools.

— Napoleon

Jack was the first to break the uncomfortable silence. "Of course, we do not keep any records concerning our ammunition factory here. They are kept at the plant in Wickenburg."

"Yes, I drove out there and they would not let me enter. Could I get a written statement from you allowing me to look at those records?"

Jack pressed an intercom button and said, "Molly, would you type a statement to the effect of allowing Mr. Burke, is it Jeff?" nodding to Jeff.

"Yes."

"It's Mr. Jeff Burke — giving him permission to look at our records at the Wickenburg plant. I'll sign it. Address it to Barry Schapiro."

"Are there any problems?" Jack eyed Jeff for an answer.

"No, not really. I'm going to start helping Tony Blake do some auditing of your tax return. I want to start with the ammunition plant in order to get a *larger* refund." Jeff was trying to get some incriminating evidence from Jack Rosenbaum.

"I don't understand. I thought IRS agents always tried to get more money from us. Is this a new policy?"

"Mr. Rosenbaum, I have talked to Tony. I understand the arrangement. You have nothing to fear from me."

"Seriously, Mr. Burke, I do not understand what you are talking about. What 'arrangement' are you referring to?" Rosenbaum's right hand smoothed his black mustache.

At that moment the secretary walked in carrying a letter which she handed to Jack.

"Thank you, Molly. Was Tony Blake the young IRS agent that audited our tax return last year?"

"Yes, I believe it was. Do you want me to check the files?"

"No, that won't be necessary." Jack read the short letter and then said, "The letter is fine, Molly."

Molly turned and left the room.

"Mr. Burke, there must be some mistake. You must have our firm mistaken with another company. Mr. Blake did audit our return last year, but found only some minor corrections. I believe we had what is called a 'clean return.' I will be glad to call our counsel in here and let you discuss this matter with him." Jack rose to indicate that the interview was finished.

"No, that will not be necessary. I'll talk to Tony." Jeff rose and shook Jack's strong hand. "Could I have the permission letter?"

Jack gave Jeff the letter, and Jeff made a graceful exit.

Jeff drove away for a short distance, but returned to a parking lot across the street from the coin company. He entered a bookstore directly across the street and began to watch the parking lot and the coin company entrance.

Jeff's instincts had been correct. Within an hour Tony Blake arrived and entered the coin company. He stayed for about twenty minutes and left.

Jeff followed him in his rental car. The revenue agent took Route 89 North to North Wickenburg. Jeff followed at a safe distance until they passed through Wickenburg and the agent turned onto the small road which led to Vulture Peak and the ammunition plant. Jeff waited about five minutes until Tony was out of sight and then he drove toward the ammunition plant. A jackrabbit dashed across the road and the dust and heat was irritating to Jeff's eyes.

When Jeff spotted the ammunition plant he parked in a side parking lot and waited. After an hour's wait Jeff saw Tony leave the plant, get in his white car, and drive toward Wickenburg.

Jeff locked his car and walked to the entrance to the plant. He gave Rosenbaum's letter to a broad-shouldered guard and asked for instructions how to locate the main office.

The guard read the letter, turned and went to the small guardhouse and made a phone call.

The guard came back and said, "I'm sorry but we had a personal phone call from Mr. Jack Rosenbaum and he indicated that you are not allowed to enter. Do you have a summons or search warrant?"

Jeff shook his head and shouted, "What is wrong with this company? I have a letter from your president and you still will not allow me to enter. You people will pay through the nose."

"Sorry," was the response. "We are not sure you are a Revenue Agent. I have called the Wickenburg police so please stay until they arrive. Maybe then we can clear up this matter."

Jeff turned to walk away. Jeff heard the guard draw his gun from his holster.

"Please halt or I'll shoot."

Jeff continued to walk. It was a gamble.

"Halt! If you do not stop, I'll shoot," the guard shouted.

The guard did not shoot. Jeff was perspiring when he reached his hot car.

Jeff was able to catch up to Tony and he followed the agent for the rest of the day. He followed him home and watched his house until ten-thirty that evening.

CHAPTER 18

There will come a time when the poor man will not be able to wash his shirt without paying a tax.
— A congressman in 1790

The next morning Jeff was watching as Tony left his home and drove to the Federal Building on North First Avenue. Jeff followed him to his IRS office.

Around noon Tony left his office and drove to the Pepper Tree. Once inside Jeff saw that it was a very large building with a variety of restaurants. There were Mexican, Italian, Chinese, German, a deli, and many other small diners and restaurants. Tony ordered a roast beef sandwich at the deli and sat down.

Jeff purchased a small sausage pizza and a glass of light beer. He sat down about two tables away from the agent. Shortly Jeff put his hand to his head in order to shield his face. He saw Jack Rosenbaum come over and place his tray of Chinese food on Tony's table. They began to talk softly. Jeff could not understand what they were saying, but the expressions on their faces indicated they were angry.

They began to glance and talk to a gentleman wearing dark sunglasses and a straw hat sitting alone at a table next to them. It was not a casual conversation. The man talking to them was vaguely familiar to Jeff but he could not place the face.

Jeff wished he had an electronic device to overhear the conversation. Of course, Jeff knew that the use of a mechanical, electronic or other device to overhear or record a non-telephonic conversation had to be with the consent of at least one party of the conversation. Further, such activity must be approved in advance by the Attorney General. A court order or search warrant is not needed for the transmission or recording of a conversation when done with the consent of one of the parties.

Jeff casually walked over and purchased another light beer. From the small restaurant he had a good view of the third man. Jeff took a small surveillance camera and snapped several shots of the third person.

Abruptly the third man rose and walked toward the exit carrying a briefcase. Jeff followed him on a hunch. Outside the man hailed a taxi. Jeff noted the number on the taxi and raced to his car.

Jeff was able to catch up with the cab and follow it to the airport. The taxi stopped in front of the United Airlines terminal, and the man wearing the sunglasses and hat went into the terminal.

After he parked his car, Jeff rushed into the same terminal. But he could not find the unknown man with the briefcase. He had disappeared. Jeff walked around the Sky Harbor airport for one and a half hours.

But no luck. The only faint ray of hope was the film in his camera. Now he had two mysteries. He was looking for a hit woman with the name of Deidre Moore. He also wanted to know the name of the man who disappeared in the airport.

Jeff was at his wit's end. He did not know what to do. He returned his rental car and bought a ticket to Lexington, Kentucky.

One of the newspaper clippings found by his secretary indicated that a Professor Gregory in the Psychology Department at the University of Kentucky had conducted some subliminal research in the early eighties. His secretary had not found any clippings concerning Deidre Moore.

The quiet, soft-spoken Dr. Paul M. Gregory indicated that he had conducted a number of classroom experiments in 1985 and 1986 on subliminal suggestions.

The elderly, thin professor sat behind his desk in his modest book-cluttered office, and he described his experiments and results to Jeff. Jeff listened politely, noticing the numerous accomplishments, certificates, and educational degrees that were framed and hung on the white walls.

"I published the results of my experiments in several journals so almost anyone could have read about them," continued the professor.

"That's interesting," replied Jeff as he rubbed the tip of his nose. "Do you have a list of the students who participated in your experiment?"

"That's some time ago," shrugged the professor. "We only have to keep exams for three years."

Professor Gregory slid his chair back, put on his glasses, and walked over to one of the bookcases that was crammed with books.

"But you are lucky. I have a record of every grade I have given. That would be around 1985," the professor mumbled to himself. He searched through a number of grade books. "Ah, here it is," he said as he turned around smiling. "Six classes participated in that particular experiment — about 360 students. I've thrown away their questionnaires, but I do have the names of the participating students. I could photocopy the names of these students. Of course, I can't give you their grades. That would be against the law."

"The names are fine," replied a delighted Jeff. "Do you have the student yearbooks for 1985 and 1986?"

"No, but you can find them in the campus archives."

Jeff took a copy of the list of students and almost ran to the archives. He found the 1985 and 1986 student yearbooks in the library. He began looking at the photographs of each of the students in Professor Gregory's roll book.

After about two hundred and seventy photographs, Jeff saw her — Debra Sweeney. She was a woman in her late thirties, Jeff guessed. She was the Deidre Moore for whom he was searching. Jeff's hands began to shake slightly and his palms became sweaty. She was an ordinary, attractive woman. He remembered that night well.

Jeff pulled out the map to the University of Kentucky's campus, found the location of the Alumni Office, and ran part of the way to the office. He hardly noticed the students going to and from classes.

"Hi, I'm Jeff Burke, a former student. I'm looking for the current address of one of my classmates, Debra Sweeney. Can you help me?"

The lady rewarded Jeff with a smile. "Oh, we probably can. Let me look in our files."

After several minutes she returned with her perpetual smile. "She now lives in Pikesville, Kentucky. I've written her address and telephone number down." She handed an envelope to Jeff. "Would you take this envelope and consider making a donation to the University? It takes a lot of money to send a student to college now."

Jeff took the envelope and said, "I'll check with my wife. She controls the budget."

When Jeff arrived on his flight to Williamson, Kentucky, he rented another compact car and drove to Pikesville, Kentucky, a three-time All-Kentucky city. The coal town had a population of about six thousand. This Model City was laid out like a winding snake along the Chesapeake and Ohio Railroad. Although it was late in the evening, Jeff located Debra Sweeney's two-story house. On the mailbox with black letters was "John Sweeney."

Later in the evening Jeff called one of the guys on his softball team and asked him to check the computer console the next morning. "I'll call you around 9:45. Let me know any information about John and Debra Sweeney, 1121 Shady Lane, Pikesville, Kentucky."

Next Jeff called Rick Garrison, the Washington detective. Jeff said that he needed help in following the suspect since she could recognize him. The detective indicated that he would be in Pikesville sometime tomorrow.

The telephone conversation the next morning with his third baseman provided Jeff with the information that 1) John Sweeney was a Baptist minister, 2) Debra Sweeney was a housewife, 3) they reported a moderate amount of taxable income, 4) their two children were away at college, and 5) Debra reported a modest amount of income writing children's books.

As he waited in his car near her house Jeff wondered if he had been mistaken about the photograph in the yearbook. Maybe she had a twin sister. At 11:45 a.m. Debra Sweeney emerged from her home. Watching with small black binoculars, Jeff saw Debra Sweeney wearing striped slacks, a blue blouse, a navy jacket and leather boots come out of her home. She drove towards Pikesville. The woman looked just like the lady he had slept with at the Hilton convention. He still remembered the black negligee.

Debra stopped at a phone booth on the way to town and made a short telephone call. Jeff noted the time and the location of the phone booth. She then drove to the Baptist Church and went to lunch with her husband, apparently. She certainly did not fit the pattern of a professional killer.

The First Bank and Trust was the only bank in Pikesville. The manager was quite surprised when Jeff indicated that he wanted to see the bank records of John and Debra Sweeney.

"Do you mean Reverend John Sweeney?" was the puzzled response.

"Yes," was Jeff's simple answer.

Jeff spent several hours checking signature cards, deposit slips, ledger sheets, teller's proof sheets, safe deposit records and other records. He found nothing out of the ordinary. Rev. and Mrs. Sweeney seemed to be a typical American family living in a small town. In three years he found only two overdrawn checks — certainly no Bert Lance.

Debra Sweeney had deposited some rather large checks, normally at the end of March and September of each year. Jeff reasoned that these amounts were royalties from her children's books. He noted, also, the rather large checks written to support the two children in college. The son was at Princeton and the daughter was enrolled in Yale.

Rather disappointed, Jeff left the bank and intended to go back to his motel. Instead he stopped off at the public library. He noticed the "Please Be Quiet" sign as he entered the old library. The sign was not heeded. The library was located in the YMCA and kids were running around shouting and arguing.

A rather elderly lady was behind the counter. She looked up from her book when Jeff said, "May I see several books written by Debra Sweeney?"

"Oh, our only author in Pikesville. Sure, we have them over there on display." The stoop-shouldered lady pointed to four books that were prominently on display. She immediately began reading her romance novel again.

Jeff walked over to the four books on display. He was not impressed. They were short. But aren't all children's books short? "She makes money off of these easy books. Maybe I should start writing children's books," Jeff thought.

He jotted down the publishers of the books. Three of the books were published by Kids Publishing Co. (New York) and the other book was published by Banage Publishing Co. (New York).

Jeff went back to his plain motel room and waited. At four-thirty Detective Rick Garrison arrived. Garrison was a tall man in his mid-thirties. As he removed his rumpled overcoat, dandruff fell from his untidy blond hair. A restless, gregarious detective, he grinned as he shook Jeff's hand in a firm grip. His hand was calloused and hard like a laborer's.

"How are you, Mr. Burke? Have you found our killer?"

"I believe so. The real name of the woman who picked me up in Baltimore is Debra Sweeney. She's the wife of a Baptist minister. She doesn't look like a professional killer. Maybe her hair just happened to be on the model plane which hit Jake," shrugged Jeff. "I just don't know. She writes books for children."

"Where does she live?"

"1121 Shady Lane. We'll go out there now. You follow me. I'm going to try to get a flight back to Baltimore tonight. There's not much I can do here. If she sees me with you, that will blow your cover. What do you suggest we do?"

"Well, I suppose follow her for several days. If she did it, someone is paying her. We need to find out who hired her. I'll put a tap on her phone. Eventually I will want to get into her home and get some materials from her workroom."

"By the way, on the way into town today to meet her husband, she stopped at a pay telephone and made a call. Did you get a copy of her handwriting at the Hilton?"

"Yes," replied Rick.

"Good," replied Jeff. "We can force her to produce handwriting exemplars to prove she was in Baltimore. The Fifth Amendment will not shield her from the compelled production of handwriting or voice exemplars."

After showing Rick the Sweeneys' house and the telephone booth, Jeff hit patches of ice and snow on his drive back to Williamson, Kentucky. The snow-capped peaks of the mountains did not look inviting. He was able to get a late flight into Dulles.

After waking from a short nap, Jeff felt better. Sleep had removed some of the fatigue from his face. He had arrived at the Dulles airport very early in the morning. But by the time he hit his bed, he was asleep.

At ten o'clock the next morning when he got back to his office several of his agent friends were grinning. He should have guessed. Above his desk next to his framed motto by Thomas Edison and Albert Einstein: "Genius is 99% perspiration and 1% inspiration," was a new addition. During his absence he had been awarded the infamous Special Agent's oath. The oath read as follows:

I am proud to be a Special Agent. I will be true to the trust and will fulfill the responsibilities placed in me by the Service and my Country. I will dedicate myself to the policies of the Service and in all my activities will uphold the provisions of the Constitution of the U.S.

The Oath had a rough history. Initially each Special Agent had been given a framed copy of the oath in order to improve the morale of the Special Agents. But the oath became a laughing joke among the agents. Eventually the group supervisors took back the oath from each agent. Instead each office got one copy to be given each week to the best agent for the past week.

Even the weekly award did not work. The agents did not want to receive the award. So if an agent was out of the office for several days, he would come back and find the oath over his desk. Jeff would have to find out which of the agents was out of the office today and hang the oath above the missing agent's desk.

His desk had a pile of mail. Included in the stack of correspondence was a fingerprint report on the practice run of the gambling numbers which he had found in the garbage dumpster. He forwarded the report to Hank Brown. Jeff wondered if Hank had found any incriminating evidence on Flesher's porno bookstore and aircraft business.

Jeff had just glanced through a second *U.S. Tax Week* when the phone rang. "Hello," answered Jeff. He suppressed a yawn.

"Hi, Jeff, would you come into my office?" It was Jeff's supervisor, Sam Westley.

"Sure," was Jeff's response.

Sam was Jeff's boss. He was a typical product of the Civil Service System. Sam had not been an outstanding agent. He merely had seniority. He was promoted because the time-in-grade indicated that it was time for him to be promoted. Since Sam was only an average agent, he had stayed out of trouble. He never found any fraud cases which always slowed the productivity of an agent. Thus, when Sam's supervisor had retired, Sam was a noncontroversial replacement.

Sam was the epitome of the "Peter Principle." In any organization an individual is promoted until he reaches his level of incompetence. Sam clearly had reached his level of incompetence.

On the way to Sam's office, Jeff dropped off the film which he had taken in Phoenix to be developed. He knocked on Sam's office door and then entered.

Even before he sat down, Sam looked up and asked, "Where have you been?"

"Well, I flew to Phoenix to check on the Rosenbaum coin company and on the way back I stopped off in Kentucky. I may have found Jake's killer."

"Did it have to do with the Onner affair?"

"Yes, I believe all of these people are involved in a conspiracy to . . ."

"I thought I told you to drop the Onner affair," Sam barked back. Sam was clearly angry and upset.

Jeff shot back, "Look, Jake was my friend. You would not even tell me who was placed in charge of Jake's investigation." Jeff's scowl indicated that he was as angry as Sam.

Jeff's aggressive outburst apparently decreased Sam's hostility. Calmly, Sam replied, "Look, Rosenbaum made some significant political contributions during the last campaign. Some powerful individuals owe him favors.

"I hate to do this, but I'm terminating you for at least two weeks. I'm having to do this." In a softer voice he said, "If you leave this affair alone, I believe I can get you reinstated in two weeks. You have a good record. Don't blow it. Let the cops find Jake's murderer. Leave the Rosenbaum and Onner affair alone."

Jeff turned and walked out. Someone very important in the IRS was involved. Why else would so much pressure be placed on Sam? Jeff did have a good record and normally had a good relationship with Sam.

Back at his desk Jeff called Jake's supervisor. "Hello, this is Jeff Burke, Jake's friend. I called you last week indicating my suspicions that Richard Onner, an IRS employee, and the Rosenbaum Coin Company were somehow connected with

Jake's death. I now have found enough fraud to close down the Rosenbaum operations. I have a photo of an IRS agent meeting with Jack Rosenbaum and an unknown person in Phoenix.

"I would like to inventory Onner's safe deposit box and audit the Rosenbaum coin shop in Martinsburg. I believe Onner buys rare coins from the company each week. But I've been suspended for at least two weeks. Someone very high in the IRS is trying to shut me up. By the way, I left a Washington Detective Garrison in Pikesville. He is shadowing a woman we believe was Jake's killer. Could you meet me at two o'clock at the Martinsburg Bank and Trust, 1210 Main Street?"

"Yes, I'll be there."

Next Jeff called Kids Publishing Company in New York. After going through the switchboard, he was finally connected to an employee in the accounting department. He found out that Debra Sweeney earned very few royalties from the three children's books. She earned less than three hundred dollars per year.

His conversation with Banage Publishing Company was even more informative. This company was a vanity publisher. True, the company published her other children's book. But she paid them to publish the book.

Jeff reasoned that Debra Sweeney was using the children's books as a screen to hide her outside, illegal payments. Maybe she was a professional killer after all.

CHAPTER 19

Estate planning is social work among the rich.
— Robert Brosterman

At two-thirty Jeff met Jake's supervisor, Jason Pabst, inside the front door of the Martinsburg Bank and Trust. He had waited for the strike force supervisor for thirty minutes. Outside the bank the temperature was 31 degrees and falling in a cold wind. Jeff recalled reading that some people are habitually late because they are expressing an unconscious hostility. The individual shows how unconsciously angry he is by forcing the other person to wait. Since Jeff really didn't know the supervisor, Jeff assumed that he was not angry with him.

"Hello, Jeff."

"Hi."

"Sorry I'm late. I ran into some heavy traffic on the way here. Have you talked to anyone?"

"No, as an ex-IRS agent I need your authority," answered Jeff. "I did make an appointment with the manager, Mr. Michaelson, for two o'clock."

Jason did not look like an IRS agent. He was short, plump, and slightly balding. He looked like an ordinary accountant rather than a strike force agent charged with the responsibility of finding corruption within the federal government.

"Okay, let's go to work." Jason turned, walked over, and spoke to a woman behind the nearest desk. "Where is Mr. Michaelson?"

"He's in the second office right over there," pointing to the right side of the bank lobby. "You'll have to ask his secretary."

"Hello," Jason said to the attractive, brunette secretary. "Could we please speak to Mr. Michaelson?"

"Do you have an appointment?"

"Yes. Mr. Burke made an appointment for two o'clock. Obviously, we are late, but I ran into some difficult traffic. I'm Mr. Pabst. This is Mr. Burke," said Jason turning toward Jeff.

The brunette looked at the telephone lights. "Mr. Michaelson is on the phone. Would you wait in those seats? He'll be with you in a moment."

By the time Jason and Jeff had sat down, the secretary picked up the phone and buzzed the manager. "Mr. Burke and Mr. Pabst are here to see you."

Even before the secretary had hung up the phone, the manager came striding out of his office.

"Hi there, I'm Brett Michaelson. Won't you come in." He led Jason and Jeff into his office.

"Mr. Michaelson, I'm Jason Pabst and this is Jeff Burke. I'm a special strike force agent with the Treasury Department. We suspect one of your customers, Richard Onner. We'd like to inventory his safe deposit box.

"You or your employees are not to inform Mr. Onner of this inventory. We will need one of your employees to stay with us to ascertain that we do not take anything from his box. Are there any questions?"

"Is this legal? Do you have a written request?"

"Yes, it is legal. Here is a written request." Jason handed the manager a written letter. He read it rapidly and turned and put it on his desk. "I will observe you myself."

When the big box was opened, Jeff whistled softly when he saw so many rare coins. At the top of the box was a list of rare coins with the dates of purchase. There was a sale column. Entries had been made in this column for some of the coins. All of the coins had been purchased from Rosenbaum Coin and Stamp Shop on Main Street.

They immediately began a written inventory showing the date of entry, box number, name of bank, and owner. In the presence of the manager they made a list of all of the rare coins. There were several rare stamps in the box. Once the inventory was taken, Jeff took several photographs of the entire contents. The manager was requested to initial all pages of the inventory and to sign the last page as acknowledgment that the contents were returned to the rental box. They made a copy of the list of coins that had apparently been prepared by Onner.

After thanking the manager for his cooperation and encouraging his silence, Jason and Jeff left. Outside the shop Jason said, "I think we should hit the Rosenbaum Coin Shop now."

"I agree," smiled Jeff. They went directly to the Rosenbaum Coin and Stamp Shop on Main Street.

As they entered the coin shop, Jeff noticed a new sign:

"If you don't know your coins, know your dealer! Rosenbaum cares!"

The smiling shop manager greeted them warmly. "May I help you?"

Jason returned the smile and said, "I'm a special strike force agent for the Treasury Department. We would like to see your invoices involving any rare coin sales to a Mr. Richard Onner. We are here at closing time so that we will not disrupt your business. However, we would like for you to get these invoices this evening." Jason flashed his Treasury Commission.

The smile disappeared from the shop manager's face. "But I'm going to a play tonight!"

"If you hurry and get those invoices, you'll be able to see it."

"How do I know you are really Treasury Agents? You may be crooks."

Jason took out his card again and handed it to the manager. "Jeff, let him see your badge." Jeff handed the manager his badge.

"I believe I should call my lawyer," the manager replied in a broken voice as he read the cards.

"Look, we just want to see a few invoices. If you give us any trouble, we'll get a court order and audit your whole blasted store. What's it going to be — a little trouble or some *real* trouble?"

Reluctantly the manager turned and went into a back room. Jason and Jeff followed him. He pulled several boxes down from a shelf. "You're lucky. I give all of my customers a written guarantee and I file them in alphabetical order." He gave Jason a stack of papers.

"Great, do you have a copy machine? We'll pay you for the copies."

"No, but the store next door has one. They're probably still open."

"Also, could you give us the invoices for a customer whose name begins with an S or a T?"

Although the shop manager looked puzzled, he gave Jason a small stack of invoices for a customer with the last name of Stern.

Once copies were made of the invoices, Jeff purchased a copy of *Coin World*. They left the coin shop and found a motel. That evening Jason and Jeff prepared a schedule showing the list price, the value of the rare coins on the sale date, and the difference. In each case they noticed that Onner had been able to obtain a nice paper profit on each purchase. On only those items which they looked up in *Coin World* newspaper, Onner had made a profit of about $15,000.

	Invoice Price	Price	Profit
1793 Wreath cent	$10,850	$14,750	$3,900
1795 Flowing hair half dime	1,600	2,700	1,100
1806 Draped bust half dollar	1,800	2,500	700
1814 Caped bust dime	1,420	2,200	780
1802/1 $2 1/2 gold piece	1,200	2,960	1,760
1873 Three dollar gold (closed date)	650	1,390	740
1894-O $5 gold piece	425	725	300
1875-CC $20 gold piece	640	1,010	370
1876-CC $20 gold piece	570	895	325

	Invoice Price	Price	Profit
1815 Capped bust quarter	$2,200	$3,195	$995
1942/1 Overdate Mercury dime	275	475	200
1937-D 3-legged Buffalo nickel	565	925	360
1919 Walking Liberty half dollar	975	1,625	650
1892-S Barber half dollar	1,175	1,850	675
1920-S Walking Liberty half dollar	1,325	2,250	925
1794 Flowing hair half dime	1,110	1,820	710
			$14,490

The profit was not really paper profit. Of the rare coins which Onner had purchased from Rosenbaum, he had sold about one third of them. He had made a nice profit on each of these sales.

Jason and Jeff noticed that the coin shop would often list the coin sold to Onner as an almost uncirculated coin (AU) whereas the rare coin was listed as uncirculated (UNC.) on the coin folder.

Jason collected coins. He told Jeff that an uncirculated coin is a newly minted coin which shows no evidence of circulation, but is not necessarily brilliant. A coin can have some nicks and scratches and still be uncirculated. Abrasions may occur when the struck coin falls into the hopper or when the coins are bagged for shipment. More abrasions may occur outside the mint from roll-wrapping techniques and coin-counting machines used by banks. As a general rule, the heavier the coin, the more scratches and nicks it may have.

Jason explained to Jeff that the grade of a coin has a significant effect on its price. For example, an uncirculated 1846 Liberty Seated dollar may sell for $750, whereas the same coin in almost uncirculated condition may sell for only $200. "Obviously Onner is being paid by the Rosenbaum company through purchases of rare coins at a steep discount. Or Onner is paying the price of an almost uncirculated coin, but is receiving a more valuable uncirculated coin. When Onner needs money, he merely sells the rare coins to other dealers at much higher prices."

Jeff then explained to Jason how all of the 1,500 coin shops were obtaining illegal refunds. How no one was auditing the small coin shops.

Jason was silent for a moment. "Notice that in both cases, the customer is paying for the coin under the installment method. I wonder if Onner is paying anything for the rare coins? Also, in comparing Stern's invoices to Onner's invoices, Onner always got a bigger discount on his coin purchases than Stern did.

"When I went through his bank records, he had many checks written to Rosenbaum's shop. I believe he's paying up front."

Jason paused for another moment. Jeff noticed that Jason seemed to look to the right when thinking. Jeff knew that this trait indicated that the left hemisphere of Jason's brain was dominant. A left-hemisphere dominance indicated that Jason had a pleasant and optimistic view of life. A person with a right-hemisphere dominance was more prone to depression.

"I remember a case several years ago when a large corporation was deferring about twenty million dollars of taxes illegally through the installment method. Can you imagine how much tax money is being deferred if the fifteen hundred shops are collecting their sales up front and are reporting the income using the installment method? This case could be the ultimate rip-off. How could anyone even spend that much money?"

After Jeff explained again to Jason how the many coin shops were obtaining illegal refunds, Jason agreed with Jeff that they had enough evidence to close the whole organization down. "We certainly have enough evidence to get Onner," Jason indicated. "But there are people much higher up in the organization involved if they can force your supervisor to suspend you. Suppose we sit tight, do nothing until we hear from the Washington detective. Maybe your hit woman will lead us to the guilty parties."

CHAPTER 20

The first great commandment is, don't let them [IRS agents] scare you.

— Elmer Davis

His drive back to Baltimore was uneventful. There was a chill in the wind. He only occasionally glanced at the bare-branched trees whipping by his car.

Jeff was up early the next morning. He didn't know why. He had read that short sleepers were energetic, ambitious people who worked hard and kept busy. They did not worry. Jeff was worried. He wondered if he would get his job back.

He tried to read a novel. Finally he phoned Hank Brown — the Special Agent working on the Flesher case.

"Hello, Hank, this is Jeff Burke. What's new?"

"Not much. Same old stuff. Did you hear about the revenue agent in the Washington office — Rod Taylor, I believe? He was convicted of filing false returns and using the mail to defraud the government . . . a thirteen count indictment."

"You mean he didn't file his own tax returns? How stupid."

"No, no. It's more involved than that. Apparently he obtained the names of eight taxpayers and filed fraudulent income tax returns in their names. He even sent in W-2 withholding forms showing them working for Acme Industries."

"Very original company," smiled Jeff.

"Anyway, the returns each claimed partnership losses sufficient to entitle the taxpayer a refund ranging from $12,000 to $16,000. The fake returns gave false addresses to rooming houses and transient hotels where rooms had been rented in the taxpayers' names."

"How did the agent get the money?" asked Jeff.

"The revenue agent had his brother and another accomplice working with him on the scheme. The refund checks were picked up by his brother and deposited in bank accounts opened in the taxpayers' names at four banks. Later the money was withdrawn."

"How did they catch the agent?"

"I don't know. Maybe an informant. But the accomplice testified against him in court. And they used the agent's own tax return against him."

"How?"

"Man, don't ask so many questions. I'll tell you the whole story. Your suspension has got you up a tree, huh?"

Jeff didn't respond.

Hank continued. "His handwriting on the bodies of the tax returns was used as exemplars of his handwriting and gave the experts a chance to say that the fake returns were prepared by the agent. Apparently he wrote all of the tax returns in block capitals like on his personal forms."

"He was a dummy," Jeff responded. "Why didn't the agent argue that the admission of his tax return into evidence was prohibited by the confidentiality provisions?"

"He did argue that, but lost. Why did you call?"

"Oh, just to catch up on the Flesher case. What's happening?"

"Not much," replied Hank. "We have not been able to touch B.W. We did find out that he has an interest in a rare coin shop."

"Which one?" Jeff almost shouted.

"A Rosenbaum shop in the northeast section. Why?"

"This Rosenbaum shop is a member of a chain of about 1,500 rare coin and stamp stores all over the U.S. I believe they are not only paying no taxes, but are ripping off refunds of about $150,000 each year. If organized crime is into the action. . ."

"Holy cow!" exclaimed Hank. "How?"

"Don't ask so many questions," Jeff mocked, followed by a controlled chuckle.

"Cut the crap, Jeff."

"Okay, okay. Each shop indicates to the regional offices that they are filing a separate return and each obtains a refund. The headquarters in Phoenix is filing a consolidated return and offsets all of these 1,500 net operating losses against the parent company's income."

"Pretty good," replied Hank. "Why aren't they caught?"

"I'll tell you if you'll let me work with you. I'll stake out the coin shop B.W. owns."

"I don't know. You're trouble."

"Come on."

"You'll have to do it on your own. I'll keep you informed. But I'll deny having anything to do with you if there's trouble. Is that satisfactory?"

"Fine. There's a computer fellow in Martinsburg who is covering up the fraud."

"Have you reported him to the Internal Security Division?"

"Yes. I'm working closely with Jason Pabst. He was Jake Anderson's supervisor before Jake was killed by the model plane explosion. I believe his killing is involved with the Onner affair."

"Please stay away from me! I'm too young to die."

"What connection does B.W. have with the rare coin shop?" Jeff asked.

"B.W. only owns 20% of the coin shop, but he actually does much of the buying. He's a coin freak. A numismatist, I believe they are called."

"Do you think they are using the shop to launder their illegal profits?" asked Jeff.

"Could be. I hadn't thought about that. Do you know what B.W. looks like?"

"Yes, I've seen photos of him. I'll start watching him today. Here's an idea. Could you get your supervisor to furnish you with an estate made up of rare coins — say 20? I could sell the estate to the coin shop, and we could follow the coins through their accounting system to see if they are laundering money."

"I don't know. He wants to catch B.W. for sure. Let me check with him. I'll call you tonight."

Jeff immediately called Jason Pabst and told him about the possible organized crime connection with the Rosenbaum coin company.

"I'm going to start shadowing B.W. Flesher this afternoon," Jeff told Jason.

"Be careful," was all that Jason said.

The Rosenbaum Coin and Stamp shop was in a large shopping center off of the freeway. It was a very small shop, but located near heavy walking traffic.

Jeff went up to the entrance, but the door was locked. A sign indicated to ring the bell. Jeff punched the bell with his index finger. A short, sandy-haired man in his mid-thirties looked up and pushed a lever behind a counter which unlocked the door.

"Hi there," was the friendly response from the handsome man behind the counter.

"Are you afraid someone is going to get in?" joked Jeff.

"Actually, it's there to slow anyone down who wants to get out. I won't let you out until you buy something," laughed the man. "Can I help you?"

"Well, I would like to sell some coins."

"Good, we buy them, too. Did you bring them?"

"No, my father died several months ago and left them to me. I have them in my safe deposit box."

"I'm sorry about your father. I'll have to get Mr. Flesher to look at the coins. He does most of our buying. Could you give me your name and telephone number? He'll set up an appointment and meet you at the safe deposit box."

"I'll be out of town the next several days. Can I call him instead?"

"Sure. Here's his card. His office and home telephone numbers are listed. What is your name?"

"Burke. May I look around?"

"Help yourself. Do you know anything about coins?" asked the young man.

"Not really," replied Jeff as he strolled around the small shop. It was quite similar to the Rosenbaum shop in Martinsburg. Finally he walked over to the door to get out. He couldn't — it was locked.

The young man looked at Jeff and smiled. "You haven't bought anything yet." He reached down behind the counter and pushed a button. Jeff walked out. He mentally jotted down a notice that he had seen on the small bulletin board: Important Coin Show, Sheraton Convention Center, Lanham, Maryland, 7:30. Two weeks from then.

That evening Hank called.

"We're in luck. My boss will get a coin collection — about 20 coins. But you'll have to sell them close to the cost value to the department. Where do you bank? Do you have a safe deposit box?"

"Municipal Bank & Trust. No box. I don't have anything to save. But I'll get one tomorrow."

"Then call me after lunch tomorrow and I'll bring the coins to your bank. We're going out on the limb working with you. Don't mess up. My bosses don't know this might involve the Onner affair. So keep your mouth shut. We'll have accurate descriptions of each of the coins. Should I mark each coin with an anthracene pencil?"

Jeff thought for a moment. "Yes, put your initials on the coins. Surely they don't check all of the coins they buy. Will your boss pay for the safe deposit box?"

"Good grief, Burke. Save your receipt. See you tomorrow. Don't take any wooden nickels." Hank was laughing loudly as he hung up the phone.

Jeff was up early the next morning. He was at the public library when the doors opened and he checked out five books on coin collecting.

Back at his apartment he began reading. He made only three calls during the day. One was to his bank to reserve a small safe deposit box. The second one was to B.W. Flesher to set up an appointment at 2:00 the next afternoon in order for him to appraise the rare coins — he used the name Burke Jefferies. The third call was to Hank. He met Hank at the Municipal Bank where they deposited the rare coins. Their total wholesale value was approximately $16,000.

That evening and the next morning Jeff continued to read about coin collecting. He read how coins are minted from a master die. He read about silver dollars, commemorative coins, trade dollars, Eagle gold coins, $3 gold pieces, type coins, half cents, large cents, half dimes, Liberty Seated half dollars, coin rolls, the *Red Book*, 1917 Matte Proof Nickel, proof sets, the Charlotte mint, and much more.

He read about the end of inflation in Germany in 1923. After seven years of constantly accelerating inflation, the German mark finally stabilized at the rate of four trillion, two billion (4,002,000,000,000) to one U.S. gold dollar. Jeff knew that the U.S. dollar was no longer backed by gold.

Jeff was at the bank early. He made arrangements to get to his safe deposit box and waited for B.W. Flesher to arrive.

B.W. was a husky, well-dressed man with the build of a highly trained athlete. He did not fit the stereotype image of an organized crime member. Of course, they never do. Jeff recognized B.W. Flesher when he entered the bank.

Jeff walked over and introduced himself. "Hello, Mr. Flesher. I'm Burke Jefferies. I'm glad you could come."

"Oh, I'm always happy to look at rare coins, my son. I'm sorry I was late. Got behind in some slow traffic. What do you have for me?"

"There are about 20 coins. I'm not exactly sure what I have. As I mentioned on the phone, my father left them to me."

"There is nothing better than the inheritance of rare coins. Sorry about your father."

Jeff and Mr. Flesher followed a pretty, red-headed bank employee into the vault. She wore a tight skirt and a loose, light blue blouse. She smiled as she opened the box and said in a sweet voice, "Call me when you are finished, gentlemen."

Jeff carried the metal box over to a small room for privacy. They had to leave the door open slightly because the room was not big enough for two people.

"By the way, Mr. Jefferies, my name is Wayne. May I call you Burke?"

"Yes, please do."

B.W.'s eyes seemed to glitter as he saw the coins in the box as Jeff opened it. B.W. picked up the first coin and looked at it very closely. "Your father was a connoisseur. Most of these are gold coins. The Arabs continue to trade their billions of dollars of oil for gold. They understand inflation. Did you know that the Germans took the entire nation of Italy out of hock for *gold*?"

B.W. didn't wait for a response to his question. "Are you a numismatist?"

"Not really. I know a little about coins."

"See this five dollar half edge? A draped bust left. Magnificent! An 1809 over 8." B.W. was very carefully holding the coin on its edges for Jeff to see. He was really talking to himself, not Jeff.

"Notice the 8 within the 9. Here, look through the glass. Can you see the 8?"

"Yes. Is that good or bad? Is a defective coin worth more or less?"

"Worth much more, my young man. The denticles on the obverse in the area above Miss Liberty are practically non-existent."

B.W. picked up another coin. "An 1849 $10 eagle, no motto. Only about 650 of these coins were minted." B.W. did not look at Jeff as he talked.

"Here's a double eagle 1879-O twenty dollar piece. The 'O' mint mark means that it was minted in New Orleans. It's the only New Orleans mint double eagle with motto. Breathtaking!"

B.W. took out a pad of paper from his brown leather briefcase and began to write down a list of the coins and their conditions. After making the inventory, he took out a gray looking newsletter and began to look for prices.

"Are those gray sheets?" Jeff asked.

"Why, yes." B.W. looked a little confused. "I thought you knew little about coins?"

Jeff didn't respond. He knew that the "gray sheets" gave the wholesale price of the coins — both a "bid" and an "ask" price. Somewhat like over-the-counter stock.

Jeff watched as B.W. marked prices for each coins which he had listed. Finally B.W. looked up and said, "You are a very lucky young man. There are several very good coins here. But some of the coins are in poor condition. I'm willing to offer you $14,250 for all of them. Notice that I'll take the ones in poor condition from you also."

Jeff paused as if he were thinking about the offer. Then he said, "Mr. Flesher, another dealer has offered me $14,750."

"Call me Wayne, please," B.W. said softly. "Gold is the instrument of gamblers and speculators, and the idol of the miser and the thief."

"What?" was Jeff's puzzled response.

"Just an old saying, Burke. You know, of course, that gold is the metal that men dig out of holes for dentists and governments to put back in." B.W. paused and then continued. "I'm merely joking. What is your occupation?"

"I'm a bookkeeper," Jeff lied.

"Really, I just lost my bookkeeper. Who do you work for?"

"No one really. I'm an independent contractor. I do jobs for a number of clients."

"Are you good?"

"I believe so."

"It's much better to have your gold in the hand than in the heart. I'll give you $14,900 for the coins. Can you get me some references? I need to hire a part-time bookkeeper."

Jeff smiled. "It's a sale — for the first question. And yes, I can get you references with respect to the second question."

"Good, then it's a deal." B.W. stuck out his hand and Jeff

shook it. B.W.'s grip was very muscular. "Will you accept one-half of the amount by check and the other half in cash?"

"Will the check bounce?"

"No."

"Are you going to carry the coins out now?"

B.W. patted under his left shoulder. "I have a weapon." B.W. wrote the check, and counted out 75 $100 bills. He then put the coins in his briefcase. "The receipt of cash can help you out taxwise. Do you understand?" Jeff shook his head. "Don't forget to call and give me some references."

Jeff later watched as B.W. drove off in his light blue Lincoln Continental. He then opened up a bank account with the $7,500 cash and the $7,400 Rosenbaum check.

One hour later Jeff called Hank. "Hey, Hank. I made the coin collection sale for $14,900."

"What? That's $1,100 below wholesale value," moaned Hank.

"But that's not all. I can get a part-time job working on his books. He needs a bookkeeper."

"You can't add 12 and 12. But, on the bright side, your paychecks can be used to make up the difference you lost on the coins."

"Can we line up some references for me? I told B.W. — uh, Wayne — that I was an independent contractor. I used the name Burke Jefferies."

"That's original. I'll get you a social security number under that name. That's easier than trying to find three people who would recommend you even for dog catcher. Do you know how to keep books?"

"I'm offended. Old accountants never die, they just lose their balance. I got a degree in accounting from Penn State."

"Is that in the United States?"

"Get back to work," Jeff responded.

CHAPTER 21

Another difference between death and taxes is that death
is frequently painless.

— Anonymous

For the next several weeks Jeff Burke (using the name Burke
Jefferies) spent a number of hours on the books and records of
Rosenbaum Coin and Stamp Shop. Jeff was able to work with
B.W., who managed to drop by the shop daily.

On the first working day he had to take a lie detector test,
and he had to agree to take such a test every two months.

Jeff reported regularly to Hank as to what he observed, heard,
and read in the coin shop. He had free access to the entire shop
— it wasn't large. He read materials on or in the desks and
elsewhere in the shop. He asked questions of the other
employees as to how the business was conducted.

From the young man whom Jeff had talked to during his
first visit to the coin shop, Jeff learned that although the
Rosenbaum Company owned eighty percent of the shop, B.W.
Flesher exerted very much power for a 20% owner.

While posting the financial transactions and watching the
flow of money, Jeff found out how B.W. was laundering his
illegal profits through the coin shop. B.W. did almost all of the
buying of the rare coins.

B.W. was understating most purchases. For example, of the
$14,900 purchase from Jeff, only $7,400 came through the coin
shop. Jeff reasoned that the $7,500 difference came from cash
from B.W.'s other illegal businesses.

Understatement of purchases, of course, overstated the final income figure of the coin shop. But since the coin shop was paying no taxes because of the computer manipulation of Richard Onner, "dirty money" was turned into "clean money" in a "legit" coin business.

During the second week of undercover employment, Jeff talked B.W. into taking him to the Lanham Coin Show. Jeff met B.W. at the Sheraton Convention Center in Lanham, Maryland, around 10:00 Wednesday morning.

"Hello, Burke. Did you have any trouble finding the place?"

"No, not really."

"Suppose we go to the bourse area first. The auction starts at 12:30. You stick close to me, and you'll learn something about coins."

In the bourse area there were approximately 300 eight-foot bourse tables. Behind each table was a dealer in either coins, stamps, silver, gold, and other collectibles — or some combination. It was a large coin show.

Jeff was amazed as B.W. effectively went from one table to the next looking for something to buy. He bought a draped bust 1801 half dollar (Type III) at one table; a brilliant uncirculated 1856 flying eagle small cent from another dealer after he argued convincingly that the coin was a slider (i.e., not really uncirculated).

For most of the coins, B.W. paid cash. Occasionally, he would write a Rosenbaum check for a particular coin. For the more expensive coins he normally paid cash. At one table he paid 16 one-hundred-dollar bills for a 1874-S Gem B.U. $20 Liberty Gold piece. B.W. told Jeff that the S mint mark stood for San Francisco.

At another table he gave 45 $100 bills for a 1934-S uncirculated Peace dollar. Here, as in most situations, B.W. was able to get the dealer to reduce his selling price by $500.

By 12:20 they had covered only about 100 tables. Jeff had noticed dealers such as New England Rare Coin Galleries, Gobal Rare Coins, Nunemaker's, J.J. Teaparty, Royal Enterprises, Max Hirschhorn, Carolina Coins & Stamp, Paramount

International, Deep South Rare Coins, First Coinvestors, Nevada Coin Mart, Kagin's, Perera Fifth Avenue, Bower & Ruddy Galleries, and other "blue chip" coin dealers.

At one table Jeff almost bought a "Hide It." This item was a secret book safe. It looked just like any real book, but opened to reveal a combination lock safe. Jeff thought it was big enough to hold all of the bribes he had accepted — exactly zero. But B.W. tapped him on the shoulder and said, "Let's get a coke and hot dog and go to the auction."

The auction was the "Breen VI Auction Sale" presented by the Pine Tree Auction Galleries. The pamphlet explaining the sale indicated that there were more than 1,600 lots. It seemed that B.W. bid on at least half of them, from Colonial coins, U.S. Type coins, Morgan silver dollars, Peace dollars (Jeff wondered if this should have been spelled Piece), gold coins, to mint sets.

B.W. certainly knew how to handle himself at the auction. The auctioneer apparently knew B.W. because he only had to move his pencil to bid. Jeff could not always follow the bidding, but B.W. seemed to know exactly what was happening. The auctioneer talked too fast for Jeff. He seemed to have a speeded-up, dry drawl of someone from the Southwest.

Around 4:00 p.m. Jeff whispered to B.W., "I'm going outside to get something to eat. My tail is getting tired."

B.W. waved him out. "Go on and see the exhibits. Only a coinaholic could sit in here all afternoon." He was deeply engrossed in the next coin up for bid. Outside the auction room Jeff reached down and picked up a brochure. It was an invitation to join the Society of Bearded Numismatists.

After glancing at the humorous poem entitled "On Being Invited to Join S.O.B. Numismatists," Jeff turned the brochure over and began to jot down as many of the purchases that B.W. had made in the bourse area and during the auction as he could recall. He was able to list 12 with prices and 16 more without prices. The books which he had read in the past several weeks on rare coins had helped him to recall a reasonable description of the coin purchases.

Jeff bought some light beer and another hot dog. He started watching a slide-illustrated program on the "History of the Philippines Money and the Japanese Occupational Notes." He left before it was over. Next he glanced at a 10-panel exhibit of the coinage of the world from ancient to modern times.

As he was perusing the crowd, unconsciously looking for the blonde head of Debra Sweeney, B.W. came up and tapped him on the shoulder. "Can you follow me to my home? I have a small fortune in this briefcase. I have a safe at home."

"Be glad to."

"Do you want to attend the auction tomorrow morning?"

"Yes, if you don't mind. I'm really getting interested in coins."

"Okay."

Jeff followed B.W. to his home in the northeast of Baltimore. It was a modest home with a swimming pool. But there was also a tennis court. Still, the house did look incongruous with a light blue Lincoln and a light tan Cadillac sitting in front of it.

Jeff was not invited into B.W.'s house.

The next day Jeff sat through the entire auction with B.W. He later watched B.W. pay for the coins with more one-hundred-dollar bills. Afterward Jeff recorded for future reference 16 items with prices and 12 coins without prices which B.W. had purchased at the auction. He had purchased many high-priced coins.

During the next several days following the auction, B.W. brought most of the rare coins into the inventory of the coin shop. They were recorded on the books at very low purchase prices. The coins were then sold at reasonable prices to investors and dealers (including many to the other Rosenbaum shops).

Late Thursday Jeff called Hank Brown from his apartment. "Hank, I believe I have about as much evidence as I am going to get on B.W. The longer I hang around, the higher the odds are that someone is going to recognize me. I believe we should do our thing."

"Can you make photocopies of his books and records?" asked Hank.

"I doubt it. There's no copier in the store. It would be too risky taking the records out of the store at night to be copied. Once they suspect something they'll destroy the books."

"Could you use a camera?"

"Not really. Someone would see me for sure."

"So we are going to have to seize his books and records," Hank concluded.

"Probably. I don't know any other way."

"Could you prepare an affidavit tonight with the information you have gathered? We'll take it to a magistrate tomorrow morning at 10:30 and get a search warrant. We can hit Flesher's coin shop in the afternoon."

"It's Rosenbaum Coins and Stamps," Jeff interjected.

"Sure, sure. See you at 10:30."

Jeff's affidavit was convincing, and the magistrate provided a search warrant.

The short, sandy-haired employee, Jesse, looked up when Jeff rang the buzzer. He automatically pushed the button and Hank Brown followed Jeff into the small shop.

"B.W. is in the back, Burke," Jesse advised.

"Jesse, this is Special Agent Hank Brown. I'm also a Special Agent, Jeff Burke."

Hank handed the young man the search warrant and said, "We would like to see all of the books and records that are here."

The employee was shocked. He slowly read the front part of the search warrant. Finally he turned and shouted, "Mr. Flesher, you better come out here."

B.W. walked out, smiled, and said, "I wasn't expecting you today, Burke."

"Mr. Flesher, he's — he's an IRS agent."

For a moment B.W. didn't move. He merely shot an angry, gunmetal stare at Jeff. He regained some composure and said, "How can I help you gentlemen?"

The employee gave the search warrant to B.W., who read it slowly. He looked up at Jeff and said, "You creep." He waved his arm and sat down in a chair. "Jesse, call my lawyer and tell him to get over here fast." Turning to Hank, he said, "Please wait until my lawyer gets here."

"I'm sorry, Mr. Flesher, there is no need for a lawyer. Where are your books and records?" Hank asked.

"Burke knows where they are," shot back B.W. "Or whatever his name is."

"My real name is Jeff Burke, Mr. Flesher."

B.W. Flesher did not respond. He was tired. He didn't know what to do.

Hank and Jeff made a thorough search of the entire coin shop. They seized all of the books and records, over the angry objections of B.W. Flesher.

Two days later Hank called Jeff.

"Flesher has had his lawyers working overtime. He has filed an action seeking money damages, the return of his books and records, and an injunction on the use of his documents in any future *criminal* proceedings."

"What money damages?" asked Jeff.

"He maintains we violated his Fourth Amendment rights. Plus he wants compensation for his books and records."

"Fine. Make copies of his real books and records and give them back to him. That'll do away with any real monetary damages. He might get some nominal damages for the invasion of his privacy. But will he not go to jail? He can use the nominal damages to buy cigarettes. What about the injunction?"

"Our lawyers believe the injunction is premature. If we bring a *civil* tax suit against him, there's no problem. Such an injunction in a civil action is a premature claim. In a future *criminal* proceeding against him, the injunction may be proper."

"So do our lawyers think we have him?" asked Jeff.

"They believe so. You did a good job."

"Don't forget to send me the reimbursement for the safe deposit box."

"You'll be lucky if you are not locked up with Flesher. Good luck on the outcome of your suspension. If there is any way I can help, seriously, give me a call.

"Wait a minute," said Hank as an afterthought. "There was a memo distributed today which may interest you. Here it is. Let me read it.

"Special Agents who pursue tax criminals are advised to fit auto hoods and gasoline tank caps with locks. Violators on occasion sabotage government cars by putting emery dust, sugar and similar substances in the crankcase and gasoline tank.

"How does that grab you?"
"Gee, thanks. That's all I need," replied Jeff.

* * *

"Hello, is this Box 20011?"
"Yes," was the crisp response.
"The additional money is in your account. You must terminate the two parties within 48 hours. Why is it taking you so long on the first party?" The male caller was clearly disturbed.
"Just problems, that's all. It will be done." Click.

* * *

Later that night Jeff received an important phone call from Rick Garrison.

"Jeff, this is Rick Garrison. Debra Sweeney is on the move again. She contacted someone in Washington on the pay telephone. I taped her conversation. She received new instructions. She must kill you within 48 hours along with someone named Jason Pabst," continued Garrison in a very rapid voice.

"Figures. Pabst is the internal security inspector working with me. Her contact really has an almost instantaneous information flow. Who could it be?" asked Jeff almost to himself.

"We are at the airport now. She's catching a plane to Washington in about twenty minutes. Call this Pabst fellow and let him know the danger. I'm going to follow her."

Jeff tried until he fell asleep to call Jason Pabst. He had no success. He had placed a chair against his doorknob. His bedfellow that night was a .38 revolver within easy reach. Washington was only a short drive from Baltimore.

The ringing in his ears made him jump. It was only the phone. The glow of his clock indicated that it was only 6:14 a.m.

"Hello," mumbled Jeff.

"I lost her," shouted Garrison into the phone. "I lost her cab when she drove into Washington. Did you contact Pabst?"

"No, I couldn't get him on the phone. No one would answer."

"Debra's contact gave her his address. I'll try to beat her there."

"Did you recognize her contact?"

"No, it was a male caller. Keep calling Pabst."

Jeff dialed Pabst's number. There was no answer. He dialed information to check to make sure he had the right number. He did, and called again several times. There was no answer.

CHAPTER 22

Collecting more taxes than is absolutely necessary is legalized robbery.

— Calvin Coolidge

Debra Sweeney was in a distressed mood. She had attempted to eliminate Jeff Burke three times; she had failed three times. Why had he not drunk the coffee and eaten the Danish she left for him at the Hilton? The poison would have killed him in three minutes.

Her contact in Washington had given her a time limitation. She did not like to work under a deadline. There was more chance of a fatal mistake. But on the bright side, the extra assignment meant a larger payoff.

She did not know who had hired her. The first contact had been by a typed letter with instructions to her code-name mail box in Elkhorn City. Her mother still lived there. She could vividly remember her abused early childhood. After the initial contact she had used a pay telephone, calling a pay telephone at a certain time in Washington, D.C.

Debra had gotten into her financially rewarding business by accident. When her husband had a church in Ashland, Kentucky, she had hit a man walking along the side of the road with her car late in the evening. She had panicked and left the scene of the accident. Although the man died, she was never caught.

Her older child was beginning his freshman year at Princeton. A minister's salary simply was not enough to pay the tuition. But they were not poor enough for her son to receive financial support from the university. One evening she was watching a movie about a "hit woman." Almost as a joke she sent a short advertisement to an underground Los Angeles newspaper:

Very personal extermination service. Quick and inexpensive. Write Box 20011, Elkhorn, KY. Send a pay phone number and a specific time when you can be called.

The ad ran for four weeks. During the third week she received a response. She called the respondent who apparently wanted a labor union official eliminated. She stalled, indicating that she had already accepted too many jobs. However, she made arrangements to call the respondent in three weeks.

She established a bank account in Lausanne, Switzerland. When she returned the call, she instructed the male caller to deposit ten thousand dollars in her numbered account. She told him to send a photograph of the intended victim along with pertinent data.

When the money was deposited, Debra intended to keep the money and forget about the hit. But she flew to San Diego for an Aeronautics Convention. She drove to Long Beach, and followed the union official for about two days. She shot the man at point blank range with a pistol. The Los Angeles papers indicated that the assassination was part of a gangland war.

Each subsequent hit became easier and easier. Her trademark was to vary the manner of terminating the victim in order to confuse the authorities. She had not advertised for several years. As she became more efficient, word of mouth advertising brought in enough work to send two children to expensive universities. She now had a Swiss bank account of about $290,000.

To disguise the source of income from her husband, Debra began writing children's books. Since she handled the finances in her family, it was fairly easy to report to her husband that she had received a "fat" royalty check from her publisher. Her husband was continually encouraging her to write more books. He was especially proud of the ten percent tithe which she gave to the church from her "royalties."

Debra had flown to Washington and taken a taxi to a non-descript motel. She did not want to rush her work. Fewer mistakes were made when a contract was planned carefully.

A slight tinge of excitement raced through her body as she worked in her motel room that night. She had a special termination technique for Jason Pabst. She had an extract from the tree *Unonopsis veneficiorum* which grew in the upper Amazon region. Indian tribes used this poison to tip their blowgun darts and arrows.

This compound into which she was dipping the small dart would prevent nerve impulses from activating skeletal and voluntary muscles. An injection would first affect the muscles of the ears, eyes and toes, then those of the limbs and neck, and finally the respiratory muscles. Respiratory paralysis would eventually cause a painless death.

As for Jeff Burke — the man with three lives — she had a special exotic death planned.

Ironically, on the night stand next to the telephone was a Gideon Bible. Someone had left the Bible open to Chapter 10 of Matthew. Verse 26 had been underlined.

There is nothing covered that shall not be revealed; and hid that shall not be known.

In her navy-tailored suit, white blouse, brown wig, and wide-rimmed glasses, Debra was watching as Jason Pabst emerged from his apartment house. A tall gentleman in his mid-thirties was with Mr. Pabst. The man seemed vaguely familiar to Debra.

Although both men seemed to be glancing from side to side, they did not see Debra in her car. It was very cold. She followed them to a subway parking lot. She got on the same subway, but in a different car. When they emerged from the underground subway near Constitution Avenue, she followed at a safe distance. They walked toward the IRS building.

About one block from their destination, she walked up rapidly behind them as they stopped at a crosswalk. There were about eight people waiting at the crosswalk. She removed her mirror and the blowgun from her purse. While pretending to put on lipstick, she aimed the long lipstick tube at Jason's neck. She blew the poisonous dart. Rather than hitting his neck, the dart hit his left shoulder blade.

Debra turned right and walked away as the "walk" light began blinking. She knew that the dart had probably penetrated his overcoat. Time would complete this half of her contract. Surprisingly Jason Pabst was still walking as he entered 1111 Constitution Avenue. His overcoat may have slowed the effect of the poison.

Rick Garrison and Jason Pabst walked to Jason's office on the third floor.

"She didn't get me this morning," said Jason as he walked over to his coat rack. He wiped several small beads of sweat from his forehead.

"Just a second, there's a bug or something on your coat," commanded Rick. He walked over and pulled something from Jason's coat. "It's a dart! Have your children been using your coat as a dart board?"

"We don't have any darts," replied Jason.

"Wait a minute. Maybe she did get to you. This could be a poison dart. The strap on your bullet-proof vest must have kept the point from reaching your body."

"Here, put that thing in this envelope, and we'll have it analyzed by the Intelligence Division. We have got to find her. Am I glad you talked me into wearing this vest," responded Jason as he shook his head slowly.

"You know what we should do? She had instructions to kill you within forty-eight hours. Someone important wants you rubbed out. Why don't I call an ambulance and take you to the hospital? We can then shadow Burke and try to get her before she kills him."

"I don't know," replied Jason.

"Look, I feel responsible. I should have arrested her in Pikesville. If she knocks both of you off, how do you think I'm going to feel? Call your wife and let her know what is happening. We can call Burke and warn him. We need to let him know what has transpired."

"Okay, if you insist."

When the ambulance arrived at the front of the IRS building, two attendants hurried to the third floor and carried Jason back to the waiting vehicle. A small crowd watched the ambulance move down Constitution Avenue with its siren screaming. Once the ambulance disappeared, Debra walked down the street and caught a taxi to the airport.

In the late evening newspaper, there was a small notice on page 25:

Jason Pabst, an Internal Revenue Service Agent, died today on arrival at St. Mary's Hospital. Cause of death is unknown. Funeral arrangements are pending.

Jeff had waited in his apartment until Rick Garrison and Jason Pabst had arrived. After the staged ride in the ambulance, Jeff and Jason had driven to Jeff's apartment in Baltimore.

The plan was for Garrison to stay with Jeff. Jason was to follow at a safe distance in the hopes of observing Debra Sweeney following Jeff. Jason looked ridiculous in sunglasses and an Orioles baseball hat.

After some discussion, Jeff and Garrison left in order to drive to Jeff's office. Upon leaving his apartment, Jeff placed a small piece of transparent tape on the top of his door attached to the doorframe. If Debra came into his apartment she would disturb the tape.

When he parked his car in Baltimore, Jeff took the same precautions. He locked both doors and placed a small piece of transparent tape at the bottom of each door, attached to the frame of the car.

Once at his office, Jeff picked up the photographs he had taken in Phoenix. He was spreading them out on his desk showing them to Rick when Jason entered his office.

"Well, did you see her following us?" inquired Jeff, looking up from the pictures.

"Nope, not a glimpse," replied Jason. He had already removed the sunglasses and baseball hat. He walked over and looked at the photos.

"Hmm, interesting," said Jason as he scratched his forehead. "Would you believe that your mysterious conspirator looks somewhat like Commissioner Callaway! Mind you, not much evidence because of the straw hat and glasses, but if it is Jimmy Callaway, that would explain why you were relieved of duty for two weeks. We may have found a big can of snakes. I probably have a termination notice back at my office."

"I thought he looked familiar," exclaimed Jeff. "I just couldn't place his face."

Jason turned to Jeff. "Did you get a list of the telephone calls made to and from the pay phone that Debra used?"

"No, I never got around to it," replied Jeff.

"Can I use your phone, Jeff?" asked Jason. "I'll call and have those phone numbers sent to you."

"Sure. Dial nine to get outside."

Both Jeff and Rick sat down while Jason made arrangements for the telephone numbers to be mailed to Jeff's home address.

When Jason hung up, Jeff spoke to him. "How much power do you have? We are in big trouble if Callaway is involved."

"Theoretically I'm supposed to report directly to the Commissioner. Under the circumstances I probably should report the matter to Secretary of the Treasury Clyde Hickey. To protect us I should sit down and type a short letter to the Secretary, explaining our suspicions. Where's your typewriter?"

"Why don't you dictate it." Jeff pointed to the dictating machine on his side desk.

"I can type it just as quick, and there won't be a secretary to spread our unsupported theories to your group supervisor."

"You're right. Ask my secretary to take you to a vacant word processor."

After Jason left, Jeff turned to Rick. "What do we do now?"

"Beats me!"

"If we can't find Debra, we probably should get Onner. He's the computer employee at Martinsburg who is helping the Rosenbaum Company obtain about $225 million of illegal tax refunds each year."

"Forget about finding Debra. She'll find you," said Rick. "You better hope we see her first. I wonder *how* and *when* she is going to try and kill you?"

Jeff sat silent for several minutes. He wondered if it was worth the trouble of being a Special Agent. He could always take a safe job such as a barber or an accountant. He could probably make more money, too. He had never heard of a barber or an accountant being shot by a professional killer.

Jason interrupted Jeff's thoughts as he entered the office. "Here, how does it sound?" Jason handed both Jeff and Rick a copy of the letter he had typed. "I'm going to send Attorney General Ben Gibson a copy since the Justice Department will eventually have to prosecute."

Honorable Clyde Hickey
Secretary of the Treasury
1111 Constitution Avenue
Washington, D.C. 20013

Dear Mr. Hickey:

I am a member of the Internal Security office which investigates corruption within the IRS. Special Agent Jeff Burke (Baltimore) and Detective Rick Garrison (Washington, D.C.), and I believe that Commissioner Jimmy Callaway may be involved with Richard Onner (IRS computer employee — Martinsburg, W.V.) and other unknown parties in a massive fraud within the IRS.

The fraud involves approximately 1,500 coin shops controlled by Rosenbaum Company (headquarters in Phoenix, Arizona). One of my special strike force agents (Jake Anderson) has already been killed, apparently by Debra Sweeney (Pikesville, KY), a professional killer. Sweeney has also made an attempt on my life. I staged my death and am now working closely with Jeff Burke. Detective Garrison intercepted a telephone message from an unknown individual to Debra Sweeney with instructions to kill Jeff Burke and myself within 48 hours.

An individual who appears to be Commissioner Callaway met with Jack Rosenbaum and Tony Blake (Phoenix IRS agent) in the Pepper Tree establishment in Phoenix approximately two weeks ago. Enclosed is a photo of this meeting. Other photos and negatives may be obtained from Jeff Burke.

Due to the sensitive nature of this matter, only yourself, Jeff Burke, Rick Garrison, and Attorney General Gibson have received copies of this letter.

Sincerely,

Jason Pabst
Group Supervisor
"Clean House" Strike Force

JP:jp

cc: Attorney General Ben Gibson
    Jeff Burke
    Rick Garrison

'Looks good to me," said Jeff.

"Same here," agreed Rick, handing the copy of the letter back to Jason.

"Both of you keep a copy of the letter. I'll keep a copy and mail the original to the Secretary today."

After Jeff had filed away his copy, Jason spoke to him. "If you are going to be our guinea pig, we should leave for your apartment. If we avoid the rush on the streets, we should have a better chance of spotting Debra. Rick, you stick on him like a flea. I'll follow close behind." Jason put on his sunglasses, his ridiculous baseball hat and overcoat and walked out the door first.

CHAPTER 23

There are seven species of the Genus Naja — the cobra. A cobra is quick and agile. When annoyed or frightened, a cobra rears and spreads his hood as a warning. A cobra can strike with rapidity and has a tendency to hold on after biting a victim.

The Cape cobra, *Naja Nivea*, is found in the Cape Province and certain areas of Southwestern Africa. It is probably the most dangerous of all cobras. The Cape cobra is courageous and will face its foe. Its potent venom will cause death within a few hours. Its bite can kill a 6,000-pound elephant. Less than two drops of *Naja Nivea* venom is sufficient to kill an average-sized man. This cobra can produce 15 drops with ease. This poison is so deadly that the only thing you can do if you've been bitten is to die.

*　　*　　*

Jeff's walk to his auto was uneventful. Jeff and Rick saw Jason drop his letters to the Secretary of the Treasury and the Attorney General in a mail box. Before Jeff and Rick got into the car, they checked the transparent tape on both doors. The tape had not been disturbed. Before entering his apartment,

Jeff checked and saw that the transparent tape on his door had not been disturbed. Jason parked some distance from Jeff's apartment and waited about thirty minutes before he knocked and entered Jeff's apartment.

That evening they decided to go to the Justice Department the next morning to make arrangements for arresting Richard Onner. They also needed to start action against the Rosenbaum Company. They did not know what to do about the Commissioner. Maybe Onner or Jack Rosenbaum would implicate Commissioner Callaway.

Very early in the morning Debra Sweeney placed a reed basket on the ground near a car. Within a minute she was able to open the door on the driver's side. She put some work gloves on. Gingerly she removed the top from the basket and shook a four-foot long cobra on the back floor of the dirty automobile. With a long curved rod she was able to force the snake under the front seat. The alarming hiss and flaring hood of the cobra would bring the taste of fear even to a hardened criminal. Another minute fled by and Debra locked the door, carefully replaced the tape on the door, and disappeared.

Around seven thirty Jeff awoke from his dreams. He went into his kitchen, removed a box of Raisin Bran from a cabinet and a gallon of milk from his refrigerator. His movements awoke Rick and Jason, who came into the kitchen to eat.

"Do you have any Pop Tarts?" asked Jason.

"No, cereal is all I have," replied Jeff. "I do have some orange juice."

They ate in silence.

Jason was the first to leave. He left by the back door. He went around to the front of the apartment wearing his sunglasses and the Orioles' hat. Nothing appeared to be out of the ordinary. Jason unlocked his car door and got in so as to watch when Jeff and Rick left. Jason had not left any transparent tape on his car doors.

Rick was the first to come out of the apartment door. He looked around and then motioned for Jeff to come out. Jeff locked his door and placed some more tape at the top of his front door.

Once at his car, Jeff checked both doors. The tape was still there. After unlocking the doors, Jeff and Rick got into the car.

Jeff drove through the parking lot and stopped at the entrance. He glanced in the rear view mirror and saw Jason driving up behind him.

"Hey, what do you have in your car?" shouted Rick. His left leg jerked forward, and he reached down and slapped at his leg. The sharp pain stopped in his leg, but something bit him on his left hand. "Damn!" bellowed Rick.

Jeff looked over at Rick. A snake was holding on to Rick's hand. The sight of the snake made his flesh crawl.

Rick began shaking his left arm. He hit at the snake with his right hand. Rick jumped out of the car at about the same time Jeff crawled out.

By the time Jeff got around to the other side of the car, Rick was jumping up and down shouting, "Turn me loose!" The snake was still attached to his left hand.

Jeff drew his gun and shouted, "Be still; I'll shoot it."

Surprisingly Rick stood almost like a statue. Jeff shot twice. The second bullet hit the snake, and it dropped.

"Get into the car," Jeff ordered Rick. Jeff turned to Jason and shouted, "Put the snake in your trunk and follow me to the hospital. Look around and see if Debra is near here."

"I'll call ahead to the hospital and get them ready," Jason shouted back. He jumped out with his umbrella and opened up his car trunk. He picked up the snake carefully on the end of his umbrella and threw it into his trunk.

Rick's muscular activity and the increase in his heart action when he had been jumping up and down trying to free himself from the snake had accelerated the spread of venom. Once back in the car Rick looked at the wound on his hand. There were two small punctures about three quarters of an inch apart. Two large drops of a clear serous-like fluid tinged with blood oozed from the two punctures. He did not even bother to look at the wounds on his leg.

There was a burning pain around the wounds on his hand and leg. The pain rapidly increased in intensity and extended in a circular fashion around the wounds.

About fifteen minutes passed before Jeff entered the emergency entrance of St. Joseph's Hospital. Rick was complaining about pains shooting up his leg and arm. "I'm beginning to feel dizzy," cried Rick.

Jeff kept wondering how Debra Sweeney had been able to get into his car without disturbing the tape. She must have seen him putting it on the car door. Now Rick was having to pay! He should have had at least one more safeguard on his car to prevent anyone from entering without his knowledge.

By the time the attendants at the hospital helped Rick from the car, he began to lose control of his leg muscles and he staggered when left unsupported.

Once in the hospital there was some confusion. No one could initially identify the snake Jason brought into the hospital and flung on the floor. Finally one nurse mentioned that the snake had a hood. "Maybe it's a cobra. I saw a man kiss a cobra at a snake show last year."

Finally, a short doctor came into the emergency room. His five-foot-seven-inch height made him hard to spot in a crowd, but he took control. He gave Rick a shot of antivenom.

About forty minutes after the snakebite, the paralysis of Rick's arms and legs increased. His lower jaw began to fall, and frothy viscid saliva oozed from his mouth. He began to moan, shaking his head from side to side. He spoke as if he were drunk.

Rick's breathing gradually became slower and finally ceased forty minutes after he was bitten. His death occurred forty-two minutes after the infliction of the first bite.

Jeff Burke had cheated death again. But this time fate had taken someone else in his place.

When Jeff got home he was depressed, but a telephone call shifted his attention to another matter. It was Hank Brown.

"Do you remember Rob Fowler?"

"Who could forget him. We couldn't tie him to the Flesher operation. What's he up to?"

"He got busted on a marijuana rap. The cops called me. Rob wants to talk to you and me about trading some information. I'm going to see him at 5:45. I know you've been canned, but do you want to be there when I talk to Rob?"

"Yes, I'll be there. Which station?"

"The one on St. Paul Street. I'll see you there."

Jeff was waiting with Hank at the police station to see Rob. "They caught him with about a ton of pot in a horse trailer. The police have seized his truck, horse trailer, $4,575 cash and the ton of illegal weed. Apparently he purchased it at the Mexican border and drove it to Baltimore. The way I figure it —" Hank was interrupted by a policeman leading Rob into the small room.

"Hello, Rob," Hank rose and shook Rob's hand. "This is Jeff Burke."

"Yeah, I know him. You and him caught my old lady at the Flesher plumbing outlet."

Jeff smiled slightly as he remembered Hank putting holes in Rob's condoms at the time they searched his home.

"You guys put me in here," Rob continued. "You cut off my money. They tell me I can get ten years. I don't want to rot in prison. I can give you some important information about a big man in the IRS if you'll help me beat this rap."

"Look, Rob, you have more problems than you think. I made some calculations on the way over here. The way I figure it, you owe taxes of about $137,000."

"What?" Rob looked surprised and stared at Hank.

"This is probably not the first load you've sold. Assume you sold only one other load. You probably grossed $780,000 from the pot sales. Say we allow a deduction of about $682,000 including $280,000 for the cost of the weed, $320,000 sales commissions, and $40,000 of the driver's expenses. That leaves a net profit of $137,000."

"Wait a minute, Hank," Jeff interrupted. "For a drug-related issue, a taxpayer is only allowed to deduct cost of goods sold."

"Look, guys, that was my first load. I don't owe any taxes. I'm an honest man. I don't need any trouble with you guys. But I can help you. I know some juicy gossip about your fancy Commissioner — Callaway is his name. But you guys have got to help me. Will you?" His voice was unsteady.

Hank's eyes involuntarily swung toward Jeff when Rob mentioned the name Callaway. He leaned forward in his straight chair and said slowly, "How do *you* know Commissioner Callaway?"

"I know some information about him." Rob looked more confident now. He had seen both Hank and Jeff's sudden interest when he mentioned the name Callaway. "Now can you help me?"

"I am currently working with the supervisor of a special strike force which deals with corruption in the federal government. I believe I can help you *if* your information is worthwhile." Jeff spoke for the first time.

Rob turned to Jeff and said, "I knew Tish Scarbourg, a girlfriend of Richard Onner. He's an IRS employee. I lived with her before she met Onner."

"Really!" exclaimed Hank.

"So, anyway, Tish worked for this Commissioner Callaway. She broke up with Onner for several months and started fooling with Callaway. She learned that Callaway sometimes employs a hit woman." Rob hesitated to dramatically allow this disclosure to have its full impact on his two listeners.

"Surely Callaway didn't just tell Tish such damaging information," Hank said.

"Apparently Callaway got drunk or careless one night and called this hit woman from Tish's apartment. Tish overheard him, became jealous of his calling another woman, and threatened to tell his wife about their affair. To pacify her, Callaway told Tish the truth — that the woman was a professional killer."

"How did you find out about this?" asked Hank in a disbelieving tone.

"Tish got into trouble. She got caught with some crack and wound up in jail. She couldn't find Onner, and she called me. I helped her get out of the pokey, and I stayed with her the rest of the weekend. She told me about the incident with the phone.

"Somehow Onner and Callaway got to know one another through Tish. Onner was able to get Callaway to transfer him to Martinsburg, Virginia."

"That's West Virginia," corrected Hank.

"What?"

"Martinsburg is in West Virginia."

"Okay, West Virginia. Tish still lives with Onner in Martinsburg. She calls me every once in a while when she gets mad at Onner."

"Would you testify to this in court?" asked Jeff.

"Sure, if you get me off."

"That's no good, Rob," said Hank. "How do we know you're not making this up to get out of the slammer? Besides, it's hearsay evidence. It's worthless. We have to get this Tish woman. Sorry, Rob."

Hank rose and said, "Come on, Jeff. He's wasting our time."

"Wait a minute," Rob pleaded, obviously scared. "I can help you get Tish. If I get her for you, will you help me?"

"Come on, Rob. You're going to testify that she smoked some pot. That's not going to help us."

"No! That's not it." Rob was squeezing the arms of the chair very firmly. "I worked with Tish about five years ago in a confidence game. I'm sure she didn't report any of the income."

"Well, now, Rob. You may have something." Hank's eyebrows lifted as he sat back down into his chair. "Tell us more."

Rob seemed to regain some confidence as he sat more erect in his chair. His deep-set brown eyes flashed at Hank. "I'm involved; so you'll have to get me immunity. Can you? Can you help me beat this drug rap?"

"Rob, we would not be worth our IRS salt if we could not help you," replied Hank.

Rob turned and gave Jeff a quizzical look.

Jeff nodded in agreement.

"She was involved in a Ponzi scheme," Rob began. "She and I both were in Los Angeles then. She was a nurse, and started going with an intern. I met them both at the same hospital. Due to their expertise and connections in the first aid field, we — they represented to friends, acquaintances, and various relatives that they were able to purchase ambulance shells directly from the factory, equip them, and sell the finished ambulances to municipalities or companies at a substantial profit."

Both Jeff and Hank remained silent.

"The business did not exist. They promised to share the profits with the others if they would loan them money to purchase the original vehicle. Tish — she used another name in L.A. — and Kenneth persuaded a number of investors to advance money to them in return for 25% interest. They had no intentions to repay the loans. They would promise to repay the investors within one month their original investment plus the high interest."

Rob paused for a moment and began again. "Over a two-year period they collected about $1.7 million from at least fifty-seven individuals. Throughout this period they gave different investors contradictory stories about the business, including the identity of the customers, from whom they were buying the vehicles, why they did not borrow from conventional financing sources, and why they were unable to repay investors on schedule. They had about twenty different reasons for slow payments, ranging from the need to care for a mentally ill and suicidal sister to the fact that the son of the person who was to deliver the money had been in a motorcycle accident and needed to have his arm amputated."

"What happened?" asked Hank, clearly interested.

"Tish and Kenneth left town. Vanished. Changed their names."

"I don't believe it," Jeff said, eyeing Rob coldly.

"How do you know so much?" Hank asked.

Rob sighed. "I was Kenneth."

An obviously surprised Hank said, "What happened to the money?"

"We went to Las Vegas. Tish got more money than I did. She could hustle better than me. She would promise the suckers that in addition to a return on their investment, they would receive new automobiles free or at special discounts. She would tell them the company was able to obtain these good deals because of the many purchases of ambulances from automobile manufacturers. I lost most of my money gambling in Vegas."

"Does Tish still have her money?" asked Hank.

"Some of it. She didn't gamble as much as I did."

"Rob," said Jeff, "if you called Tish, would she meet you — say for lunch? You could tell her you have another deal cooking."

"Sure she would meet me, man. She owes me a lot."

"Arrange it for Saturday. You should be out on bail by then. You'll post bail, won't you, Hank?" Jeff turned to Hank.

"Why not, it's only the IRS's money. My boss loves me — I hope."

CHAPTER 24

What is the difference between a taxidermist and a tax collector? The taxidermist takes only your skin.
— Mark Twain

Tish Scarbourg was surprised to hear from Rob. She had intentionally tried to suppress that part of her life. She still had some of the money from this stage of her life in a Cuban numbered account in Miami. She was skeptical of Rob having any type of productive scheme, except to borrow or milk money from her. Yet she really had no choice, Rob knew where too many of her skeletons were hidden.

When she came into the small restaurant she saw Rob sitting with two men at a corner table. They looked like businessmen. Tish thought that maybe Rob might be after something other than borrowing money.

Tish walked to the table confidently. She was still an attractive woman. Even with the years, she was tall and not overweight. Of course, her blonde hair was not natural, and there was some slight lines in her face. But her figure still made men take a second or third look when she passed by.

Only Rob rose when she reached the table. "Hello, Tish. Glad you could come. Is a Scotch on the rocks okay?"

"Yes, that will be fine."

Rob motioned to a passing waiter and ordered the drink.

There was an uncomfortable silence as they waited for the drink. Finally Rob said, "Tish, these gentlemen are IRS Special Agents. They know about our ambulance scam."

206

The color drained from her tanned cheeks. She took a perfunctory look at Hank's extended Special Agent badge. Then she said in a somber voice, "Anyone can have a badge like that. What are you trying to pull, Rob?"

"It's no joke, Tish. They got me on a drug charge. I had no choice. They need you to get your ex-friend the Commissioner."

"What are you talking about?" Tish tried to sound convincing. There was a sour feeling at the bottom of her stomach.

Hank spoke first. "Ms. Scarbourg, Rob has given us information about your unreported income from your ambulance operation in California. You are aware of the penalties for not reporting income."

Tish in desperation said, "But I did report it."

"Wrong, Ms. Scarbourg. I checked your tax returns this morning on the computer."

"Besides, even if I didn't report it, that was five years ago. The statute of limitations has run out. You can't get me."

"Wrong again, Ms. Scarbourg, there is no statute of limitations in the case of fraud. Suppose you calm down and listen. We are not really after you. We want the Commissioner. If what Rob has told us is correct, you can help us."

"What's in it for me?" She was slowly drumming her fingertips on the table top. Her voice was calmer and quieter. She took a sip of the Scotch after the waiter set it in front of her.

When the waiter moved away, Jeff said, "Ms. Scarbourg, the IRS can handle a taxpayer in a whimsical, unpredictable and highly personal manner. We can very easily turn you over to our collection division whose job it is to go charging after overdue money. These boys can be high handed and obnoxious."

Jeff raised his right hand and continued, "One revenue collector in my office seized a $2,000 bank account that a taxpayer had set up to pay for his wife's cancer treatment because it was the readiest asset the taxpayer had. Last year a revenue officer seized a guard dog company and sold off his dogs within two days to the taxpayer's competitor before the man had a chance to obtain the money to pay. These guys get points for seizing money from taxpayers on Social Security, on welfare, or from a pension plan. The bottom line: revenue collectors are low lifes."

What Jeff did not mention was that about 12 of these revenue collectors per week report threats and about 40 or more are assaulted per year.

Jeff turned to Hank. "Tell her about that Tracy fellow in Montana."

"Ah, yes. Mr. Tracy was a TV personality. He had a talk show and frequently invited tax protesters to his show. It seems that he openly expressed sympathy with a tax protester's statement that the IRS uses illegal methods to collect taxes. Some agents paid a visit to the TV station demanding tape recordings of his past shows. He was fired the next day.

"An unemployed Mr. Tracy wrote and published a booklet entitled 'Guide to Tax Rebellion.' Several months later agents demanded from his bank microfilm records of the names of all the people who paid for copies of the booklet by check. Sales of his book naturally took a nosedive. But Mr. Tracy was a slow learner. Later he led an anti-tax rally in front of the IRS office in Salt Lake City. Nearly 150 people stood in the pouring rain to protest excessive taxation. An IRS agent stated in public 'The IRS is going to get Sam Tracy.'

"And they did. Four days later he was taken to the Salt Lake City jail where he was detained for 14 hours without explanation. The next morning Tracy was brought in chains before a U.S. magistrate and charged with illegal possession of an IRS insignia. It seems that Tracy had displayed IRS publication No. 34, the seizure notice, at the protest rally. Any citizen can legally get this notice under the Freedom of Information Act.

"When released from custody, Tracy found that his auto, office and briefcase had been searched without a warrant. Business funds of $30,000 were missing. He was unable to recover these funds. At his trial for illegal possession of the

IRS Insignia, he was denied a jury trial and summarily found guilty by the judge. He received the maximum sentence of six months in jail." Hank stopped talking from sheer loss of breath, but he did smile in self-satisfaction.

Jeff continued. "There was a gentleman in New Jersey who filed tax returns claiming two burros as children. He might have never been caught, but he listed the names of the children as Sassafras and Happyjack. Well . . ."

Tish interrupted just as Jeff reached forward and jabbed a finger in mid-air. "Don't give me any more gestapo stories. I'm impressed. What do you want?"

Hank answered. "Would you tell us about Jimmy Callaway?"

Tish again gave Rob a hard look. "I had a thing going with Jimmy. There's no law against that. That was some time ago."

"Tell us about his hit woman."

There was a short pause, and Tish leaned forward and began. "We were at his house in Maryland. His wife was visiting her folks in North Carolina. I was his mistress and was very possessive. He had been drinking and was in the john when the telephone rang. I answered it, and it was a woman — not his wife. I left the phone off the hook and took him another phone into the bathroom. He has phone plug-ins all over the house. To make a long story short, I went back to the other phone and listened to the conversation.

"The caller was a professional killer. Jimmy made arrangements for her to kill a local politician in North Carolina who was holding up his possible appointment as the Commissioner of the IRS. She asked for $10,000 to be placed in a numbered account in Switzerland. He was to put $10,000 more in the account after the transaction was completed. She used the word 'transaction.'

"Maybe I put the phone down too soon, but Jimmy seemed to know afterwards that I had listened to the conversation. He got very angry. I told him that I had heard very little. He was so mad and angry that I left."

"Why didn't he just have you killed?" asked Hank.

"I thought about that, so I wrote up a summary of the conversation, dated it, and put it with my will in my safe deposit box. I told Jimmy the next day that I was frightened so I had written up the conversation and had given it to my lawyer to be opened in the case of my untimely death. The whole event seemed to place a chill over our affair, and we broke up several weeks later. Actually, he is the one who introduced me to Richard Onner. I really have not seen him since that time, but I do read about him infrequently in the paper. He seems to be doing well."

Jeff excitedly asked, "Did you write down the number of the Swiss bank account?"

"Yes. Initially I thought the information might be worthwhile. But Richard and Jimmy correspond frequently. They apparently are involved in several business projects. Besides, who wants to mess around blackmailing a professional killer."

"Do you know the woman's name?" spoke Hank.

"No, she didn't mention her name or address."

"Do Richard and Jimmy collect rare coins?" asked Jeff.

"Richard does. He gets some crazy junk mail. The other day he got a piece which said Doomsday! Will it be October 15, 1995? They were trying to sell a monthly advisory letter called the 'Uptight Spike.' I don't know about Jimmy. I really don't. I could ask Richard."

"No, don't," exclaimed Jeff. "Could we go and get the Swiss bank account number from your safe deposit box?"

"What are you going to do to me?" asked Tish.

"Nothing if we can get Jimmy Callaway. You may have to testify sometime in the future. But no one knows about your little ambulance episode. We'll keep it that way if you will cooperate with us. We'll need a copy of your written account of Callaway's phone conversation. Also, you should tell Onner nothing — absolutely nothing."

"I won't say a word. Jimmy would have me killed. I'll take you to get the Swiss number."

True to her word, Tish did have a Swiss bank account number and a signed statement as to a conversation between

Jimmy Callaway and an unknown woman. Jeff and Hank got a copy of the statement and they went to Hank's office.

In Hank's modest office — if it could be called an office — Jeff said, "We really have little evidence against Callaway unless we can get more evidence from Debra Sweeney. She's probably not going to help us unless we can get her money from her Swiss safe deposit box. Can we get it?"

"I believe so," said Hank. "There was a court case several years ago when an American won the Irish Sweepstakes — a cool 50,000 Irish pounds. About $140,000. When he learned he had a silent partner in his winning — the IRS — he deposited the money into a secret foreign bank on the Island of Jersey, between England and France. Well, the taxpayer was convicted of income tax evasion and went to prison. But his money was still in the foreign bank. The IRS went to court again to repatriate his assets from the foreign bank and deposit the funds with the clerk of the court. We won. The taxpayer's money came back to the U.S. They didn't know his bank account number."

"What section of the law did they use?"

Hank picked up a copy of the Internal Revenue Code of 1986 and flipped through it. "I believe it was Section 7402. Here it is — Section 7402(a)."

Jeff took the dog-eared copy of the Code from Hank and read: "The district courts of the United States at the instance of the United States shall have such jurisdiction to make and issue in civil actions, writs and orders of injunction, and of *ne exeat republica*, orders appointing receivers, and such other orders and processes, and to render such judgments and decrees as may be necessary or appropriate for the enforcement of the internal revenue laws. The remedies hereby provided are in addition to and not exclusive of any and all other remedies of the United States in such courts or otherwise to enforce such laws."

Jeff shook his head. "It doesn't say anything to me."

"Be more positive, Burke. We have to win. We are the good guys with white hats. They always win, don't they?"

EPILOGUE

The world is not the way they tell you it is.
— Adam Smith, in "The Money Game"

The Pikesville local newspaper carried the following electrifying front page headline on Wednesday: "Minister's Wife Jailed." The copyrighted story began as follows: "A mother of two, Debra Sweeney, is an alleged professional killer. Wife of a Baptist minister, her apparent idiosyncrasy was a passion for exotic 'hits' of her intended victims. Bombings, poison darts, and a cobra bite were only some of the techniques used by this mother and writer of children's books. She is apparently connected to a much wider 'Neutrongate' fraud that may involve the U.S. Treasury Department. Her bond has been set at $750,000. Reverend John Sweeney was unavailable for comment."

* * *

"Nightline" broke the story last night when an unidentified IRS agent spoke about his narrow escape from death. Apparently one agent, Jake Anderson, was allegedly killed by a flying model airplane in Washington, D.C., last month, and another Washington detective, Rick Garrison, was killed by the bite of an exotic cobra several days ago.

* * *

On Thursday, the *Phoenix News* carried this headline. "$758 Million Tax Liens Hit Phoenix Tycoon." The front page story ran as follows: "Alleged nonpayment of $758 million in income taxes has prompted federal action against Jack Rosenbaum, Phoenix businessman and personal friend of IRS Commissioner Jimmy Callaway, officials said here.

"Federal tax liens were placed against Rosenbaum's personal assets as well as his financial empire, which includes more than 1,500 coin shops throughout the country along with the world's largest mail-order coin business located in Phoenix, the Internal Revenue Service said this morning.

"Rosenbaum also controls the Rosenbaum Ammunition Plant located near Vulture Mine. The federal official indicated that much of the unpaid taxes had been used to develop a neutron bomb which has been outlawed for many years. The scam is apparently worse than the Iran-Contra affair in the eighties.

"The liens were filed with the recorder's offices in 1,570 counties where Rosenbaum owns property. This action served notice to persons doing business with Rosenbaum in any of the counties in which the IRS has a 'prior claim on any assets' owned by Rosenbaum, the spokesman said.

"The liens were filed at the same time IRS agents served Rosenbaum's attorney, Mark White, with a 'jeopardy assessment,' which the spokesman said was a harsh action. There is no notice. You pay up now.

"The spokesman said that the IRS resorts to the procedure only when the taxpayer is preparing to leave the country or go into hiding, or if the taxpayer is going to place his assets beyond government reach, or if the taxpayer's financial solvency is or appears to be imperiled.

"Rosenbaum has the 'judicial right to appeal within ninety days' the jeopardy assessment in federal civil court, the spokesman continued.

"The liens represent one of the largest income tax claims since the income tax law became effective in March, 1913. The spokesman would not say how Rosenbaum could have incurred such a huge tax liability. But other sources indicate that some well-placed IRS employees were involved in this gigantic rip-off.

"Rosenbaum reportedly raised two million dollars for President Keeney's political campaigns. The financier was not available for comment at his home in Scottsdale. A spokesman for President Keeney indicated that the President had 'no comment.'"

*　　*　　*

On Friday, the *Phoenix News* carried this follow-up story on page one. "Phoenix businessman Jack Rosenbaum assailed the Internal Revenue Service Thursday for a $758 million income tax lien filed against him and his empire.

"The fifty-five-year-old tycoon issued a statement saying that the lien is 'the most shocking display of bureaucratic power and arrogance I've ever seen leveled against an individual citizen of the United States.'

"'At some bureaucratic levels I am being attacked as a friend of President Keeney. It appears to me that some governmental zealots are anxious to develop a little Coingate in Phoenix,' he added.

"'I am, therefore, determined to take whatever steps are necessary to clear my name from these misleading and contrived actions by certain agencies of the government,' Rosenbaum pledged."

*　　*　　*

Richard Onner was arrested for tax fraud on a personal level. When it became apparent that Rosenbaum or Callaway would not help him, Onner told of his special assignment by the IRS Commissioner which allowed him to protect Rosenbaum Company. Onner spent three years in jail.

*   *   *

Debra Sweeney was confined for psychiatric observation after providing powers of attorney to information concerning her Swiss bank account. Some of the funds going into this account were traced to Callaway's personal secretary. Neutron Activation Analysis indicated that certain materials found in Debra's workshop were similar to pieces from the model plane which exploded and killed Revenue Agent Jake Anderson.

*   *   *

Rob Fowler received a suspended sentence.

*   *   *

A combination of publicity concerning the Rosenbaum tax fraud with his close association with Callaway and of publicity concerning the hit woman paid by Callaway's personal secretary almost caused a Senate investigation. Callaway quietly resigned several weeks after this publicity and the Senate Committee never met. He went back to North Carolina and practiced law for two years. Then he ran for and was elected to the North Carolina House of Representatives.

*   *   *

Rosenbaum Company was prosecuted for back taxes only, and paid the largest assessment for back taxes in U.S. history. Defense Department and CIA intervention at the Presidential level caused the new IRS Commissioner to quash any criminal proceedings against Jack Rosenbaum. The federal government quietly confiscated and destroyed a number of neutron bombs found at the Rosenbaum Ammunition Plant.

* * *

Jason Pabst was transferred to Sioux City, Iowa, and was denied an expected promotion. His career with the IRS was effectively finished.

* * *

Yvonne Talbert became a Special Agent and member of Operation Greenback, a joint effort between the IRS and Customs Special Agents. The sole purpose of Operation Greenback was to investigate CTR and CMIR violations. Special Agents are part of thirteen task forces around the nation with the sole purpose of stopping the sale of narcotics.

* * *

Jeff Burke wondered how many other companies Onner was helping to cheat the government. Jeff also wondered if there were other computer operators who were doing the same thing. He never found out. Newspaper articles began appearing such as "IRS Horror Stories Prompt Hearings on Proposed Taxpayers' 'Bill of Rights.'" An Arkansas Senator said:

> Like a bully, the IRS relies on intimidation and arm twisting to strike fear into the hearts of those it bullies. ... And they do this in the name of compliance. It is my guess that compliance could be improved not by continuing to browbeat taxpayers, but by reestablishing respect for the IRS in the manner in which it performs a difficult and unpopular task.

Former IRS employee John Smith testified in Congress:

There are a lot of outrageous and arbitrary actions by agents because of the "unchecked power" of the IRS. Contrary to claims from the national office, IRS field employees are pressured to produce statistics that show that they are doing their jobs. As the joke in the office used to go: the name of the game is quality. Lots and lots of quality. . . . The IRS equates increased production and increased seizures with increased quality.

Later, Smith admitted that:

Between 90 and 95 percent of all cases are handled properly by the Service. Given the broad scope of the IRS's mission, this error factor should be considered "perfect." What is needed is "some vehicle where the ordinary person can go" when he experiences unnecessary harassment or illegalities by a revenue or collection agent.

President Keeney asked for and the Democrat-controlled Congress passed a "Taxpayer's Bill of Rights." Internal Security Inspectors could only investigate dishonesty of IRS employees and not other governmental employees.

Within six months Jeff Burke was transferred "temporarily" to the Bureau of Alcohol, Tobacco, and Firearms. Two years later as an ATF agent he was shot in the line of duty, while trying to arrest two buttsleggers in New Jersey. The two were involved in contraband cigarette smuggling.

*   *   *

Carl Strovee fled to Caracas, Venezuela, and did not return to the United States until eight years later — under another identity.

217